FOR RYE

GAVIN GARDINER

Content compiled for publication by Richard Mayers
of *Burton Mayers Books*.
Cover design by ebooklaunch.com

First published by Burton Mayers Books 2021.
All rights reserved.

A CIP catalogue record for this book is available from
the British Library

ISBN: 1-8383459-0-7
ISBN-13: 978-1-8383459-0-7

Typeset in **Adobe Garamond**

www.BurtonMayersBooks.com

Dear reader, unto you I present the acknowledgements section, the part of the book every author expects to be immediately skipped. I'll make you a deal: grant me this one, hasty indulgence, and I'll tell you a killer joke afterwards.

I'd like to thank Richard Mayers for believing in this nightmare; George, for your peat, flotsam, and Aga expertise; Barbara, for the tomato and rice soup; and Heather, for more than I could possibly say. Further: Dad, Jamie, Hannah, John, Rayner, Angus, Kyle, Derek, Mai, Michelle, Brandi, Casey, Han, Matt, and everyone in between – I thank you all.

Finally, Mum. For better or worse, this is as much yours as it is mine. For the endless phone calls debating everything from the placement of a comma to the volume of gore required, you have my undying gratitude.

And the joke, ladies and gentlemen, is that any undertaking such as this can possibly be conquered by just one person. Without those who inspire, guide, endure, and care for the writer, the pursuit is doomed.

To everyone who's inspired, guided, endured, and cared for this writer: this one's for you.

A brutal and distressing strain of horror has been poured into the pages of this novel. Anyone reading should take a moment to consider whether this is a depth into which they should dive.

I believe it is.

To my favourite.

1

Knives.

'Madam?'

Everywhere, knives.

'Are you all right?'

Knives in the eyes of every onlooker, each glance carving red-hot rivulets of pain through her flesh.

'You'll need your ticket.'

Everywhere, knives; everywhere, eyes.

She plunged trembling fingers into her worn leather satchel. *Damned thing must be in here somewhere*, she thought in the moment before her bag fell to the concrete flooring of Stonemount Central. The ticket collector's eyes converged with her own upon the sacred square slip, tangled amongst the only other occupant of the fallen satchel: a coil of hemp rope.

They stared at the noose.

The moment lingered like an uninvited ghost. The woman fumbled the rope back into the bag and sprang to her feet, before shoving the ticket into his hand, grabbing her small suitcase, and lurching into the knives, into the eyes.

The crowd knocked past. A flickering departure board passed overhead as she wrestled through the profusion of faces, every eye a poised blade. The stare of a school uniformed boy trailing by his mother's hand fell upon her, boiling water on skin. She jerked back, failing to contain a shriek of pain. Swarms of eyes turned to look. The boy sniggered. She pulled her duffle coat tight and pushed onward.

The hordes obscured her line of sight; the exit had to be nearby, somewhere through these eyes of agony. She prayed the detective – no, no more praying – she *hoped* the detective would be waiting outside to drive her, as promised. One last leg of the journey, out of the city of Stonemount and back to her childhood home after nearly thirty years.

Back to Millbury Peak.

She stumbled into a standing suitcase. The eyes of its owner tore at her flesh as she knocked it over and scrambled to regain her footing. She dared not look back as she struggled away, silently cursing the letter to have dragged her back to this unfamiliar hell, to have ripped her from her haven hundreds of miles away, forcing her to trade her cottage on that bleak, storm-soaked island for a town she hadn't called home for decades. Not since the accident. Not since the seventeen-year-old had found in white corridors and hospital beds a new home. But this wasn't about her. No, this was about an elderly lady, butchered. She was returning to Millbury Peak for her mother, her sweet, slaughtered mother. She slipped a hand into the leather satchel—

It would have held.

—and felt the coarse hemp of the noose against her fingers. She shouldn't be here. She would have been gone—

It was strong, solid.

—had it not been for the detective's letter. Gone to nowhere, forever. No more knives, no more eyes. She'd planned to be gone. She should have been gone.

The beam would have held. It was strong, solid. It would

have held.

With desperation she glanced around, the exit to this damned train station still hidden from view. She spotted a gap in the bodies. Through this gap she spied solitude: the open door of a bookshop, deserted. She went to it.

The woman lunged through the door, the teenage cashier behind the counter glancing up momentarily before returning to her magazine, uninterested. She shuffled between the rows of bookcases and backed into an obscured, shadowy corner to calm herself. She passed her hands over her bunned hair, quickly checking the headful of clips and clasps before once again reaching into the satchel. She closed her eyes as she ran her fingers over the coiled noose. The knives, the eyes, the faces. Soon, they'd all be gone.

Soon, she'd be gone.

She was turning to leave the bookshop when a thought came to her. A gift for her father, how nice.

just bruises

After all, they were separated by decades from their last meeting. Yes, she'd see if she could pick up one of her novels for him. How lovely, how *nice*.

My love, they're just bruises. He would never hurt us, not really.

She was tiptoeing through the bookcases searching for the romance section when, upon turning a corner, she found herself in the midst of a towering dark figure. She reeled back, before realising the figure was a cardboard cut-out. The blood-red shelving of its book display fanned around the figure, macabre imagery making it obvious as to which genre it subscribed. The man depicted in the life-size cut-out wore a dark turtleneck and tweed blazer, an expression of calculated theatricality staring through thick horn-rimmed glasses. The sign above read:

HORROR HAS A NAME:
QUENTIN C. RYE
CHOOSE YOUR NIGHTMARE – IF YOU DARE

The display's centrepiece was a pseudo-altar upon which sat the author's latest release, a hardback titled *Midnight Oil*. She was turning from the display when her eye caught a thin volume squeezed between spines of increasingly doom-laden type, many screaming the words *NOW A MAJOR MOTION PICTURE*. The novel calling to her had only two words trailing its spine, two words that seemed to speak to a place buried deep within her. She reached for the book.

Its cover depicted a woman standing in the middle of a road, an emerald green dress flowing behind her in the fog. This road was empty but for one vehicle: a rust-coated pickup truck from which flames billowed, flying in its wake like tin cans from a wedding car. It tore towards the mysterious woman, who stood fearless in the face of the hurling metal. *Horror Highway*, the title read.

Suddenly, blinding pain.

The paperback dropped from her hands. Agony flashed through her head, tearing like a claw, then fell away as quickly as it had risen. She looked down to find her knuckles white around a wheel that was not there. Struggling for breath, she released her imaginary grip as a stray strand of hair floated into her vision. In a panic, she picked a fresh kirby grip from the handful in her duffle pocket and fastened it amongst the mass already intricately fixed. A loose strand meant something out of place. Something out of place meant disorder. Disorder meant disaster. She closed her eyes and thought of those long white corridors, sterile and simple, everything in its place. Her breathing settled. She'd never really left hospital, or maybe hospital had never left her. She slowly opened her eyes and turned from the Quentin C. Rye display. Find the book – it'll be *nice* – then get out of here.

...he would never hurt us.

ROMANCE read faded lettering above a shelving unit at the far end. She stepped towards the unassuming section and traced a finger along the alphabetised volumes towards W.

The cashier scanned the book's barcode, offering the woman not a glimmer of recognition.

Just how she liked it.

'From one writer to another, being spotted with your own book ain't the most flattering of images.'

The voice materialised from many. She stood at the pick-up spot on the street outside the station, hesitating before looking around to the source of the voice. She glanced instead at the book in her hands as if to remind herself of whom the voice spoke:

A Love Encased
The latest in the Adelaide Addington series
Renata Wakefield

'Miss Wakefield,' the voice said with a New England twang, 'it's a pleasure. Big fan.'

She turned to find a pair of thick horn-rimmed glasses watching her, the same glasses from the Quentin C. Rye display. The same face from the Quentin C. Rye display.

Quentin C. Rye.

'My wife is anyway – ex-wife, that is.'

Her mouth refused to open. The burning pickup truck and emerald green dress filled her head.

'Didn't mean to startle you, Renata,' he said, slipping a fat leather notebook back into his blazer. He ran his fingers through slicked back hair shot with streaks of grey, then held out a hand. 'Don't mind if I call you Renata?'

So many years avoiding human interaction and it should be this American to greet her upon resurfacing? Of all people, of all eyes, why were *his* welcoming her back to the place she hadn't called home for three decades? You couldn't write it. She should know.

Renata stared at the outstretched hand.

'Your work's kinda outside my field of expertise,' he continued, twirling a pen between the fingers of his other hand, 'but I've been assured you're quite the talent.'

'I'm sorry, I—'

'Name's Quentin. The local cops asked me to help with the investigation after your Mom's…uh…' His brown frames glanced over her shoulder. 'Detective! How's it going? You guys know each other, right?'

The bulky detective stepped towards Renata, his wrinkles multiplying as he strained against the afternoon sun. 'We did a long time ago.' He smoothed his long navy raincoat, chewing on a toothpick straight from a forties noir. 'Maybe long enough for you to have forgotten. It's Hector, Detective Hector O'Connell.' He held out a hand. This one she shook, noticing its slight tremble. She risked a glance at the man. He was right: she barely remembered this greying face in front of her, but she did recognise something pained in that deep-set gaze. Not the beginnings of jaundice-yellowing looking back at her, but something else, something that stared from every mirror

6

she'd ever gazed into. Whatever it was, it didn't stab with the same ferocity as those in the station.

She looked away.

'Your parents have been friends of mine since you were a girl, Miss Wakefield,' he rumbled, scratching his sweat-stricken bald head. 'I'm the officer who contacted you following your mother's death.' Then, lowering his voice, 'This must be a lot to take in. There'll be time to talk in the car, but know that Sylvia Wakefield was loved by everyone in Millbury Peak. We'll find her killer.'

Millbury Peak: a name both vague and clear as crystal.

'I'll follow,' said Quentin. A cigarette had replaced the pen twirling between his fingers. 'Listen, I've rented a little place on the same side of town as your dad's house—' *Little place*. The bestselling horror novelist of all-time had rented a *little place*. Renata glanced at the detective, sensing from him the same cynicism. '—so I'll be nearby if you need anything. Besides, I'll see you at the funeral tomorrow.' He pulled a crumpled packet from his blazer pocket. 'Kola Kube, Ren?'

Ren…?

'Mr Rye,' Hector began, 'I'd ask we reconvene after the service. Sensitivity is paramount at this time, and your presence at Sylvia's funeral may be unwise.'

Quentin nodded, stuffing the packet back into his pocket.

The detective took Renata's meagre suitcase and led her to a battered Vauxhall estate, as tired and worn as its owner. A carpet of empty whisky bottles, no effort having been made to hide them, clinked by her feet on the floor of the passenger side. His sweat-laden brow, trembling hands, and yellowing jaundice eyes suddenly made sense. She looked warily out at Hector.

'Small suitcase, Miss Wakefield. Travelling light?'

'I won't be around long.'

The detective smiled and gently closed the passenger door as she stuffed the book bearing her name into her satchel. Rope brushed her finger.

It would have held. The beam, it would have held.

The slam of the driver's door made her jump, causing further clinking at her feet. Hector glanced at the glass carpet. 'You should know, I just quit,' he said. 'Still to clear those out.' He pulled an old pocket watch from his tatty waistcoat – navy, like the raincoat, shirt, trousers, and every other article of clothing besides his shoes – and popped the cover's broken release switch with his toothpick. 'It made me slow, sloppy. The drink, I mean.' He gazed at the timepiece. 'Going to have to sharpen up if we want justice for your mother.' He stared at the pocket watch a moment longer, then closed the cover and slipped it back into his waistcoat. There was a roar from behind. 'These Hollywood bigshots,' he grunted, pulling himself back to reality as he wrestled the car into first gear, 'need to be seen and heard wherever they go.' Quentin's motorbike revved again. 'Never thought I'd have a Harley tailing this rust bucket.' The estate coughed to life and dragged itself from the car park.

The main road to Millbury Peak passed through twelve miles of lush English countryside beyond the city of Stonemount. Their route ran alongside the ambling River Crove, its waters losing interest intermittently to swerve off course before re-emerging from behind the oaks and sycamores. Renata gazed at the rolling fields. The air, smell, and purity of the green expanses reached to the girl she once was. Her reverie was shaken by the bellowing of Quentin's bike from behind, begging for tarmac.

Hector yanked the gearstick, a cough hacking from his throat. 'It's been decades, I understand that. If I had my way you wouldn't have been called back to Millbury Peak at all. Still, procedure's procedure, as Mr Rye kept telling me.'

'Why wouldn't you want me called back?' Renata tensed. Was she doing this right? She curled her fingers, pushing her long nails into the palms of her hands. 'I'm sorry, it's just...well, I've been away a long time, but she was still my mother.' She hesitated. 'And may I ask, Detective...why is a horror author assisting in a murder investigation?'

Hector jabbed his teeth with the toothpick. 'I was thankful for us having this time together before the funeral tomorrow, Miss Wakefield. There's things you need to hear.' He wiped the pick on the torn polyester upholstery. 'I'd like to be the one to explain the circumstances of your mother's death. I'd rather you had a reliable account to weigh any rumours against. The manner in which your mother passed was somewhat...'

His bulk shifted.

'...brutal.'

Now it was she who shifted. What 'brutal' end could Sylvia Wakefield possibly have met? Locking her eyes on the asphalt streaming beneath them, she cobbled together a mental image of her mother's face. So many memories washed away piece by piece with every passing year, but Sylvia's face remained, even after all these decades. Still, it had been so long. Why had she let the death of a virtual stranger postpone her suicide? How could her end to end all ends possibly get sidetracked by some woman she hadn't even seen in—

Promise you'll be there for him if anything happens to me.

She clenched her fists.

'As for Mr Rye,' Hector continued, 'you have every right to ask why he's here. The nature of the murder requires his presence, Miss Wakefield. You see, from the evidence available at this time, it seems the incident was…how can I put this?' He paused. 'Inspired by him.'

Renata looked up.

'Not that he's a suspect.' He rolled his shoulders as if preparing to jump the tired Vauxhall over a ravine. 'I'll be straight with you. Sylvia – that is, Mrs Wakefield – was found in the church across the fields from their house, the same house you grew up in. You remember the church, yes? The one with the clock tower?'

Clock tower. Renata's lips hinted a smile.

'Miss Wakefield, we have reason to believe whoever's responsible for your mother's death was making a statement.'

She felt like a patient being drip fed. Suddenly she knew how the crawling Harley behind them felt. She took a deep breath. 'Detective O'Connell, yes?'

'That's right, Miss Wakefield. Or Hector, whichever you'd prefer.'

She picked at her beige Aran knit. 'Detective O'Connell, I've come a long way to say goodbye to my mother and to make sure my father's in good hands.' *…my love, they're just bruises…* 'If you don't mind, I'd ask one more thing on top of the kindness you've already shown.' A strand of wool came loose. 'Be straight with me.'

For a fleeting moment she allowed his stained eyes to meet her own. She'd spent a lifetime filling pages with other people's emotions, yet, living the life of a recluse, she had little personal experience of such things. Somehow, through second-hand knowledge gained in a childhood lost to books, her writings had become like the voice-over in a nature documentary, expert narration on something she could see but never touch. That same narrator gave a name to the thing behind this man's eyes, muttering it in her ear: sadness.

'Yes, I apologise,' he said. She felt him flatten the throttle. 'Your mother was found bound on the church altar. I'm afraid...well, I'm afraid she met her end by way of...' He cleared his throat. '...fire.'

The estate lurched as if the man had just broken the news to himself.

'What are you telling me? She was burned?'

'Yes.' The detective straightened. 'The remains of Sylvia Wakefield indicate she was restrained and set alight. However, I must add there's no evidence to suggest she was conscious throughout. No gag of any kind was recovered, implying there was no need to prevent unwanted attention by way of, well, screaming. For this reason I surmise she was rendered unconscious or passed away before her...' He swallowed. '...lighting.'

Her stomach cartwheeled, then whispered: *That's your mother he's talking about, the woman who raised you. Burnt. Like a witch.*

'A note was found near her body, Miss Wakefield. It's this note that links the crime to Mr Rye. His most recent novel, a thriller by the name of *Midnight Oil*, features the strikingly similar scenario of a woman being bound and set alight upon an altar by the story's antagonist, who recites a rhyme throughout the murder. Aside from the method of execution, it is this rhyme that connects your mother's death to Mr Rye's latest work.'

'The note,' she said, eyes cemented to the grey conveyor belt passing beneath, 'my mother's killer left the rhyme at the scene?'

'Midnight, midnight…'

His voice lowered.

'…it's your turn. Clock strikes twelve…'

Her breath caught in her throat.

'…burn…'

She felt her hands tighten around that imaginary wheel.

'…burn…'

She thought of the flames.

'…burn.'

White light exploded from infinite points. She gasped as the pain tore through her head.

'Miss Wakefield, are you all right?' Hector asked. 'I said too much. You understand I just wanted you to hear the truth from a reliable source.'

The motorbike lost patience and powered past them. Renata ran her fingers over the coiled noose in her satchel, stroking the coarse hemp like a cat in her lap. Soon she'd be gone.

Her breathing levelled.

'Sorry, no. I mean, it's alright,' she stammered. 'I'm just tired from the journey.' Her hand stilled on the rope. 'Has Mr Rye been questioned?'

'Yes,' said Hector between chesty coughs. 'He cooperated fully and his alibi checks out. Poor man. Years spent writing the damned thing and some psycho comes along only to use it as a how-to manual.'

Poor man, indeed. Forges a career in torture porn, makes millions of dollars, and finally inspires someone to set fire to an old lady.

'Yes, pity,' she agreed.

'Anyway, he's devastated at the thought of his work having played a part in all this. Personally, I can't stand what he does, but I respect his efforts to put things right. He rented his…' Hector smiled. '…*little place*, and has done everything he can to help with the investigation. He's become quite the regular around Millbury Peak.'

'And my father?' Renata asked hesitantly, rubbing her wrist. 'What's he got to say about Mr Rye?'

The detective's smile faded. 'Still wears that same old vicar garb, but don't be fooled: he hasn't much positive to say about anything these days. That's another reason I wanted to explain to you the circumstances of Sylvia's – I'm sorry, Mrs Wakefield's – death. It's better coming from me than him, I think you'll come to agree.'

She already did. Her entire adult life lay between this day and the last time she'd seen her father, and yet the spectre of Thomas Wakefield had always loomed, like the ghost of a man not yet dead. Through the vast void of time, his fist forever reached.

She squeezed the noose.

…he would never hurt us.

The afternoon sun slid down a cool autumn sky as the Crove, in all its fickle meanderings, finally reconvened with the lurching Vauxhall. Quentin's Harley had long since shrank into the horizon, leaving behind only the coughs and splutters of Renata's ride. She gradually began to notice the lush fields and clear sky lighten in tone.

They were driving into a haze of mist.

Detective O'Connell switched to full beams and squinted through the windscreen. 'Not far now, Miss Wakefield,' he said. 'Just as well. Can't see a bloody thing.'

Shapes formed in the fog. Tight-knit ensembles of cross-gabled cottages and Tudor ex-priories emerged around them, triggering neural pathways long since

13

redundant in Renata. The town was a snapshot dragged into present day, some kind of Medieval-Victorian lovechild refusing to bow to the whims of natural progression. You could practically sense from the rough brickwork and uneven cobbled roads the stubbornness with which this town opposed modernisation of any kind. It was stuck in the past, and perfectly content. The familiar forms of Renata's childhood, of this frozen town, assembled themselves as Millbury Peak unfolded in the mist.

Yet there were still gaps in her memory, scenes spliced beyond repair. There was just one thing of which she was sure: she shouldn't be here. She'd come back on the strength of a promise made when she was just a damned child. What had she been *thinking*? By now, it should all have been over.

It would have held.

'That's Mr Rye's rented house on the left.' He pointed to the Georgian manor rolling past, Quentin's Harley already leant against a side wall. 'I can tell he meant what he said. He really does want to help if you need anything.'

'I'm sure my father and I will be fine, Detective.'

Their route was leading out the east side of Millbury Peak when she spotted a stone finger pointing to the sky. Renata's eyes widened. The clock tower dominated the fog-drenched fields.

Hector glanced over. 'Must be a lot of memories.'

'Yes,' she replied.

And yet so few.

Detective O'Connell shut the engine off outside the house and heaved the handbrake with both hands. Renata pulled the book from her satchel.

'A gift?' asked Hector.

She looked at the thin paperback. 'I thought my father might like to see one of my novels.'

She felt the detective's gaze linger on the book in her hands. He scratched his stubble. 'Like I said, your parents are old friends of mine. I watched your father's health decline, his body wither, the untreated cataracts turn him blind. Thomas is not the man you knew. Although in many ways...' He glanced at the house. '...he's exactly the same.'

She stuffed the novel back into her bag and smiled at the dashboard. 'Well, I suppose I can't expect a blind man to get too excited over a book.'

'I wouldn't expect your father to get excited over anything, at least not in a good way.'

She stepped out of the passenger door onto the gravel track and stared at the towering monstrosity before her, part of her begging to get back in the car and escape to somewhere else – anywhere else. She tightened her coat.

It was a memory made real. The two-storey Victorian farmhouse had been acquired long ago by the parish for use as the town vicarage, lying conveniently close to both Millbury Peak and the church a few fields over. The struts of the wrap-around porch had seemed past their prime when Renata was a girl; now, the boards and beams resembled mildew-ridden sponges, with each of the roof's wooden shingles seemingly ready to fall to the ground with a splat.

The entrance, bay windows, veranda: all irrationally tall. The entire house looked stretched like an absurdist caricature. It dominated the fields, both a monument and a tomb. Most of all, the thing was spooky, an image of cut-and-paste cliché from a Quentin C. Rye dust jacket. *The*

Dreaded Ghost House of Doom. Or something.

Hector set down Renata's suitcase and joined her in the shadow of the house. 'I won't get in the way of your reunion,' he said. 'I'll be over to drive you to the funeral tomorrow.'

She stole a glance. *Sadness*, that expert narrator muttered again. She jerked her gaze back to the house.

'I really am sorry,' he said, voice low. 'Sylvia was an admirable woman. Mr Rye does want to assist any way he can, and I'd like to extend the same offer.'

'Thank you, Detective. I'll remember that.'

'You have a life outside of Millbury Peak, Miss Wakefield,' he whispered. 'No one will judge if you return home after the funeral.'

'I have to ensure my father's wellbeing,' said Renata, rubbing her hands. They were clammy from the journey and could do with a good wash. 'Once my brother and I have arranged care for him, I'll be leaving.'

It'll hold.

Hector's eyes dropped. 'Miss Wakefield, Noah won't be coming.'

She straightened. 'He won't be attending the service?'

'Actually, it's unclear whether your brother will be coming to Millbury Peak at all.'

She bit her lip. 'Why?'

'It was another officer who spoke with him, so I didn't get all the details. Family commitments or something.'

As excuses to dodge your own mother's funeral went, 'family commitments' was pretty rich. Like everything else in this town, her memories of Noah were vague. There was enough, however, to render this behaviour all too believable.

'I see,' she said through clenched teeth. 'Nevertheless,

16

I'm glad you understand I may not be staying long.'

She felt him level his gaze.

'Yes. You should leave.'

A sharp wind blew up her back. Before she could respond, the stocky detective was trudging back to his car, slamming the driver's door, and turning on the ignition. He rolled down the window.

'My regards to Mr Wakefield,' he said. Then, in a hushed tone, 'Remember, I'm here.' The rusted estate lurched into the fog. She took a deep breath.

The woman looked up at the house.

2

The house looks down at the girl.

It's like a scary face, maybe even scarier than Mr Farquharson's when she hadn't done her homework, or Mrs Crombie's when she caught her snooping around her garden, or Father's when he's having an angry day. Come to think of it, maybe not scarier than Father's. His could get SUPER scary.

But the house is like a scary face, that's for sure. There's loads of windows – not too many to count, but maybe too many to count on one hand. There's two above the porch, glaring at the little girl like a pair of eyes. The front door is a mouth, ready to gobble her up.

Anyway, it's definitely scary, and not the kind of surprise she was hoping for when Mother said Father was waiting in the car to take them somewhere. No ice cream, no penny chews, no trip to the funfair. They have popcorn at the funfair, that's what she's heard. Not that she knows much of that kind of thing, but the funfair would definitely be better than this big weird house. Besides, she might only be five-and-a-half, but she still hasn't missed the fact everything's been packed into cardboard boxes the past few weeks. She has a pretty good idea what's happening, has done for a while. She just wishes they'd spill the beans instead of treating her like…well, a five-and-a-half-year-old.

SURPRISE!

Nope, that's not what Father had said, maybe like you'd say to a five-and-a-half-year-old when you're about to take her to the circus or the beach or the funfair with the popcorn.

Instead he'd just made that gruff snorting noise that always made her nervous but also snigger a little inside 'cause that's the noise donkeys make 'cause she'd seen one in a field near school once and she even thought Father looked a bit like a big stern donkey sometimes but she wouldn't say that to his face 'cause she knew what happened when you said much of anything to his face 'cause Mother sometimes did and one time the little girl had been hit by the netball at school and it really hurt and that's probably what Father did to make the bruises appear on Mother's face – a big fat netball right on the nose. Bop.

'What do you think, love?' asks Mother with that wide encouraging smile of hers. The girl marvels at the woman's perfectly arranged hair. How does she get it so perfect? Mother squeezes her hand. The girl loves it when she squeezes her hand. 'What a big house! Think of all the places to play!'

There's a duck pond at the other house, the house called home, and she's wondering if it's coming with them. She's too scared to ask so she just pops a big smile on her face and peers around, trying to find a good pond-spot for when it gets unpacked. She says a quick little prayer in her head, asking Jesus to make sure the pond is brought along.

Father seems more interested in the big glass crucifix that usually sits on the table where other kids might have a TV but where Father has a big glass crucifix. The boxes were thrown in the back of the car like Mr Chisolm throws the squishy mats back into storage after gym class, but that big glass crucifix, oh, it sat in Father's lap the whole way here. That's what he seemed to care about most on the drive. That, and the big creepy painting of the water and the sad faces. She was pretty disappointed to see that hadn't been forgotten. If he was going to leave anything, it should've been that. Or the stupid bookcase he'd had moved in before they even got to see the place.

'Looks lovely, Mother!'

Father sets down the big glass crucifix and fiddles with the front door, his hands twitching and quivering – always twitching and quivering. Soon, the house's mouth is all wide open like a big old train tunnel. Steam trains go straight into those tunnels, they don't even slow down! The girl always found that funny 'cause she slows down whenever she goes through a door 'cause of that time she went through one too fast and BAM, there was Mother crying and Father yelling and who wants to see that? Then again, steam trains probably don't have mothers and fathers, so they don't care.

Father's red hair is all shiny in the sun. He stands next to the big old open mouth with the big glass crucifix next to him on the ground. He's looking down at her, tapping a single finger against the side of his thigh, and he wants her to go in and the little girl wishes she had a steam train 'cause right now she's not feeling too cheery about walking into that big old mouth.

Trains are brave. Maybe she'll be brave.

Maybe she'll be a train.

So Mother squeezes the little steam train's hand and off she goes, full steam ahead, 'cause that's the only direction big brave trains go.

Choo-choo!

Soon the little engine is puff-puff-puffing ahead and nope, Mother's not even holding her hand any more 'cause she's chug-chug-chugging all on her own, heading straight for that big tunnel. Trains are brave. Trains aren't afraid of some stupid old house.

The little train tears up the porch's three steps 'cause that's what trains do. Well, they don't really go up steps, but this is a special train. Three steps is nothing!

Except there's a fourth.

The little engine clips her wheel and tumbles to the ground. She bashed her whistle on the step but that's okay 'cause the whole thing's sort of funny anyway.

Oh, and she fell into the crucifix. It's in a zillion pieces now.

That's not so funny.

The gruff old donkey starts huffing and puffing and his jaw is sticking out further and further and his hands are quivering more and more and his face is turning red as a balloon and he scoops the trembling little train under one arm and off they go into that big old mouth and Mother's shouting but Father slams the house's mouth shut and it's locked now so Mother stays outside and the little steam train's on the floor and Father's staring down at her and she doesn't feel much like a brave little train no more. There he is, see? Standing over her, fists clenched.

'New house, new rules,' he says.

Gruff-gruff goes the donkey.

'By the Holy Book, by the sacred plight of our Lord and Saviour, that woman shall give me a son. And YOU shall bring upon yourself the solemnity of the meek.'

Bang-bang goes the door.

'Do you have any idea how long it took her to give me YOU?'

Waah-waah goes Mother.

'Lower thy head.' He presses her face into the rough wooden floorboards. 'Lower thy spirit before God, child, and offer upon Him a change in will, a strengthening of service.'

Flutter-flutter goes a little moth, landing next to her face.

'Change in will, strength of service. SAY IT.'

No more coal for this little engine.

'Chay-chay-change in...Father, please! You're hurting—'

'CHANGE IN WILL, STRENGTH OF SERVICE.'

'Change in...in will...'

'STRENGTH. OF. SERVICE.'

'Streh-streh...' The girl chokes on the floorboards. *'...strength of service.'*

'Yes.' Her father lowers his face to hers, his red hair not so shiny out of the sun. *'Humble thyself before His will, girl. This house shall be our salvation. Here, our family will grow. Once she finally fulfils her function, once she gives me my son, he shall grow into a man under this blessed roof.'*

His eyes cut into her.

'And YOU, my child...'

Like knives.

'...shall learn your place amongst the meek.'

Why are they like knives?!

'Now, get up. But forever keep your head to the ground. Find your place amongst the meek, girl, where you belong.' He raises a twitching, quivering hand, its fingers slowly clenching.

'Tell me you see, Renata.'

Choo-choo goes the fist.

3

There was a constant in Millbury Peak: pure, wholesome tradition, running through the town's history and into its present like an arrow. Change was not on the menu. The small but fervent council had devoted three years to challenging and eventually overruling the proposed development of an industrial estate on its south-east corner, an orgy of concrete that was the complete antithesis to this thread of tradition so vehemently held by its residents. The rabid little consortium never once backed down, tirelessly standing guard over the town like a pride over its cubs.

Traditional values kept Millbury Peak on the straight and narrow as generations of townsfolk dogmatically followed in the footsteps of their forefathers, at times fanatically defensive over their treasured sense of unity. Don't come a-knockin' with anything on your mind other than the local crochet club or the biannual gardening gala and you'll get on just fine.

And today, as autumn sank and winter rose, something neither regular nor rare for the East Midlands maintained a stubborn watch over the town and its surrounding grassy planes: the mist remained.

The small congregation huddled tight as crowds of headstones kept a solemn watch through low-hanging fog. The group would have liked to be larger, but Thomas Wakefield, his unseeing eyes gazing aimlessly into the mist from his rusty wheelchair by Renata's side, insisted on a modest gathering. He also demanded the service be held in the cemetery surrounding the decrepit, now abandoned church in which he'd spent his life giving impassioned sermons before retirement. This was all in spite of the still pimple-faced Edwin Ramsay's – Thomas's successor as town vicar – protestations, for whom the newly built replacement in the heart of town was Millbury Peak's ticket to modernisation. A wish shared by no one.

The eager young cleric had taken over as vicar after Mr Wakefield's declining health tore him from his charge. The new church, which replaced the crumbling relic overlooking today's humble burial, was Ramsay's brainchild; five minutes with the rosy-cheeked clergyman was enough to witness his pride in the pale, plasterboard facility bubble over like champagne. Thomas Wakefield's glass, however, was very much empty. His decision regarding the ceremony's venue had been final. He insisted on a great many things on a great many days, usually from his loyal wife, Sylvia – until she'd been burnt alive upon an altar barely thirty yards away.

Every breath Renata drew was a terror, with so much as a twitch of her finger feeling like an announcement of her presence. She kept her gaze fixed on the rippling grass, away from the eyes – those carving knife-eyes – eyes that speculated, judged, concluded.

Where's she been all these years?
Is she even bothered?
She could at least shed a tear.

Not for the first time during the service, she risked a glance above to make sure the clock tower remained. Sure enough, her childhood friend was still there, looming over the crowd. It hadn't abandoned her, not like the others.

The vicar's monotonous drawl droned on while the

police tape over the church's sealed entrance fluttered noisily in the wind, a hyena cackling from the sidelines.

'As in life, so in death, Sylvia Wakefield shall inspire us to live our lives fully and with courage…'

The coffin sunk with a terrible creak.

'…and upon those who adored her most, let God grant solace in His promise of reunion. For in all the Wakefield family have endured, all they have lost—'

Thomas snorted, his blind eyes locking on Ramsay.

'—uh, their place in Heaven is ensured. I ask the friends and family of this cherished woman to bow their heads for Sylvia Wakefield's favourite prayer.'

There was a bellowing roar.

The Harley skidded to a halt on the track, spraying dirt into the face of a stone cherub. Despite Thomas's drowning in the fraying, black robes of his old cassock, Renata was still able to detect the tightening of his emaciated frame. His face glowed red.

Like a balloon.

'What is that accursed racket?' he spat.

Quentin stepped off the bike and approached the congregation amid tutting and shaking heads. He knelt in front of the elderly man. 'Mr Wakefield,' he announced with clichéd US theatricality, 'sorry for interrupting. I'm here to pay my respects to what I'm told was an awe-inspiring woman, an angel who—'

'Get this *beast OUT OF HERE*,' roared Thomas. Spit dotted Quentin's glasses.

The young vicar lowered his prayer book. 'Mr Wakefield,' he said, 'Mr Rye consulted with me before the funeral and I gave him my blessing. He feels profound remorse for his novel playing any part in Sylvia's death, and has expressed a deep desire to—'

'The man's a damned *hatemonger*, Ramsay!' Trembling fingers tugged at his yellowed clerical collar as he spoke. 'With God as my witness I want this foul soul *away* from my wife.'

Quentin rose, wiping his glasses. 'Mr Wakefield's wish is my command,' he said, smiling at the shocked faces. 'I'll leave you folks to it. But know this.' He scooped a handful of dirt and held it over the open grave. 'I'm gonna do everything I can. Sure, I don't know who did this, and I can't give Thomas and Renata back their beloved Sylvia...' The dirt trickled from his fingers. '...but that doesn't mean I can't help make things right.'

He looked to his audience, shaking the remaining dirt from his hand.

'I'm keeping on my rented accommodation in Millbury Peak. My production company's gonna film the latest movie adaptation of my work right here in your magnificent town.'

Jaws dropped.

'We're talking big-budget here, guys. Trade, jobs, recognition. It'll bring all these things to Millbury Peak. Nothing can replace Sylvia,' he looked at Renata, 'but that won't stop me giving something back.'

'Out...*NOW*,' exploded Thomas, before breaking into a coughing fit. Chatter erupted.

'He can't do this—'
'Nobody wants him here—'
'Mr Wakefield's wife just died—'

Renata, paralysed with terror, watched Quentin walk silently to his bike. The prattle was suddenly decimated by another roar, this time from the tower as its bell tolled noon. She turned her eyes to the great clock face of the stately stone column, then, glancing back down, met

Quentin's eyes as he revved the engine. He flashed a gentle smile before tearing down the track back towards Millbury Peak.

'Father,' she'd said, 'it's been a long time.'

Their reunion had been blunt. She'd found Thomas alone in front of the dead fireplace, save for the decrepit grey mongrel in an immobile heap by his side. The rusted tag hanging from its collar read the name 'Samson', the same name transferred to every grey mongrel Thomas had owned through the years. She wondered what number he must have been on now. Samson Mark VI? Grey mongrel replaced by grey mongrel. If only everything in life was as simple as Samson.

Ramsay had been taking care for the former vicar prior to Renata's arrival, before terminating his duty and leaving the responsibility of her welcome home party to the old man and his senile canine companion. She'd froze before approaching the gaunt figure in the wheelchair, horrified at the pastiche of memories that was her childhood home – or, more specifically, horrified at what now encased the home.

The minimal décor still functioned only in painting a picture of a home, not creating one. In this respect, little had been removed or added since she last stood in these wide open rooms, with mainstays such as the heavy doors and thick oak shutters having proved immutable through the passing decades, not to mention the grandfather clock by the door, its hands now dead, the eternal ticking of its pendulum silenced. The main divergence from memory, and the source of Renata's horror, was the house's state of uncleanliness. Corners where Sylvia's duster once obsessively frequented were now pinned with festering cobwebs, while dust floated from the Persian rug as Renata crossed the hall. The door handles even left a sticky residue on her fingers, a thin scum presumably covering much of the house. She'd frantically wiped her hand on her long pleated skirt.

So much out of place.

The week since her mother's passing wouldn't have been sufficient for this degree of filth to take hold; Sylvia Wakefield had quit her compulsive cleaning long ago. Aside from her mother's obvious abandonment of a once manic cleaning habit, the damp-plagued ceiling and mildew-stained walls betrayed the presence of issues beyond the neglect of routine housekeeping duties. The house was a shadow of its former self.

Two whitened orbs had shot at her, glaring blankly, then resumed their vacant lazing in their eye sockets as she'd approached the armchair. The blindness of his eyes should have been a relief, but Thomas Wakefield didn't need sight to put her on edge.

'It's good to see you,' she'd said, dropping *A Love Encased* into a brimming wastepaper basket. Her pale face tightened in disgust as a cockroach scuttled over the binned book. She'd closed her eyes and thought of those white walls. So clean, so orderly. Everything in place.

'I was sorry to hear what happened,' she'd continued, eyes still shut. 'Mother's at peace now.' Peering through half-closed eyelids, she'd seen the man's face twitch, more as if recalling a forgotten detail than his deceased wife. 'I'm going to care for you, Father,' she'd continued, 'until we can arrange something more permanent.'

Was now the time to ask about her brother, Noah? Her father's leathery lips pursed. As part of a lifelong habit, one of his ragged fingernails tapped and scraped out some frantic pattern on the arm of his chair like a confusion of meaningless Morse code.

The lips tightened. The finger sped up.

Perhaps later.

She'd finally managed to coax something from the old man when enquiring as to the following day's funeral arrangements – who would speak, was he acquainted with the minister, why hold it a stone's throw from where his wife's flesh melted from her bones just a week prior (well, maybe not that part) – to which he'd grunted some names and times and Bible verse numbers. His biblical utterances made her shudder. Bible studies had ended for Renata long ago, Baby Jesus having checked out of her life the same time as everyone else. That didn't stop his mention jolting her like a defibrillator.

Suddenly she'd noticed the ghostly condensation following her father's words. Her disgust at the state of the place had seemingly overwritten her sense of temperature. She'd knelt by the hearth, Samson watching through one half-open eye, and started a fresh fire. Flames lit the musty room, giving the man's cracked face a warm glow. It was then the reality of whom she was knelt before dawned upon her.

Despite the atrophied muscles of his trembling, cadaverous form, the core of Thomas Wakefield remained, the part which caused grown men to hold their tongues and divert their gaze. The underbite protruded even further in his old age, seemingly reaching up for those wild, arched eyebrows – eyebrows of the same faded copper as the thin smattering of hair on his scabby head. His face looked like it had been smashed then glued back together, a roadmap of wrinkles consuming every inch of skin. As for his once-broad shoulders, they'd shrivelled to resemble a scrawny clothes hanger upon which sat his quivering head in place of a hook. The tattered clerical collar hung loose around his throat, beneath which threadbare robes sagged over a wasted body. Youth had abandoned Thomas totally. Although his shell was in tatters, the same man from her childhood lurked inside, fingers forever locked in that twitching fist. Her mother had made her promise to take care of this man should anything ever happen to her, but all Renata saw in that reeking armchair was a monster.

And tonight, the crispy remains of Sylvia Wakefield cast to the earth, here they were, father and daughter. With the carrots cut and potatoes peeled, Renata stood simmering water over the hot stove, staring into a bubbling oblivion. She stepped to the sink and turned the tap. Rubbing her hands under steaming water, she thought of the coffin, pressed down this very moment by six feet of soil. That sweet six feet should have been hers, it was meant to be hers, yet somehow her mother had taken her place, and she'd taken her mother's place: by the stove, cooking for a monster.

It would have held.

Stonemount Central crept back into her mind. The thought of those eyes – those watching, scrutinising eyes – caused her heartbeat to quicken, her mouth to dry. She forced her thoughts back to those long, white corridors. Those sweet, serene corridors…

She calmed.

It hadn't always been this way. Once, she'd been indifferent to the presence of others. She'd lived happily outside the waters of her mind, introversion a concept of no consequence. Everything had changed when her father moved them to the new house. The first time he'd raised his fist to the girl marked her permanent relocation to these waters, the never-ending narrative of her thoughts becoming her only place of peace.

Time marched on and reality transposed from the outside in. Thoughts and dreams and stories became the only plane in which she felt sane, her head breaking the water's surface only when unavoidable.

Will you please pay attention in class?

The waters would part.

What did you learn in school today, girl?

She'd peer out.

My love, they're just bruises. He would never hurt us, not really.

Back under she'd go.

It was this introversion she had to thank for her profession; her life as a novelist was down entirely to the waters of her mind, her font of fiction. This career in romantic literature was, in turn, to thank for her life of reclusion. It was also responsible for her sole experience of that thing called *love* – not that *that* had ever shown itself outside the pages of her paperbacks.

By the time they'd told her she was finally well enough to conclude her years in hospital following the crash, it had been obvious to all she was destined to live apart from the world, away from the pain that plagued her when around other human beings. Five of her novels had been published before even leaving care, and these provided her with sizeable unspent savings. *Options*, her doctors had called them. The option she'd suggested had been received surprisingly well, so long as she found her way back for regular checkups when instructed. What she'd proposed may even be *for the best*, they'd said. They were right. It had been for the best.

A two-hundred-year-old cottage on a secluded, unpopulated island in the Outer Hebrides off the west coast of Scotland – unnamed, save for the unofficial title afforded by neighbouring islands: Neo-Thorrach. Gaelic for 'infertile', the nickname originally referred the island's inability to grow anything of any value to anyone, leading to its lack of habitation. Once word got around of the strange hermit lady in residence upon Neo-Thorrach, the name took on a dual meaning as the bored children of the islands concocted stories of the woman. The 'Neo-Thorrach Buidseach', she came to be called. The 'Infertile Witch'. She was no witch, though. Far less glamorous. The sole inhabitant of Neo-Thorrach was nothing more than a second-rate romance writer who needed to be alone with her thoughts and live out her days at her Adler typewriter. Away from the eyes.

Now, in the presence of just two blind eyes, Renata and her father dined in silence. She ate little, her decade and a half of hospital food having permanently crippled her appetite in the years since. Her courage to mention Noah remained as absent as her hunger.

Thomas's shaking grew worse as the evening wore on. She sat watching his trembling frame, curling her fingers into a fist to stab uncut nails into the palms of her hands. She looked at his twisting, yellowed talons. Maybe they weren't so different, after all. Had she intended to give herself a few more decades, could this have been a window into the future she'd planned to abandon? It didn't matter. Soon, nothing would matter. Disease and degeneration had picked away at her father through the years like a fussy eater, but something with a far greater appetite had torn into Renata. Thomas's flesh was on a steady decline, but Renata's once creative mind was ravaged; somewhere along the line, her gift for writing had flown from the tiny island of Neo-Thorrach, never to be seen again. For days at a time she'd sat at that typewriter, the rain and gales battering the stone walls of her cottage as doggedly as her publisher's written demands for more cheap romance.

There was no escaping it. Inspiration had abandoned her.

As her ability to write had dissolved, so had her bank balance. Inhabiting an uninhabitable island was an expensive deal. Generator and purifier repairs were costly, not to mention food and fuel deliveries, forever left in an agreed location away from the cottage so as to maintain her reclusion. A private courier had even been required so as to be able to correspond with her agent and publisher. Manuscripts out, cheques in. That had been the arrangement, until the manuscripts stopped sprouting from her aged Adler. Then the cheques were replaced with demands for contract fulfilment. A couple of failed novels and the correspondence finally ended following one final 'don't write us, we'll write you'.

And that was that. The writing ended and the debts began. She'd tied that noose as an alternative to being forced into bankruptcy, into offices and appointments, into repayment plans and probably a job in the *real world*. But the noose was put on hold following the detective's letter. She'd have skipped the funeral had it not been for the promise. Her mother had gone through years of hell for her, and the responsibility of honouring the dead woman had possessed her like a demon. But where had that damned promise landed her? Back in this house after nearly thirty years with one of the parents who'd left her to rot in that hospital. She shouldn't be here. She ran a finger over the outline of the rope crammed into the front pocket of her mother's apron.

It'll hold.

She knelt by the hearth, considering whether to restart the fire as Thomas's unseeing eyes bored into the back of her head from his armchair. She turned and flicked a dirty-grey moth from a cushion before perching on the sofa. The moths had been a staple of the house for as long as she could remember, an enduring torment for Sylvia whose relentless cleaning had done nothing to dissuade their stubborn residency. Their place of nesting had always remained an enduring mystery, the pursuit of which her father strictly forbade.

She cast her eyes to the sprawling oil painting above the mantelpiece. The imposing spectacle had been a childhood horror; waves clawed at screaming men and women as they fought for higher ground, their expressions of dread detailed to perfection. As a girl, Thomas had ensured her complete understanding of the scene's depiction: the Great Flood, rising to rip the accursed mortal coils from these vile sinners.

Her father was infatuated with the thing. He reserved a special look of adoration for the painting, one which only his beloved Noah, and maybe the latest Samson, ever found themselves on the receiving end. However, behind that wooden, fixed smile, Renata's mother had held a very different sentiment for the framed flood, a sentiment which idled just outside the facility of Renata's recollection.

Her thoughts were interrupted by Thomas's spluttering. They'd sat in silence for hours, the fire now reduced to glimmering embers. She instinctively glanced at the grandfather clock, only to find its hands frozen in the same place as when she'd arrived.

'It's late,' she said, working an antiseptic wipe over her hands. 'Sorry, Father. I don't know where the time went. I'll get your medication.'

Renata made for the hallway and ascended the creaking wooden staircase, cringing as the hem of her ankle-length skirt hung dangerously close to the grimy steps. She glanced down the gloomy hall to Noah's room at the far end, then squeezed into the small lavatory on the landing. She took the opportunity to give her hands a quick wash and adjust her hair grips, then opened the medicine cabinet. A pharmacy's worth of bottles and blister packs awaited her, many of which bore the same name: Dexlatine. The muscle relaxant, as a note left by Ramsay had explained, was less a sedative and more a paralysis potion, a single pill having the ability to calm Thomas's shaking body and, once the drug had time to take effect, subtly freeze his muscles into a motionless state. A tub of Vicks, bottles of painkillers, and packets of sleeping pills filled the remainder of the shelves, the latter of which would ease the mind inhabiting the paralysed nerves into unconsciousness. The medications were a drastic measure, but his temper was savage enough at the best of times. No one wanted to see how much worse it could get when sleep deprived.

Renata hurried back to the living room with Thomas's dose of Dexlatine. She hoped it would ease the journey to the master bedroom, but she was slight of frame and the steep stairs proved a struggle. It was like carrying a downed climber the wrong direction to safety; how her mother accomplished the feat she'd never know. Stored on the landing was a second wheelchair in which she wheeled him to the bathroom. She had no trouble translating the scorching scowl he gave her at the offer of assistance.

The transfer of Thomas into his nightclothes was an awkward affair, during which he kept his cloudy eyes locked straight ahead on the discoloured wallpaper behind Renata. She pulled the sheets over him, wincing at the feel of the filthy fabric, and sat on the end of the bed, watching the quivering covers settle.

She placed a sleeping pill in his mouth and held a glass of water to his coarse lips. He swallowed then let out a long, rasping sigh. She looked down at the blister pack and bottle of pills in her hands. Her mind wandered back to hospital, back to that pure, perfect white. How she missed those corridors, those empty, endless—

'What is it?' he croaked suddenly.

Renata looked at him. 'Father?'

'Tell me what it is you want to say, girl. You've been stuttering like a freak all evening.' Saliva hung from his lips like liquid stalactites. 'Out with it.'

She glimpsed the man she used to know, still manning the cockpit of this ruined vessel. 'I...well, Father, I...'

'Lord, have mercy,' he said. 'The girl babbles like her mother.' Renata jolted as dynamite suddenly exploded from the frail old man's mouth. '*SPEAK.*'

She took a deep breath and threw a fresh shovel-load into the little engine's furnace.

Choo-choo.

'Father,' she began, fingering her jersey, 'sorry, but...I was hoping to ask you about, well...' Another shovel-load. '...about Noah.'

In a Quentin C. Rye scary story, such a scene may have been embellished with the pattering of rain against the window, maybe some thunder and lightning for good measure, or the shadows of branches reaching across the room like bony claws. In this scary story, however, the evening was calm and fresh, the room well-lit and claw-free, yet the moment froze as if on a triple dose of Dexlatine. Within this paralysed second, she waited.

'I expect you'd like to know when he'll be joining us. I expect you'd like to know when he'll be arriving…'

'Well, I mean—'

'…so YOU can leave.'

'I'm sorry, Father. I just—'

'Let me tell you what *I'd* like to know, girl.' He struggled to his elbows, fighting the paralysis already taking hold. '*I'd* like to know why God gave me a *girl*, one who soiled my family with nothing but anguish and misery.'

She stepped back as the monster emerged.

'*I'd* like to know,' he snarled, 'why after all these years of service, our heavenly Father took from me the only righteous thing in my life.' His crooked fingers tried to reach for her but were held back by the medication, an invisible protector. 'Except I already know the answers, child. I know because the Almighty has granted them upon me through the unfolding of tragedy – the tragedy of my family.'

Renata stumbled into the half-open door.

'He has revealed to me that this family…' His milky eyes swelled towards her, a torment on her flesh. '…is *forsaken*.'

Outside, the fields swayed gently in the placid breeze. Although it would return, the mist eased its watch for the night, the clear, crisp moonlight blanketing the calm comings and goings of the meadows surrounding the house. The clock tower was audible from across the pastures, tolling the midnight hour.

Renata's hand gripped the doorframe. She watched in

terror as the skeletal shape of Thomas Wakefield gave off a violent spasm, before finally sinking into the mattress. He stretched his face in her direction as he deflated, his jaw extending with unnatural elasticity.

'Change in *will*…' he hissed.

Tears stung.

'…strength of *service*.'

4

One

She flattened the pedal.

Two

Flames flew past. Her hands, dripping with some sort of slick, jet-black oil, tightened around the wheel as she bore witness to the dying throes of all, a world collapsing.

Three

A white light of pain struck with every count, that old familiar pickaxe to her brain. She pushed the engine through fire.

Four

A clatter from beneath as chunks of chassis broke free. The sound of tumbling metal faded behind her.

Five

The flesh of her blackened hands melted into burning vinyl.

Six

She threw the vehicle into a blank canvas of fog. She looked at the passenger seat. Sure enough, there was the spade, red as blood.

Seven

The air became searing smoke.

Eight

She glanced at the lava crawling on the floor beneath her seat.

Nine

The windows smashed, glass flying in scorching shards. She craned her neck to the sky. The magma now raged like waves across the curvature of the atmosphere.

Ten

She whipped her head back inside as fire rained from above. The surrounding fields erupted.

Eleven

Then the shape appeared, right on cue. That vague, fluid, yellow shape. It loomed in the fog ahead, unmoving. Her entire being thrust the engine harder into the mist, yet the spectre remained fixed and unwavering from its station.

It began to resemble a figure.

Twelve

She recoiled in agony as the ice pick inside her head continued swinging with each count.

The blazing sky became an ocean of flames falling from the heavens, a mighty, incurved belly finally released in a parachute of fire. The car broke apart around her, falling away piece by piece. The spade gave itself to the inferno as the vehicle's frame crumbled, retiring into its own fiery wake. Her hands continued to drip their black, sappy liquid.

And still she flew towards the yellow apparition.

Thirteen

Renata awoke.

She lay on the child-sized bed in her old room, feet sticking out the end. She stared at the ceiling. Soaked in sweat and gasping for air, she thought of the dream.

Too many years to count: that's how long it had dominated her nights. Its intensity was overpowering, always leaving a vivid trauma upon awakening. Worst of all were the stabbing pains in her head throughout. Thirteen, always thirteen.

She'd put the apocalyptic nightmares down to a cognitive remnant of the crash, fractured memories haunting her. Her doctors had told her it was only natural considering how little memory of the accident her amnesia had allowed. A day trip to the coastal village of Hadwell-on-Sea gone wrong, she'd learnt. Then she'd had her run-in with the Quentin C. Rye display at Stonemount Central.

Horror Highway. Glimpsed by chance as a little girl, she hadn't thought of the book for an eternity, but with its burning pickup truck and phantom in the fog, it seemed like a closer fit than anything else. And yet the dream, besides the fire and brimstone, was different – *felt* different. The nightmare didn't feel like a retelling of images from some cheap horror.

She rubbed her eyes then checked the clasped bun at the back of her head, before resetting the usual mass of grips and clips in her black hair. She squinted around the room, dragging the heaped boxes into focus. These four walls once housed columns of precariously stacked romance novels, until one day, along with her mother's collection, they'd vanished. Their sudden removal hadn't been questioned, as was best for everyone.

The cramped space was now a storage room, with overflowing cardboard boxes, crates, and trunks littering nearly all available floor space. A brief investigation had confirmed the missing books of her youth were not included within these assortments of unwanted kitchen appliances, children's toys, and threadbare clothing. It had never felt like her bedroom without the books, but it had never really felt like it with them, either. Likewise, she'd never been able to convince herself this house was home. Decades later, she was still unconvinced.

You didn't forget a thirty-year-old dream, but you learnt to live with it. Besides, reality has a habit of stealing your attention from the artefacts of sleep, particularly when there's an earthquake outside your bedroom window.

It started as a distant growl, but soon grew to seismic rumbling. Quentin's bike? No, too...vast. Broken springs creaked as she rose from the bed and padded across bare floorboards to the window.

The earthquake was a convoy of articulated lorries, struggling along the winding track that led past the Wakefield house. Renata made out the company name plastered across the side of the leading eighteen-wheeler:

RYE PRODUCTIONS

Obviously a man of his word, Quentin appeared to be kick-starting the project he'd promised the people of Millbury Peak. Although now a stranger to the town, Renata still knew the uproar this invasion would cause.

Suddenly, an explosion of light.

She cursed her cranial pains before realising, agony as they were, they'd never thrown her across a room or caused windows to smash.

She gasped with pain at the broken glass pressing into her hands as she sat up. The room was surprisingly silent, apart from the high-pitched buzzing; she swatted at the moth in her ear, until it dawned on her moths don't buzz. Her overdriven eardrums calmed, the chaotic sounds outside replacing the ringing in her head. She struggled to her feet and peered out the broken window, heart racing.

It was a warzone. Flames billowed from the back of the largest articulated lorry at the tail end of the convoy, the drivers and passengers of the remaining vehicles running to aid the two men trapped in its cabin. Renata stood frozen as the panic unfolded, until a second explosion from the same truck forced her back, screaming. She whipped her head round as banging came from downstairs. She threw on her mother's dressing gown and raced for the front door.

'Ren...I mean, Miss Wakefield,' Quentin stammered, standing in the doorway, 'I...I don't...those guys, they're still in the truck. The thing...it just—'

'Mr Rye, I know. I saw everything. What on earth's happening?'

Quentin glanced over his shoulder. 'I got no idea. I was up front riding with one of the sound guys, then I heard the explosion at the back of the convoy. It's Dwayne and Rich, Ren. They're stuck in the cabin.' He placed a foot in the threshold. 'Please, we gotta help them. Your phone...the emergency services, we have to—'

'Mr Rye...'

'Call me Quentin, please.'

A small fire extinguisher sprayed into the inferno, its effect akin to the throwing of a glass of water into a volcano. Howling came from the trapped men inside the cabin as members of the production team tugged on the unmoving doors.

Renata took a breath.

'Come inside, Quentin.'

'If ever a sign were needed,' Thomas choked from his wheelchair at the top of the stairs, 'let this be it.' A droll of biblical mutterings followed, eventually fading down the corridor back to the master bedroom. The grey, immobile hound by the fireplace remained as uninterested as a rug.

Renata handed Quentin a mug of cocoa. 'Sorry about my father,' she said.

'After all I've put his family through? Come on, he could throw me his best right hook and I'd only thank him.' He smiled and crossed his legs. Mickey Mouse socks peeked out from beneath his brown corduroys. 'Luckily for me he doesn't look like he has much of a right hook on him.'

Renata flinched.

Quentin, recrossing his legs, lowered his voice. 'Seems all I've done recently is bring pain to you folks.'

'None of this is your fault.'

More sirens screamed down the country tracks. The cause of the explosion was yet to be identified, but what had been established was that the hoses were only angering the flames further. All efforts seemed to do nothing but goad the fire.

'I can't believe this,' said Quentin, jiggling his foot. 'First Sylvia, now this. I mean, thank God they managed to get those guys out, but they're gonna be messed up.' The mug trembled in his hand. 'They were right, I shouldn't have come here. I did this, Ren.'

She took his cocoa and set it on the table.

People. She was surprised to find she seemed to have a fairly good idea how to act around them. What to say, where to look, how to react; there was nothing natural about it, but really it was nothing more than going through the motions, like writing a character, so long as she could keep a lid on her anxiety. As a teenager she'd thought she hated people, then it dawned on her that she just didn't care for them. Most of all, it was their mindless clamouring for individuality, like children fighting for a place in the spotlight, a feral pack she had no interest in

44

joining.

And yet, inadvertently, she'd claimed a small portion of that spotlight for herself. She'd been an author – a *professional* author. It should have felt good put like that but, despite her passion, it had really been no more than a means to an end, the end in question being the means to live alone on an empty rock surrounded by crashing waves.

And now a simple letter from a simple detective in a simple town regarding a not-so-simple murder had pulled her off that rock and onto a couch next to this man. He, too, was an author, but one whose share of the spotlight vastly dwarfed her own. His writing had been the vehicle for an empire of horror, and with it fame and fortune.

Inspired and poetic, that's how her writing had begun, artistic in its flair and technique – until sales dwindled, leading to her publisher identifying the corner of the market in which Renata could realistically shift most units.

Units. She'd been shocked by the word, but had come to associate it, and the money attached, with the possibility of avoiding a real job with real people. Those 'units' had afforded her the life of a hermit.

Dumb it down, Ms Wakefield! the letter from Damian Abbott at Highacre House Publishing had read, written, she'd imagined, from behind the horizon of a sprawling desk at the top of a skyscraper. *That's the secret. I can see you know what they want, it's just that in your stories, what they want is a little...overshadowed.*

Substance, she'd thought. Overshadowed by *substance*. She'd been won over in the end by this little niche he'd identified for her scrawny romance texts. She'd gone on to turn this dumbing down of which he'd spoke into a veritable art form.

She looked at Quentin, a man on the verge of tears,

and began to wonder if they weren't so different, after all. He dealt in death, she traded in dumbed-down romantic tripe, yet they may as well have been hookers under the same pimp.

Maybe she'd never even had any talent to start with. Her career might just have been the law of averages playing out. Sit a monkey in front of a typewriter and let infinity play out, and the thing'll fart out an airport potboiler eventually. As for all the conversations she'd avoided over the years, all the potential friendships and relationships from which she'd hid, this guy was backdating the whole damn lot. Hell, forty-five and she'd never even been with a man. She'd practically lived the life of a nun.

A tear rolled down Quentin's cheek. He had passion, she'd give him that, but there was something missing in those eyes. What was it?

'Detective O'Connell was right,' she said, fiddling with her sleeve. 'You're doing a good thing by staying, even if my father can't see it.'

Their eyes met.

As an ambulance screamed to a halt by the blast site, as the warzone fizzled down to a by the book clean-up operation, two writers sat side by side on a dusty, worn couch, their eyes meeting for a moment that seemed to stretch beyond time. And as the endlessness of that moment reached on, it dawned on Renata what was missing in these eyes.

No knives.

5

The shouting had reached its climax just before midnight. There'd been a crash from downstairs, followed by an unnerving hush, until the clock tower finally did its thing across the fields. Footsteps creaking up the stairs, the slam of a door, and only a couple more hours of pulling the tear-sodden pillow over her face before the night settled into its silent slumber.

She dare not read. The mere thought of her father spotting the light from her bedroom window upon the grass outside was too grim to bear. What about the curtains? Nah, he might still see it under the door. That brave little choo-choo was decommissioned years ago, now rusting in a junkyard somewhere.

Stupid kid.

Once the yelling had yelled itself to sleep, and from the stomping there wasn't a peep, then the light could go on. Young Renata could finally slip from this world into the pages of a story, except her current novel had run dry during playtime today. She hugs the book to her chest as if it's a kitten trying to leap from her arms. She considers settling for scribbling in her silk-bound diary, the one Mother gave her when she turned nine last year, but that can't offer the escape a story can. Tonight she needs escape.

She hugs the book tighter. The kitten behaves. Instead of just grabbing a new one from the bookcase in the living room, she prefers making a sly exchange. Less attention drawn. She never makes the exchange while her father is still up. The books aren't even his, but still, less attention drawn.

More meek.

She eases open the bedroom door and slips onto the dim landing with all the stealth of one entering a lion enclosure.

Our Father, who art in heaven...

The journey downstairs and into the lounge seems like a Himalayan trek, the staircase an Everest descent. She reminds herself that going down a mountain is easy-peasy. You fly like a kid on a sledge. Definitely the easiest bit.

Or was it the hardest?

...Hallowed be thy name...

In her mind a roadmap long committed to memory emerges from the steps. The staircase is a minefield, the map providing safe navigation through its most treacherous points. One wrong move and it wouldn't be blown limbs flying through the air, but the scream of creaking steps. Then you'd get your blown limbs.

...Thy kingdom come...

The ritual was always the same: hold the book under your chin so you can press your hands against the walls on either side of the staircase in an attempt to somehow displace your weight. Just don't think about dropping the book. Don't think about it, but also don't forget to keep pressing that chin. If the book falls, every landmine littering this wooden Everest blows.

Also, don't forget to pray.

...Thy will be done, on earth as it is in heaven...

She grins as her bare feet touch down silently on the fluffy Persian rug at the foot of the mountain. To the girl, the rug is a field of undisturbed snow, not unlike the kind you'd find at the end of your Himalayan descent. Hers are the first footprints on this winter field, an invisible imperfection imposed upon perfection. She gropes for the living room door, oak and heavy as a bank vault.

...Give us this day our daily bread...

Having turned its handle as quietly as a cat burglar, she prepares to pull.

Change in will.

She swallows.

Strength of service.

What if it creaks? What if it cracks? What if it pops? What if it bashes the wall and wakes Father and...

She swings the stupid thing open.

The light's on.

Her heart hurls up her throat as she's filled with the impending horror of being discovered. Too late to run, too late to hide. The soldier navigated the minefield beautifully, but met her end by accidently shooting herself once home free.

'Rennie?'

'Mother?'

She squints through the low light and sees the woman perched, pouring over some funny looking machine. The vicar's wife quickly adjusts her posture so she's sitting neatly. Every iota of her being is arranged to perfection as assiduously as the house, her clothing impeccable and not a hair out of place. As for that smile, that sweet, rehearsed smile, it never falters. She motions her daughter over. The girl carefully closes the door and tiptoes to the chair in which her mother sits, pregnant belly like a beach ball in her lap.

'Are you trying to wake your father, Rennie?'

She locks her gaze onto her mother's flawless hair and then the woman's tired eyes, trying her best to ignore the bruises. 'No, Mother. I'm thirsty. Wanted some water from the kitchen.' She looks at the machine. 'What's that?'

'This is a typewriter,' she says. 'I write stories with it. Your father doesn't like them much, so let's keep this between us, okay?'

'Can I have a shot?'

The woman pauses. 'You can type one line. No more.'

The girl's fingers poise above the keys, then cautiously begin tapping.

CHANGE IN WILL STREN

Her mother stops her, then gently moves her hands from the keyboard. They stare silently at the keys, the grandfather clock by the door ticking away in the silence, always ticking.

'I'm glad we got this time together, Rennie,' she says. 'Your father went to the doctor about his shaking hands. It seems he has nothing to worry about for now, but things will get worse in years to come.' She runs her fingers through the girl's soft black hair. 'He might need our help in the future, when his condition worsens.'

The girl can resist no longer. She looks at the bruises. 'Like he helps us now, Mother?'

The fingers stop. The smile wavers. 'My love, these are just bruises. He would never hurt us, not really.'

The girl looks down, fiddling with her pyjama sleeves. 'They don't hurt?'

The woman turns her swollen eyelids to the oil painting hanging above the fireplace. Waves lash up like flames at wailing faces. 'You know what that painting is, Rennie?'

'Yes, Mother. It's the Great Flood. I learnt all about it in Sunday school.'

She nods. 'That's right, dear. And you know why God sent the flood?'

The girl flips her Sunday school switch. 'Yeah. Then the Lord saw that the…uh…wickedness of man was great in the earth, and that every in–intent? of the thoughts of his heart was only evil continually. And the Lord was…uh…'

'Rennie, no,' she interrupts. 'That isn't knowing.' The girl looks at her. 'Your grandmother loved art, you know.'

'Your mother or Father's mother?'

'You know your father doesn't speak about his family.' She looks back at the faces screaming skyward. 'My mother. You never knew her, but she was a clever woman. She told me inside every painting there's a thousand more; that, like everything in life, there's lots of ways to see the same thing. That's what makes art such fun, you see?'

The girl's eyebrows arch in pained confusion.

'Listen, Rennie, between you and me, it's a pretty scary painting, isn't it?' A smile surfaces on the girl's face. 'Not to me, because I see one of the other thousand paintings inside it. Your father wouldn't like me saying, but I believe the story of the flood was teaching us something less…scary. I believe in God, but whether "the waters prevailed on the Earth one hundred and fifty days", I can't say. Some would call me blasphemous, most would call me naïve, but I believe the Bible's teaching us something different. Maybe the flood's meant to show us not how to reshape the world with destruction…' She takes her daughter's hand. '…but with love.'

The girl's eyes widen.

'Rennie, precious Rennie, I believe love can reshape a thousand more worlds than some silly flood ever could. A thousand worlds, just like those thousand paintings.'

Her mother's arms feel strong around her, her eyes shining with a courage that hypnotises the girl. The bruises seem to dissolve before her.

'Love, Rennie. Like a flood. That's what gives us real strength. Maybe we all have a little flood in us.'

The girl stares, transfixed.

'So you see, my darling, they're just bruises. He'll never hurt us, not really. Because he can't.'

She pauses, then pulls the girl closer before continuing.

'He wasn't always like this, not when we first married, and he won't be like this forever. He's just like the painting: scary, but the good bits are still in there. Rennie, promise you'll be there for him if anything happens to me. When you grow up you'll leave this town, have your own family, your own life, but he still might need you one day.'

Her mother squeezes her hand. Always at the right times she squeezes her hand.

'The flood, Rennie,' she says. 'Remember the flood, remember the love. Promise you'll be there for him if anything happens to me.'

'Yes, Mother,' the girl says. 'I promise.'

6

She stopped cutting and listened again. The chattering was distant, but unmistakably there.

The clean-up operation had rid the blast site of the shrapnel sprayed from the back of the articulated lorry. Although being treated for third-degree burns at Millbury Peak Community Hospital, the truck's driver and passenger were both in a stable condition. A slightly blackened crater on the road was all that was left of the incident, a reminder of the madness gripping the placid town in weeks past. Thomas's babbling had continued deep into the night following the explosion. This was, his mutterings declared, the end of times. As for Renata, the memory of the blast was putting her even more on edge than usual. Every time that old familiar pain shot through her head she expected her world to erupt in light once again, but it never did. No more trucks, no more explosions.

Now, the following evening, the chaos of sirens and reporters and clattering stretchers was replaced by this far-off chit-chat. Renata set down the fabric scissors beside her needle and thread, planning to resume this tedious repair job on her father's moth-ravaged trousers later, and looked at the snoring man in the armchair.

She'd set aside Thomas's outburst from her second night at the house. Not that it hadn't upset her, but time was limited; find Noah, pass on this damned responsibility to him or his wife or his husband or whoever the hell filled her stranger-brother's life, and get out – of everywhere.

She didn't consider herself 'depressed', and she didn't hate life. The thought of suicide had materialised in her mind in much the same way Millbury Peak had emerged in the mist: first an indistinguishable shape in the fog, then total clarity. It was a tactical escape route, she'd told herself. Find her oh-so-busy brother, (Of course, Noah. It was just a small service anyway. Oh, I know, you can't abandon your commitments. I completely understand.) dump her father, (By the way, here's Dad.) and get out. Leave the debts, leave the dad, leave the knife-eyes. Leave it all. And every extra day that she hung onto, that coiled hemp snake continued its incessant whisperings:

...it would have held it would have held it would have

Laughter broke up the chattering. She stepped over the unconscious Samson to peer through the grimy window and saw two men sitting by the charred crater. After a quick glance at the snoring skeleton in the armchair, she made for the front door.

Detective O'Connell took a swig, then noticed Renata. He quickly handed Quentin the hipflask. 'Miss Wakefield, good evening. We're just—'

'I was just telling the detective the secret of what the C in my name stands for,' Quentin interjected. 'Nothing! Totally random. Just thought it sounded good.' He nudged Hector. 'Bet my ex-wife could think of something though, right?' He held out the hipflask. 'Evening tipple, Ren?'

She eased the door shut. 'How's the investigation coming?' she asked Hector, unsurprised at his return to drink. People were fickle, disappointing. She knew this.

'Well this is just a celebratory drink, actually,' he rumbled, thick fingers pawing an unshaved cheek. 'A one-off. Today was my last day on the force. I'm officially retired.' He jerked forward as a grinning Quentin thumped him on the back and passed the scotch.

'I had no idea. Congratulations, Detective,' said Renata. 'Or is it just Mr O'Connell now?'

His smile faded. He cleared his throat. 'Actually, with your permission, I intend to continue my investigation. You see, I'm afraid I wasn't so…popular within the force.'

'They thought the drink got to him,' Quentin hiccupped.

'Yes, and they were right.' He looked at the crater. 'But they weren't getting the job done and they were holding me back. I'll make better progress without them – or the drink.' He took a long look at the hipflask then passed it to Quentin.

'Forgive me,' said Renata, fingering her sleeve, 'but did you retire just to further this investigation?'

He looked up, the man's weathered face as solid as a mountain. He sighed. 'Like I said, your mother deserves justice.'

The fog thickened around the small assembly. The early evening light was soon replaced with the glow of a full moon. The blackened crater stood out before them.

Quentin stretched, then glanced at his watch. 'Well, Ren, I promised Hector I'd give you folks some alone time to go over the details of what happened yesterday.' His tone dropped as he looked back at the crater. 'I better be going.' He took one last swig before tossing Hector the hipflask. 'Happy retirement, Detective.'

Renata and Hector's efforts to slip into the house unnoticed were in vain. Thomas awoke with a gargled demand for his dead wife.

'Sylvia,' he barked, saliva swinging from his underbite, 'I need my pills. Sylvia, *my pills*.'

'Sorry, Father. It's just me,' said Renata, picking her palm. 'Hector's come to visit. He was hoping to ask us some questions about the explosion outside the house yesterday.'

'Good evening, Thomas. You're looking well,' Hector lied.

'I don't have time for this,' the old man spat. 'Go before the altar where my wife burnt, the same wife whose killer you people are too incompetent to find, and ask your questions to the good Lord.'

Further mutterings snapped from his withered lips, increasingly unintelligible in tone, until his eyelids slowly drooped over their vacant interiors.

'Sorry, don't take it personally,' whispered Renata. 'We'll talk in the kitchen.'

They left Thomas's agonal snoring. Any evening the old man was able to sleep as much as this was a good evening. 'I know it's getting late, so I won't keep you long,' Hector said, heaving his bulky body into a rickety chair by the larder door. He rubbed his hairless head, then straightened. 'Could you start by telling me exactly what you saw yesterday?'

'Well, it was early,' she began, steam rising from the sink as she gave her hands a hurried wash. 'I'd just woken up. I heard a rumbling outside my bedroom window and—'

'Your bedroom,' he interrupted, 'the same room you had as a child? Looking out the front of the house over the road?'

'Yes, I had a clear view of the trucks,' said Renata. She took a seat opposite the man. He watched her yanking at a loose strand of wool from her Aran knit. 'I saw it all, but I'm not sure I can tell you much you don't already know. The largest lorry, it just…well…' She paused, twirling the beige strand around a trembling finger. '…it blew up. I've never seen anything like it. The light, the blast. It came out of nowhere. And the trapped men…' Silence. 'I can still hear their screams,' she breathed.

'Alright,' Hector grumbled, 'I think that's enough.' He leant close enough for Renata to smell his breath. No scotch. 'I'm going to be straight with you,' he said. 'It doesn't take a genius to see the connection between your mother's death and the truck explosion.' He paused. 'Rye.'

'The flask,' she said. 'You didn't really drink from it, did you?'

'He's been nothing but cooperative, but I had to be sure.' The man sat back, toothpick sticking from his mouth. 'Criminals have been the bread and butter of my career, Miss Wakefield. You come to realise they're all the same, really. You grow antennae, develop a sense for them. I knew Mr Rye was genuine from the get-go but, like I said, I had to be sure. I needed him to drop his defences.'

She got up to close the kitchen door. 'So if Quentin has nothing to do with it, what about this connection?'

Hector frowned, stopped chewing for a moment, then recommenced his gnawing of the pick in his mouth. 'That's where it gets tricky. Of course, there is another connection: you.'

Renata blinked.

'Or rather, your family. Sylvia wasn't a random victim and your house wasn't a random blast site. The fact that your mother…' He took a breath. '…met her end on the altar of the church where your father served his whole life, the church a short walk from your family home, suggests both incidents were statements of some kind. I believe this was, as they say, personal.'

'And the note you mentioned left by the body,' said Renata, picking a nail, 'the one with the rhyme from Quentin's book.'

'Like I said,' Hector said under his breath, 'it's tricky.'

The chair creaked as he stood and stepped to the window, the kitchen tiles sticky under his shoes.

Despite his retirement, Hector O'Connell was still dressed for the part – that is, his usual part of oddly-dressed detective. His ill-fitting faded blue waistcoat and shirt buttoned up to the neck – no tie – clung to his hefty mass and made his considerable stomach look like a shrink-wrapped slab of meat. And yet here, under the tattered navy raincoat and apparent disregard for the state of his attire, was a man who moved with the pace of someone who didn't know how to rush, but was always on time. Unhurried and precise, eyes constantly darting from detail to detail, the detective still lived. The pocket watch danced in his unsteady hand.

'There's more,' he rasped between coughs. He turned from the window. 'Miss Wakefield, have you heard of nitrate film?' She shook her head. 'Movies used to be shot on stock made from a compound called nitrocellulose. The stuff was lethal, highly flammable. The lighting of a cigarette on the other side of the room was said to be enough to ignite it. Picture houses regularly went up in flames.' He sunk back into the chair opposite Renata. 'Anyway, this nitrocellulose was eventually replaced with stock made from a less flammable compound called cellulose triacetate, which had fewer self-oxidizing—' He clocked her blank expression and cut the lecture short. 'Easy to get caught up in the details of a case. Apologies.'

'No, you've obviously...done your homework. But if you're saying you think the explosion was caused by this material, then why would the truck be filled with flammable film in the first place? Sorry, what's the theory here? It was placed deliberately?'

'First off, I know the explosion was caused by nitrate film.' He swiped at a moth. 'Fragments of the wreckage have been analysed. Nitrocellulose ignition was the cause of the explosion.'

'Analysed already? It was only yesterday.'

'I wasn't unpopular with *everybody* in the force,' Hector said. 'I still have connections in forensics. I've been told there was a massive payload of the stuff in that truck.' He leant back. 'Miss Wakefield, do you know the name Sandie Rye?'

'Quentin's ex-wife?'

'No, his teenage daughter. Upcoming actress. Starred in several of his films but made the news when Mr Rye let slip to a journalist he'd had a Colt .45 stuck in her mouth for a scene – loaded. I could tell how much he loves his daughter, she seems to be his world, but he related several such decisions he's made during filming in order to...well, that's where he lost me. Something about 'truth', about wanting to introduce true danger to the production.' He cleared his throat. 'The important part is that Mr Rye himself had the nitrate film loaded onto that truck. It's meant to produce a better image or something, but his real reason for shooting with it was to bring this 'true danger' to the film, just like with the Colt. Turns out he's used the stock before. Rustled the feathers of his company's lawyers in the process, too. The question is how, and why, it ignited.'

'Insurance scam? Ignite it deliberately and claim the

loss?' she suggested. Part of her was enjoying this.

'Compared to the kind of cash he makes from his films? Unlikely. Besides, no insurance company would pay out over that kind of flammable material. The truck was effectively loaded with explosives.'

'Coincidence then,' Renata offered. 'The film was unstable, ready to explode, and it did. Just like it was bound to.'

'Safety procedures were in place,' countered Hector. 'A company like Mr Rye's has so many regulations to follow. No, I've been told all procedures were adhered to and the stock was secured to a high degree inside that truck.'

'Then…how?'

Hector reached into his jacket and pulled out what looked like a meteor fragment, charred black and melted in on itself. Hanging from its base was a severed red wire.

She looked blankly at Hector.

'It's the receiving end of a detonator, Miss Wakefield.'

'How long does it take to get an old man his pills?' Thomas demanded. She hurried through and held the glass of water to her father's lips as he struggled the Dexlatine down his tight airway, all the while tapping and scraping that finger at manic, irregular intervals on the arm of the chair.

It was late. Hector had left shortly after returning the charred detonator component to his pocket. She hadn't known what to say. Did someone want Quentin dead? Maybe they'd hit the wrong truck. Did Quentin want someone dead, or was this a publicity stunt taken too far? Maybe someone had it in for Rye Productions. Maybe the *town* had it in for Rye Productions. Could these honest townsfolk really have that kind of terrorism in them? They sure as hell didn't want him around, but they didn't seem capable of blowing a truck sky-high. Regardless, Hector's efforts all came back to the identification of Sylvia Wakefield's killer. He'd even taken early retirement in the pursuit of his cause. Despite the abandoning of his badge, Hector O'Connell was, in Renata's eyes, as much a detective as he'd ever been in their short time together, and she'd let him know:

'Goodnight, Detective,' she'd said before closing the front door. His smile warmed her.

The night was dark, and it was getting darker – just like her future. What savings she had left wouldn't last forever, and it was only a matter of time before the debt collection vultures caught wind of her absconding to Millbury Peak. It was a persistent myth that your work on the shelves of bookstores meant boundless riches, particularly when these bookstores were mostly, in fact, train station and airport newsagents. The Quentin C. Rye display had happened to share the same roof as her skinny paperbacks, but that was all they shared. No, her remaining funds wouldn't last long. More imperatively, she worried that her will to serve under the tyrant that was her father might expire even sooner. Her terror of Thomas Wakefield had never dissipated in all these years, but she was now equally terrified of abandoning him. He was a monster, a dying monster, but he was also her father. She frowned at the tedium of it, the cliché. Unconditional love: you didn't get a say in it. Biological and unstoppable, there was a circuit in her mind programming her to save this wretched creature from dying alone. Her mother, she'd had the strength to stay all those years – probably solely for Renata – and so she would find the strength too.

Had it not been for that damned promise, the rope may

well have had its way by now.

It waited patiently on her person wherever she went, a curled up serpent in her satchel offering solace; another promise, this one to herself. Once she'd arranged a babysitter for her dear old dad she could find a beam strong enough to snap her neck, nice and clean. The key to this sweet finality lay with her infernal brother, Noah. And all the while a cloak of craziness lay over Millbury Peak. A *detonator*?

The evening smiled on Thomas Wakefield, granting him a nap in the festering armchair even without the administration of his medication. Regardless, Renata still gave him his dose when he awoke. She wasn't taking any chances. The Dexlatine wrapped its invisible arms around Thomas's restless nervous system, tightening its grip on his trembling muscles.

He was calm. It was time.

'Father,' she began, chewing her lip, 'I know you don't want to discuss it, but I need to know how to get in touch with Noah. It's been great spending time with you—' she cleared her throat, choking on the lie '—but I have responsibilities, things I need to do.'

Snap, she thought. Nice and clean.

'He's not coming back,' Thomas said. 'If he was, he'd have been at his mother's funeral. He's *gone*.' A bony, liver-spotted hand, apparently still outside the influence of the medication, shot out and grabbed Renata's wrist. He pulled her in.

'Father,' she gasped, 'you're hurting me.'

His blank eyes ceased their idle rolling and locked onto her. 'You,' he breathed. She stared. He wrenched her closer. 'It should have been *you*.'

Pain flashed in her brain. She shook it off and yanked

her arm, Thomas's quivering grip slipping down her wrist. His unseeing glare burrowed into her eyes.

He smiled.

'You and I, we're the same, girl. The curse that's ravaged me is coming for you, for your mind. I feel it in your flesh.'

'Father, I—'

The breath fell from her as he jerked her closer still, their faces now inches apart. Her eyes flicked to her mother's orange fabric scissors on the couch.

'My child, this family is forsaken. The flames finally came for your mother, and death is stripping the life from me...' His leathery smile widened. '...as it will strip the life from you.'

He nodded at the monstrosity above the fireplace.

'A flood is due, girl. Our Lord has a wave reserved for the Wakefields.' His empty eyes bloated. 'It's coming, child. The flood is coming. But for now He shall settle for the souls of our blasphemous clan. We have brought this upon ourselves. This family, cowardly and sinful, has authored its own demise.'

A tear crawled from his eye.

'But my beloved Noah,' he continued fanatically, his trembling hand still locked around her wrist, 'that wave was not meant for him. It was he who was to carry this family's name from damnation. He's *gone*, you foolish girl. *GONE*. So silence that flapping tongue. Swallow those devil-sewn words.'

Soon the woman will run from her raving father like a scolded child. The words will replay endlessly in her mind – *he's gone he's gone he's gone* – as the darkness pulls her upstairs to the room at the end of the hall.

'The evils of this world are more terrible than you

know, insolent whore.' His eyes levelled beyond her, blindly fixed upon a distance unknowable, as if gazing into a hell endured long ago. The finger of his other hand tapped maniacally. 'I have seen things you could not comprehend. I give you my word, the inferno is impending. Its flames shall be that of waves, while deep within your godless core death shall sow its wild oats…'

She'll pry open the door to that room, the door upon which laughing cartoon bears and elephants still spell out the name after so many years:

NOAH

'…the hand of Hell is coming, child…'

The door will creak open to reveal the untouched, unspoilt bedroom of a seven-year-old boy.

'…the hand of *death*. And this hand, I assure you, trembles not.'

7

She doesn't want to put her foot through his skull, but she knows she has to.

Father was strangely calm during the five days Samson went missing. The dog had been let out into the back garden and never came back. As per her mother's instructions, the girl had ran into the surrounding fields calling the mongrel's name, rustling a noisy bag of chicken strips in the hope he'd come bounding through the maize and barley. But Samson hadn't heeded her calls, and the mutt hadn't turned up back at the house for two days short of a week. By that time, the dog seemed to have gone through hell and back, hobbling up to the house on a fractured leg and leaving a dotted trail of blood from his lacerated side. It turned out these injuries were the least of his worries; the real issue lay in the infected, swollen eyelid that refused to open which, Mr Milton the vet told them, had likely been torn on some rusty barbed wire while he was missing. It was (possibly) treatable, so long as they understood Samson would have to endure many months or even years of agony during his recovery. The laceration would need stitches and the leg would never properly set, meaning the dog would struggle even just to walk for the rest of his painful life.

'We'll have a think,' Father had told Mr Milton following the he-may-be-better-off-put-to-sleep conversation. The vet had to inform Mr Wakefield, in a somewhat perplexed tone, that no, he couldn't just 'take Samson home and see how he gets on' – the dog would have to undergo surgery immediately, before embarking on a long, harrowing recovery. Mr Wakefield had resolved to take Samson elsewhere in response to Mr Milton's 'antagonising tone'. The little girl had watched the vet plead with her father to let him put the dog out of his misery, passionately appealing that no animal deserves to suffer the pain that would dominate the rest of Samson's life.

In the end, Father had not taken Samson 'elsewhere'. The animal had ended up right back in the same old dog basket at home. He wouldn't move, he wouldn't eat, and the girl never even saw him properly sleep. His existence became one of shivering and whimpering.

'Why won't he let Mr Milton help Samson?' she'd asked Mother.

'Oh, I'm sure your father knows best, my love.'

Usually that was good enough for her. Usually it had to be.

Not this time.

And so, once the opportunity had presented itself, the little girl had carried the hound through the fields in her slender arms, grunting at his weight.

Her little brother or sister (Oh, let it be a sister!) was finally ready to come into this world, and so Mother had struggled out to the car whilst Father loaded the pre-packed suitcases and told the girl she was to stay in the house until he returned from the hospital. Mother had called back over her shoulder that she would telephone Mr O'Connell, their policeman friend, to come and watch her. Her father had turned to the girl as Mother made her way outside. He shook his head. 'You're on your own,' he'd said quietly. 'No one's coming. Don't go outside. There's food in the fridge.'

The car had started after a few failed attempts and trundled down the track towards town. For the first time, she'd been left on her own with the whole house to herself, *utter solitude with her thoughts and her books. It should have been a blessing, but she couldn't enjoy it. Not with Samson suffering in his basket.*

'You don't want to be here, do you, boy?' she'd whispered to him, then looked at the tag hanging from his collar – the same tag, collar, and name to be swapped from Samson to Samson year after year. The girl had assumed everyone did that with their dogs. She didn't assume, however, that every little girl felt the same twang of jealousy she felt from the way her father looked at the dog. No, that was just her. Was love really in such short supply that all he could afford to give were the looks of adoration he gave the mongrel? And what kind of love wilted away the moment the object of his affection showed signs of reaching its expiration? She'd even overheard Father enquiring with a local breeder, one Sunday morning after service, as to whether he could assist him in locating a 'replacement'.

Replacement.

The girl had looked into the creature's wretched eyes, wondering whether that was all family came down to. What about this new brother or sister? Were they a replacement? If he could be so cold about endlessly replacing the dogs he loved so much, why couldn't he be so cold about replacing a daughter he barely looked at?

'No, you don't want to be here at all,' she'd spoken into Samson's pitiful face. 'Let's get you out of here.'

And so here she is, in a woodland clearing some half hour's walk past the church and through the fields. With the firs, pines, and cedars towering on all sides, rippling in the breeze, the crippled dog lies on some flattened undergrowth with the girl standing over him, foot poised.

She doesn't want to put her foot through his skull, but she knows she has to.

It's not the jealousy, she keeps telling herself. This isn't about the jealousy. It's about putting Samson out of his misery, since she's the only one besides Mr Milton who seems to care what happens to him. It doesn't matter how much trouble she gets in, or what Father will do. She'll tell him Samson escaped again when she let him out into the back garden. Actually, she won't bother. She'll be punished no matter what she says. And besides, the thing can barely walk, let alone 'escape'. No, she'll do it and face whatever she's made to face. One quick stomp (he probably won't even feel it) and the pain will be over. She'll have saved a living creature a torturous existence.

It isn't about the jealousy.

The sun casts distorted shadows of criss-crossing branches and foliage from the forest ceiling. The girl looks around the clearing, spotting a squirrel dashing up a tree, then a magpie hopping from a fallen trunk. The tapestry of sound is soothing. Tweeting and rustling, chirping and stirring, distant squawking, and the gentle afternoon breeze flowing amongst the flora: it all moves through her with a calming influence. She lowers her gaze to the quivering creature beneath her poised foot.

Samson's one good eye looks up at her.

One...

Two...

Three...

The mongrel sighs, then lowers his head to the moss.

Nope, not happening. The girl admits defeat and eventually heaves the thing back to the house, cursing herself for thinking she'd ever be able to follow through with such a deed. Samson's suffering will just have to continue. It's because she's just a little girl – a sweet, innocent little girl. That's why she couldn't do it, not because of the terrible vision in the moments before she lowered her foot in resignation, the vision of her father's twitching fist.

Little girls aren't meant to cave in skulls, that's all.

Having returned to the back garden, the girl lowers Samson to the grass and closes the gate. She steps up to the back door which leads into the kitchen and slots the key into the lock, shaking her head at the thought of having lost an entire afternoon of reading. She opens the door, thinking about how many chapters of Doctor Zhivago *she could have torn through in the time it had taken to—*

'Father?'

'Step inside, Renata.'

The girl places the key in her father's outstretched, quivering hand, then glimpses the walk-in larder door lying ajar behind him. It's never left ajar. She lowers her gaze as he steps to the window and looks out at Samson curled on the grass.

'Couldn't do it, could you?' he says. 'I had your punishment all ready, too.' He glances through the open kitchen door to the bookcase in the lounge.

Not the Bible, please. Not again.

'I'm going back to the hospital. Your mother's due any day now.'

'Can I come, Father?'

Thomas Wakefield's eyes deepen, his face reddening as if his daughter has spoken some terrible insult. She takes a step back as his fists tighten and his chest rises. Suddenly he lashes like a cobra, grabbing her by the wrist – that agonising grip – and drags her to the larder. He swings the door open and flings the girl inside, where she trips and lands in a heap before him.

'Trust me, child,' he growls down at her, 'this is a mercy.'

He pulls her up then drives her into a wooden chair in the middle of the larder. Her eyes dart around at the towers of tinned foods, mountains of branded packets, and walls of Tupperware, indifferent and uncaring. She realises in a panic that the chair is fixed, unmoving. Looking below she sees it's bolted to the floor.

Help me Mother I'm not like you I don't have any flood in me I'm not strong I can't do it I can't I—

'I've tried so hard with you,' he says, straightening out four lengths of rope in his hands. The girl grips the arms of the chair, face white with terror. 'No matter what I teach you, no matter how many hours I make you study the holy book, you just don't learn, do you?'

She stands up then is pushed back down so hard that all the air is knocked from her lungs. Through her choking for air, she feels those clamp-like hands on one of her wrists, followed by the tightening of rope. Her other hand, frantically wiping away the tears obscuring her vision, is wrenched down and also tied in place. She thrashes her legs as her father drops to his knees, ignoring the kicking, and ties her ankles into position. The man takes a step back as she lashes and writhes against the ropes.

'I HATE YOU,' the girl screams, face red with fury. 'I'LL KILL YOU.'

Father and daughter turn to stone, he in the doorway, she bound in the chair. They stare into one another's eyes for a moment that transcends fear or anger, instead infused with some kind of tension, a promise of possibility. Something unfolds inside both of their minds – part revelation, part reminder – that in this world anything is possible.

Thomas Wakefield breaks from his daughter's stare and, in a moment the girl will never forget, drops his eyes to the floor. He steps out of the larder and slams the door.

In the pitch-darkness of this cell she will sit, alone. She will never know how long; days, of this she is sure. The blackness will pull her into an eternity of night wherein time and space twist and flatten into a never-ending expanse of madness. She will lose the ability to tell whether her eyes are open or closed, whether she's asleep or awake, dead or alive. Smells of which she'd never have imagined her body capable will rise from the places her muscles surrender their dignity, the darkness presenting to her a world in which all bodily functions occur as they do for the cows she's seen in the fields. Yes, blackness and the stench, hunger and the thirst. These will be the new laws of her existence during her time in the larder.

After a day or two, or week, or year in this perpetual black, the memory of screaming at her father will inject some unexpected strength into her. She'll remember the sensation of freedom and liberation at roaring threats in the face of this ultimate force of violence and suffering. At this, the endless dark will offer up the realisation that she has a way out.

The stories.

For some months, she'd found solace in the pages of the diary her mother had given her, the open ears of her only friend. She'd ignored the dates heading each page, preferring instead to continue the previous entry's scribbled thoughts – the words running on and on and on. The fear of her father reading the diary was too great to allow the detailing of what actually went on in the house, so she'd search her mind instead for anything else in her life, or in her head, worth committing to the page. She felt like a cave diver exploring a pitch-black underwater lagoon, arms outstretched, hunting for anything of interest.

A pitch-black underwater lagoon. Maybe that's where she is now. The girl closes her eyes and sinks into the lagoon.

Come on, there's got to be something down here.

She imagines the ropes around her wrists falling away, allowing her outstretched hands to search in the darkness. The cave diver gropes in amongst the soil and stones that make up the bed of the lagoon, knowing there's something there for her, something to carry her through this hell.

Someone reaches back.

It's a woman. She has brown hair – no, blonde hair. Her cheeks are sprinkled with freckles. She's wearing a flowing pink dress – no, buttoned blue blouse. Her lips part. She's about to tell the girl her name. (What was the name of that city in Australia where she'd sent those letters for that pen pal project at school?)

The larder door opens.

The light is unbearable. Silhouetted against the glare a figure approaches her, kneels down, and unties the rope fastenings. Gradually, her father's expressionless face falls into focus. He steps towards the open door then stops, looking back at her.

She understands.

The girl struggles to her feet, bracing herself against a shelf as her legs try to remember how to support her weight. A towel is thrown in her direction, falling to the floor by her feet. With it she wipes the worst of her mess from under her skirt, runs it over the soiled seat of the chair, sets it sheepishly on the ground, then slowly follows her father out of the larder and up the stairs into the bathroom.

Not a word is exchanged as the girl undresses. Thomas takes her clothes and returns downstairs as she slips into the pre-run bath. He reappears with a plate of dry bread, then tips the toothbrushes from their cup into the sink and fills the glass with water, setting it by the bread on the lowered toilet seat.

'Thank you, Father,' the girl croaks as he's leaving the

bathroom.

He stops and, without turning back, says, 'You stayed at a friend's.' Then, just before he closes the door behind him, he looks back into the shivering girl's eyes. 'You have a brother.'

Soon, once he's returned the larder to its previous state, she'll hear her father's car struggle to life as he leaves for the hospital to collect her mother and her new baby brother. She'll see the way he looks at the boy, while a new mutual affection opens up between her parents. She'll see her mother, her father, and this newcomer huddle together, a tighter unit than the family has ever been. She'll see friends and visitors come especially to meet the baby – an adorable baby, you simply have to meet him; oh, his little face and hands, and that beautiful red hair *– and she'll see the future, the way it's going to be. Mercifully, Samson will die within weeks, Thomas replacing him with yet another new Samson.*

A new Samson for a new beginning.

Tonight, the girl, just turned ten, will give birth to a woman with blonde hair and a blue blouse named Adelaide Addington. She'll deliver through the pencil her first creation: a person, an actual human, a character. *And she'll be real, more real than that drooling thing in the other room –* the baby you have to meet him he's got a face and hands and a nose and even an ear or two and you simply have to meet him.

Oh, Adelaide will be real. But first she has to meet her newly born baby brother.

'Rennie,' her mother will whisper, the smile on her face finally real, 'meet Noah.'

8

The broken springs of the mattress prodded into Renata's back as she listened to her father's snores. Occasionally they would mangle into fitful chokes, at one point leading to a silence she thought may have marked an end to her enduring of this place, these people, these responsibilities. She thought the choking may have signalled the dying throes of her father, the silence his expiration.

The snoring returned. She felt like she should hate herself for this moment of longing, the undeniable hope that the eternal flame of her father had finally extinguished, but she didn't.

The details of Hector's investigation swam before her. Both her mother's murder and the explosion were connected, of this the detective – yes, still a detective – was sure. As for Quentin, why were words from his novel left at the crime scene? *Midnight, midnight; it's your turn. Clock strikes twelve; burn, burn, burn.*

Was someone trying to set him up, or were they just inspired by his book?

She shouldn't care about any of it, least of all her long-lost family. They weren't her problem, just as she eventually hadn't been theirs. The teenaged Renata, following the accident, had swapped this hellhole of a home for a hospital, one that became more of a home than this house ever could have been. How reluctant she'd been to leave those white corridors. Fifteen years in care and not once had her family visited. Her mother likely had no say in this, so she didn't hold it against her. Besides, despite Renata's amnesia robbing so much from her, she did remember her relief at the lack of visitation. But it was true. She'd never stopped loving Sylvia Wakefield, the woman who'd endured so much to keep her family together.

Promise you'll be there for him if anything happens to me.

Yes, she'd stick around long enough to ensure her mother's husband was cared for before checking out, that one-way ticket all knotted and tied and ready to go. Help the monster responsible for Mother's bruises and black eyes, then snap goes the noose. Simple.

The twisted logic of her intentions knocked around her head until she could take no more. She pressed her hands over closed eyes, but the darkness behind her eyelids couldn't erase the image of what lay behind that door at the end of the hall, beyond those cheery cartoon animals still spelling his name.

NOAH

The implications of a child's bedroom kept so clinically intact all these years hadn't escaped her, and the possibility of her brother not even being an option was too much to bear. She couldn't afford to put Thomas in a home. End herself now and rely on state care? That's not what she'd promised her mother. Besides, Sylvia Wakefield's killer was still out there. Part of her felt compelled to hang around long enough to look the sweet old woman's murderer in the eyes.

She needed peace to think. She leapt from the child-sized bed.

Her father's snoring continued as she stuffed candlesticks, matches, and a packet of wet wipes into her satchel. She gave her hands a quick rinse under the kitchen tap, made a note to replace the thinning soap bar, and slipped into her duffle coat. A pile of hair clips sat on the sideboard. She fastened these in her hair for good measure, tied a woollen scarf around her neck, and eased open the front door.

The bitter night air embraced her. Then she heard the weeping. A sobbing figure sat on the curb by the blackened crater, head in hands. Quentin looked up.

'Ren,' he said, wiping the sleeve of his blazer over reddened eyes. 'I thought you'd be asleep.'

'I was,' she replied, curling her toes in her shoes until they hurt. 'I just woke up and realised I hadn't locked the house.'

He looked at her boots, coat, and satchel. 'Which house, and what mountain's it up?'

They were interrupted by the clock tower, its midnight tolls filling the vacuum of the night. They looked in its direction.

'You're going there, aren't you?' he asked, his Maine cadence still alien to Renata. 'The tower. I saw the way you looked at it during the service.'

'I…' She fished for the words. 'Sorry, yes. I am. I used to go there as a child. There was a room at the top I liked.' She paused. 'I need to get my head together.'

'That's twice you've seen me cry like a baby,' said Quentin, picking his glasses up from the curb. 'I'd be embarrassed but I'm too torn up about those guys. Third-degree burns. Had to have their seatbelts surgically removed.' The tears renewed behind his lenses. 'They have kids, Ren. They could have died and they have *kids*.' The bell ceased, leaving only the man's sobbing to fill the night.

'I'm not…the person to speak to about this, Quentin,' Renata stammered. 'Sorry, I'm just not good with people.'

She hesitated, words yet to be said balancing on her tongue. Was she really going to do this? 'The clock tower…I mean, it's kind of falling apart, but if that doesn't bother you, well…'

The horn-rimmed glasses looked up at her. His gaze was intense, but unusually calming; still no knives. Scalding water on flesh, that's what the gaze of another usually felt like. But not these eyes.

'Come with me,' she heard herself say. 'The view's impressive, if nothing else. Not that you'll see much in this fog.'

Quentin removed his glasses again and rubbed his eyes. He cleared his throat. 'Gotta be better than this. That's real kind of you, Ren. I mean, after everything I've done…you sure?'

'These people are criminalising you over a book, your production company's being sabotaged, and people are getting hurt. It's taking its toll on you. No shame in that.' She held out a hand. 'To me, you're the victim.'

He took her hand and squeezed—

always at the right times

—then got to his feet.

'Thank you, Ren.'

Stones crunched underfoot as they made their way along the gravel track. The path ran beside the road to the church, eventually straying through a knee-high stone wall that looked as ready to collapse as the church. A jumbled army of gravestones populated the cemetery grounds, marking generations of Millbury Peak's deceased.

They were trudging towards the clock tower when Renata stopped by the stone of Sylvia Wakefield. Her grave, accompanied by a wreath already beginning to wither, was meagre compared to those littering the churchyard.

Quentin knelt to pick something from the grass. 'From what I've been told,' he said, 'it sounds like she deserved a tad more than this. Maybe something more along these lines?' He nodded to a looming stone angel, then stood. 'Hey, at least she did better than this guy,' he said, gesturing to a tiny, nameless stone.

They pressed on, edging carefully around the sleeping graves. Renata could feel the man following silently behind her. The police tape covering the church's entrance had been replaced with freshly cut two-by-fours. The clock tower stood at the north end of the church, stretching into the mist and looking out towards the slumbering town. The door at its base had also been boarded over, but with planks as weathered as the headstones.

Quentin stood by her side, one hand behind his back. 'Boarded up,' he said. 'I'll need a crowbar or something.'

He watched Renata disappear around the back of the tower, then followed. He found her standing by a waist-high panel, a tight hole piercing its rotting wood where a handle had long since broken off. She picked a thin branch from the ground and fed it through the hole, pressing the stick at an angle so as to create a lever by which the panel could be prised. It opened, a sharp gust whistling from the darkness and fogging Quentin's glasses. Renata glanced at his look of apprehension.

'Too much for you, Quentin?' she smiled timidly. 'You're the horror writer. Maybe you'll get some inspiration.'

He rubbed his glasses on his corduroys. 'You're the romance writer,' he said, replacing his glasses then pulling from behind his back an improvised bouquet assembled from scraps of lichens, dandelions, and daisies. 'Maybe *you'll* get some inspiration.'

Her eyes dropped. He stepped forward and lifted her hand in his own, then placed in her fingers the bouquet.

'Right,' he said, turning to the open hatch, 'let's see this room of yours.'

She reached the top first.

In the same way Millbury Peak's emergence through the mist had reignited forgotten synaptic connections within her, so did each step spiralling up the clock tower. She remembered as a child the mental roadmap leading her safely down the creakiest steps of the house's staircase. The roadmap leading up the tower tonight, however, was a highway, ascending to the only place in Millbury Peak she'd ever found peace.

She was relieved to find the door at the top, barred vertically in bolted iron strips, not only unsealed but wide open. Decades' worth of leaves and dust had blown through the tall, narrow opening in the stone that constituted the room's only window. She ducked under the low doorframe and stepped into her past.

Moonlight poured in. The room was cold, but she was warmed by the glow of nostalgia from the ancient walls. She crossed the unassuming circular space towards the pointed, narrow lancet window, which rose glassless and open from the top of a few steps. Two rotting wooden crates sat overturned at the base of these steps, one significantly larger than the other, red lettering stencilled upside down on each. These crates had once served as the writing desk and chair for a little girl, an aspiring writer of romantic fiction. She placed her bouquet on the larger of the two crates.

She peered into a grimy pile of rubble against the wall and spotted a small, crooked shape poking from the mess, like a miniature version of one of the gravestones in the yard outside. It was a book, mouldy and waterlogged, and she immediately knew which. She shivered, not from the chill, but from a distant memory of the text within those sodden pages.

Pain flashed.

She backed away from the book. Stepping to the narrow window, she looked into the night as she rubbed the sides of her head. The mist beckoned. The ground below called.

It would be so easy.

'Christ, okay,' panted Quentin, fumbling for his Marlboros. 'You beat me.'

She turned as the match in his fingers snapped in two. He struck another but allowed the flame to sit, the unlit cigarette hanging limply from his mouth as he gawked above them at the iron bell dozing in its rusted cage.

'This was a maintenance room,' Renata said, looking up at the mechanical dinosaur. 'If I recall correctly, the bell's rope wouldn't have even passed through this space. It fed through a gap in the stonework to a chamber at the base. Would have saved the bell-ringer's ears.'

Quentin stared at the mechanism. 'Who rings it now? I've heard it every day since I got here.'

She pointed to a dirty-white control box inside the rusted cage. 'It was automated years ago. The bell's still real, but it's put into motion mechanically.' She looked back out the window again, picking at a fingernail. 'These people. Some will swear there's still a monk in here ringing it twice a day.'

'They seem pretty hung up on the past,' said Quentin,

blowing smoke up into the bell's chamber. 'Then again, here you are moping around your old childhood haunt.' He looked back through the wire mesh at the bell cradled like a hatchling in its dense machinery.

'I didn't come here for nostalgia's sake,' she said. 'I have to think things through.'

He took a step towards her and placed a finger under her chin, raising her eyes to meet his own. 'I can go.'

She felt the blood rushing to her face. A stab of inexplicable guilt shot through her stomach. Two sides battled, one telling her to run and hide and sink into the familiar waters of her mind, the other to hold his gaze.

She looked away.

The finger left her chin. Quentin turned to the door.

'Wait,' she breathed.

Renata sat on the smaller of the two crates while Quentin perched on the edge of one of the stone steps leading to the window.

'I'm glad heights don't bother you,' she said, placing the candle from her satchel on the larger crate.

Quentin sparked a match and lit the wick. 'I'd be more scared of falling through one of those crates. Taking your life in your hands there, Ren.'

She smiled. 'The only thing this place is missing is the smell of my mother's tomato and rice soup. I used to bring a flask up here without her knowing. I wonder if she still made it before she died.' Then, looking at the candle flame, 'Suppose I'll never know.'

'Tomato and rice, huh? You folks got weird taste. Hate to say it, but it might be missing a bit more than that.' He pulled his blazer tight. 'Some glass in that window for a start.'

The candle flickered.

'Tell me,' he began, the flame dancing in his glasses, 'what was it you came up here to think about?'

'Just…money stuff,' she said. 'Let's not talk about that.'

He nodded, then glanced around the littered floor. 'So I get the leaves and dirt, but what's with the paper?'

She picked up one of the crumpled yellow balls and carefully flattened out the sheet on the makeshift desk. The candlelight revealed clumsy scrawls filling every inch of the page. She ran her eyes over it, then tossed it and reached for another ball. She ran a finger over this sheet, then, satisfied, turned the paper to Quentin and pointed to a name within the scrawl: Adelaide Addington.

Quentin squinted at the words, then glanced around at the paper littering the floor, the occasional stub of worn pencil lying amongst the mess.

'So,' he said, 'this is where you learnt to write.'

She nodded, wiping her hands on her skirt. 'My father's always been this way. The anger, I mean. The writing began when I started keeping a diary, but I found it was making up stories that let me escape him. These scribbles were the only way I could get away.' She looked around the stone walls. 'And this room.'

Quentin reached for a snapped pencil. 'Writer's block that day?'

She took the broken pencil from him. 'It was starting the stories that frustrated me,' she said. 'Once I got going it was fine. But kicking things off drove me mad.'

'Same here. Like pulling teeth sometimes.' The candle quivered at a sudden gust of wind. 'I had a treehouse,' he continued, shielding the flame as he lit a cigarette. 'I could get through ten books a week in that thing. Was about as sturdy as that crate you nearly made me sit on. It's a miracle I survived.' He blew a cloud of smoke above the undulating candle. 'Did you read much up here?'

'Yes,' she said, motioning to the upside down lettering stencilled on the larger crate. He tilted his head and read the words, HARPER'S BOOKS. 'He'll be long gone now, but the man who ran that bookshop let me treat it like a library once the books in our house became…well, unavailable. I must have gotten through half his shop, until…' Her voice trailed off.

Quentin's hand dug into a plastic packet in his blazer pocket. 'Until?'

Renata hesitated. 'Mr Harper,' she began cautiously, 'he gave me free reign over any book in his store, as long as I returned them as I'd found them. I was so careful with those books, practically pried them open with tweezers, tried so hard not to—'

'*Until?* He threw a milk bottle chew into his mouth.

She took a deep breath. 'Alright, sorry. He…well, he gave me free reign over the whole shop except one section, and when he found out I'd taken one of those books without his knowledge, that free reign ended.'

Renata walked to the pile of rubble against the wall and reached for the sodden book sticking out from the leaves and dirt.

Again, pain.

She clenched her eyes, willing the pain to subside, then pulled the book from the rubble. The slimy thing was sealed shut by the damp of decades, but its cover was still clear. She held it out to Quentin. He peered through the candlelight.

He nodded. 'It was the horror section he didn't want you going in, wasn't it?'

She dropped the sodden book. The road, the burning pickup truck, the woman in the emerald green dress: *Horror Highway* stared up at Renata. Printed below the title: *Quentin C. Rye.*

'Not a fan?'

'I…well, it affected me,' she said. 'I only flicked through it, but I landed on some nasty things, as well as the scene from the cover. That pickup truck…it just tore right through her. Ripped her to bits.' Her voice wavered. 'To this day I don't know why the truck was on fire, or why the woman just stood there.' She crossed her arms tight. The walls flickered. 'And, well…I have these nightmares. Had them for years. They just feel so…real. I don't know where they come from, maybe…' The stone settled into its orange glow as the candle calmed. 'I'm sorry, Quentin. I don't mean to burden you.'

He reached into his blazer and pulled out that chunky leather notebook and pen she'd seen him with so many times already. He scribbled, then, as quick as it had emerged, the notebook was back in his pocket.

He looked up. 'Ideas, they come at any time. Usually the worst.' He stood, twirling the pen. 'Listen, your nightmares: they're useless. Just your brain pissing in the wind, coming back to slap you in the face.'

'Elegant.'

'Crude poetry aside, they're still useless. You just gotta wipe it off and get on with things, Ren. Forget that trash. There's more important things to worry about.' He removed the horn-rimmed frames and wiped their lenses on his turtleneck. 'Like the crazy shit going on around here. You know, I never wrote any of my books to hurt anyone. All I ever wanted was to find…' He replaced his glasses, then looked at her, his eyes deepening. '…*truth.*'

He lowered his voice. 'Your nightmares, that truck, Sylvia…I didn't mean for any of it to happen.'

'I know, Quentin. I told you to stop blaming yourself.'

He took her hand and squeezed.

Always at the right times.

'Ren, the money thing. I'd like to make you an offer.'

She pulled her hand away. 'Oh…Quentin, no. Really, it's—'

'My wife, Eleanor,' he interrupted. 'Well, ex-wife. Like I said, she's a fan of yours. My daughter is too, bless her heart. I caught bits here and there. To be honest, I might be a bit of a fan myself.'

'Detective O'Connell mentioned your daughter. You sound like you love her very much. Am I right on thinking she's an actress? Will she be joining you here for—'

'No.'

Silence.

'I'm continuing with our plans to film in Millbury Peak. We're getting underway soon, but there's an issue with some of the dialogue.' He kicked some leaves. 'It works in the book we're adapting, but in the script it feels a bit…inhibited. There's a hefty romance thread I feel needs a woman's touch, a woman with experience in that kind of thing.'

'Quentin, I'm sorry, but I haven't, well…written for a while, and I've no experience in film, and—'

'Your father,' he cut in, 'your financial worries concern him, right?' She looked down. 'No pressure. Total flexibility. All I need is a woman's touch.' He stepped closer. 'Your touch, Ren.'

The flame was withering, the warm glow of the small stone room fading with it. Renata glanced up into the man's eyes.

'I don't need an answer now,' he said. 'I'm only asking you to consider my offer. Tweak the dialogue, see what you can do. Your finances would be taken care of. Besides, we writers gotta stick together, right?'

His eyes were pools of electricity. Was that glimmering the spark of creativity? The spark of an artist? She didn't care for the genre in which he worked, but maybe there was more to the man than she'd thought, more to this 'truth' he claimed his writings were searching for. And his offer? Well, she was here to think things through. Now she had even more to ponder.

'It's late,' said Quentin, their faces close. That ancient, pointless guilt rose in her stomach again.

Hallowed be Thy name.

Renata turned away and pulled a fresh candlestick from her satchel. 'I think I'll stay a while longer.' She felt him placing his thick blazer over her shoulders. 'Quentin, you need that.'

'Guess you'll have to see me again to get it back to me, won't you?'

His footsteps disappeared down the spiral staircase. She went to the window and rubbed an antiseptic wipe over her hands as she watched him trudge through the graveyard, scribbling in his notebook as he went.

Her memories of Millbury Peak, this town frozen in time, had been slowly returning. Nevertheless, something told her there were memories destined never to re-emerge. She glanced at *Horror Highway*, still staring up from the stone floor. How could some cheap horror be the cause of such persistent dreams, such real dreams? She thought of this 'truth' Quentin mentioned, the truth he said his work was pursuing.

Renata stared into the blank mass of fog. It was like an impenetrable wall, a veil.

Maybe some truths were best left buried.

9

The thirteenth count stabbed.

Her trembling hands still gripped the imaginary wheel upon waking. She opened her eyes to find no fire, no brimstone, and certainly no wheel. Her hands weren't dripping with the usual sappy, jet-black oil from the dreams, and there was no road to explode behind her, no fire to pour from the sky. She sat up and massaged her temples.

The momentary agony still echoed in her head like the reverberations of a silenced orchestra. The final stab, the thirteenth, was always the worst. But they were all getting worse. Not just the pains but the dreams themselves, which were becoming more chaotic with every passing night. She groped the sweat-drenched sheets for the red spade. Of course, it remained in her dreams. She pulled the coiled noose from under her pillow and stood to look out of the window, stroking the coarse rope. The fog continued its embrace of the house, the smoky veil still in place.

She edged open the door and peered down the hallway towards the laughing elephants and bears.

NOAH

Creeping past the master bedroom, she approached the decorated door and reached for the handle.

Come in! Come in! giggled the elephant.

Time to figure this thing out! Come on in and play! chuckled the bear.

'You there, girl?' snapped Thomas from his bedroom.

'Yes, Father.'

'Pills,' he spluttered, 'I need an early dose.'

She went to the lavatory on the landing and gave her hands a swift wash. Staring into the open medicine cabinet as she turned off the tap and dried her hands, she thought back to when she'd first arrived. The cabinet's shelves had been lined with bottles and blister packs, as well as multipacks of hand soap – her own addition. Supplies were now running low, and her father's increasing demands for extra doses weren't helping.

'She dealt with that,' said Thomas when Renata had hesitantly mentioned the need for replenishment. 'Kitchen drawer, repeat prescription.' No more needed said.

Sure enough, *vend as required* had been hastily scribbled onto the slip she found in the drawer. She folded it and stuffed it into her pocket, deciding this would be the morning to restock before going to accept Quentin's offer.

'Mr Ramsay?' she said into the telephone, wiping her hands on her sweater. 'It's Renata Wakefield. Yes, Vicar…uh huh. Well, I have a favour to ask. I'm very sorry, but would you mind staying with my father for a few hours this afternoon?'

She imagined the dismay on his face.

'It's just a few errands I need to run,' she continued. 'I need to collect his medication and see to a couple of other things. I'll be straight back, but I still wouldn't want him left on his own.' She gouged her nails into her palms. 'Again, I'm really sorry.'

Renata felt within Edwin Ramsay's hesitation a groping for some way out, but there was none. The young vicar couldn't be seen to turn down the chance to spend time with the man he'd succeeded, one of Millbury Peak's most esteemed inhabitants.

'It would be a pleasure,' he surrendered.

'Thank you, Miss Wakefield,' said Mr Oakley, the elderly pharmacist. The wrinkles of his face curved around a spreading smile. 'Send my regards to your father.'

She crammed the bottles of Dexlatine and packets of hand soap into her satchel and hurried out of the chemist, hugging Quentin's grey blazer to her chest. She'd only ventured through this cobbled excuse for a high street a couple of times since her return to Millbury Peak. The stone archways and thatched roofs, anachronism at its finest, watched authoritatively over the same handful of faces scuttling out of the butcher's, popping into the bakery, or scrutinising the town noticeboard. Still, this sedate countryside settlement of barely a thousand was a thronging metropolis compared to the desolate rock of Neo-Thorrach. Creeping through the time capsule that was Millbury Peak, she felt more exposed to those eyes of knives than ever before.

She walked past Millbury Hardware, then a small locksmith, before stopping at the abandoned shell that had been Harper's Books. She checked her hair in the window's reflection before pausing to gaze through the filthy glass at the empty shelves. Mr Harper would be six feet under by now – like her mother – and she felt a twang of regret that she'd never taken the time to thank him for encouraging her love of literature. She fiddled with her hair one more time then stepped away from the window, but stopped as a sudden thought hit her. She turned back to Oakley's Pharmacy.

Mr Oakley looked up as the bell on the door tinkled. 'Miss Wakefield,' he said, flattening the sprinkling of white hair on his head, 'was there anything else I could do you for?'

'Yes, sorry, there was one last thing,' said Renata, tugging her duffle coat tight. 'You asked me to pass your regards onto my father. You know him?'

'Who doesn't!' he grinned. 'Mr Wakefield was the backbone of this town for more years than I can count. Its moral standing, its faith, worship; he was a big part of all those important things.' The aged man cleared his throat. 'Isn't that the way with every town's vicar? A fine man, your father.' He held a steaming mug to his wrinkled lips. 'A fine man indeed.'

Renata stepped closer, forcing herself to make eye contact. 'Yes, Mr Oakley. And may I ask,' she continued casually, flicking away an invisible hair, 'what of my brother, Noah? Do you know him, too?'

He sipped. 'Ah, Noah. I was going to ask you about him. I remember you both well. "Always an ill pair", that's what your mother said when the two of you moved away. Never saw it myself. Always thought you kids were the picture of health.' He wiped a drop of coffee from his chin, taking a concentrated moment of recollection. '"Fragile girl", your mother used to say once you were gone. That's all she seemed to be able to say. "Such a fragile girl. Such a sensitive girl." You were both taken away to some specialist children's hospital up north, apparently.' He cocked his head in further concentration. 'Were away for so long, so long indeed. Can't remember seeing either of you again, come to think of it. Grew up and got yourselves lives elsewhere once you got better, I suppose. That's the way these days, Miss Wakefield, isn't it now? What was wrong with the pair of you anyways?'

'You're mistaken, Mr Oakley. My brother was never in

hospital with me. He stayed in Millbury Peak.'

He looked her up and down. 'My family and I have lived here since you were a little girl, Miss Wakefield. I know everyone in this town.'

Renata's heart quickened. 'But Noah wasn't even involved in the accident, he—'

'Miss Wakefield,' the man scowled, suddenly realising he didn't need to be grilled by some big shot writer – especially a *woman*, 'I know nothing of any accident, and a man of my age doesn't care to be pushed. I'm afraid I have a busy day ahead of me. Will there be anything else?'

Renata glanced around the empty shop, then at the crossword puzzle on his desk. She stumbled back, his eyes suddenly soldering irons against her skin, knives in her flesh.

'No, no. I...' The burning was agony, the knives unbearable. She reached for the door handle. 'I'll give my father your regards.'

The air traffic control tower emerged in the mist. The fog obscuring its upper portion gave it the appearance of a skyscraper disappearing into the clouds, but this disused airfield would be nothing to Quentin. He'd come from another planet, one of cities full of real skyscrapers, and heaving streets thronging with eyes. She shivered at the thought of that sprawling Eastern Seaboard anthill an ocean away.

The airfield had served mostly as a maintenance site during the Second World War, and was surrounded by towering, corrugated iron fencing, its steely ripples having succumbed to decades of rust. Today, a small portion had been removed to make way for a temporary entrance, next to which stood a sign:

NO ENTRY!
FILMING IN PROGRESS
Rye Productions

When the production crew first arrived, a group of Millbury Peak's more active residents had taken up arms against the invasion, a small swarm of picket signs bobbing up and down around the entrance. Other matters had apparently demanded their attention as, this morning, the only faces to greet Renata were those of two potbellied young men standing guard, giggling excitedly and covered in Rye Productions attire. So these were the jobs Quentin had promised the town. They looked up from their chattering.

'Hello, sorry, I'm here to see Mr Rye,' said Renata, tugging on a sleeve and glancing around nervously. 'He told me to ask for him.'

As they were formulating an answer, a man as big as a tank stepped from behind a trailer, wide-framed and dressed all in black. 'Name,' he grunted.

It took her a moment to realise this was a question. 'Renata,' she answered, picking at her palm. 'Renata Wakefield.' The two young men lost interest and resumed their chattering. The tank glared at her. 'Mr Rye asked me to the set,' she elaborated. 'He said I should give my name.'

His face cracked a smile. 'Right this way, ma'am.'

She was led inside. The airfield was a sea of tarmac sprinkled with intermittent dustings of weeds. A large hangar stood in its centre, more 'NO ENTRY' signs plastered across its entrance. The fence snaking around the airfield's perimeter was dotted with the illegible graffiti of bored country teenagers.

The field was still being primed for production; trucks entered through a dedicated gate at the far end, delivering the means to erect a fully functioning filming location. She looked around at the swarming production crews, like bees readying the hive for their queen.

'Renata Wakefield?' The voice came from behind her. She turned to see a girl approaching, slender, blonde, and sporting denim cut-offs so meagre that for a moment Renata thought they had a streaker. She wasn't the only one who'd turned to look.

'Renata Wakefield!' repeated the beaming teenager, her US twang a high-pitched version of Quentin's. 'It's really you, isn't it?' Renata looked at the thick hardback under the girl's arm. Was that a Coleridge collection? 'I've been waiting endlessly to meet you in person, Miss Wakefield,' she said. 'What am I doing, I'm so...*boorish*.' She offered a hand, tanned, nails manicured. 'I'm Sandie.' The young actress unveiled her name with practised composure. 'Sandie Rye.'

'Ah, you're...Quentin's daughter?' Renata asked, looking everywhere but into the girl's wide, eager stare. Even the prettiest eyes could burn.

'Come on!' said Sandie as she did a little bounce. She grabbed Renata's hand and began leading her across the tarmac. The man-tank took a fearful step back. 'I'm not even in the film and the crew still gave me my own trailer. I'll show you!'

Before she could protest, Renata was pulled towards a cluster of trailers and Portakabins. Lying between the units were sealed trunks and equipment casings waiting to be unpacked, as well as marquees housing first aid stations, serving and dining areas, make-up and costume-fitting sections, and covered bulks of whirring generators, all bustling with Rye Productions crew. Sandie galloped up the steps of the largest trailer, upon which giant golden stars had been adhered. A printed sign on the entrance read SANDIE RYE. The teenager pushed open the door and lead Renata, still clutching Quentin's blazer, into the furnished living space. Sandie dashed to the kitchen area, dumped her book of poetry, and began pouring two cream sodas.

Fitted spotlights running the length of the ceiling came to life. The trailer's fixtures were dark wood, with thick carpeting underfoot and an expansive leather seating area. Sandie flicked a switch beside the wall-mounted plasma television, electronically controlled blinds lowering over the windows in response. Renata stood in the middle of the seating area, feeling like a caged animal. She felt her toes curl.

'I'm just so *jubilant* to have Renata Wakefield in my trailer!' gushed the young girl as she clattered in the fridge.

'I really do need to see your father, Sandie,' said Renata, picking at her fingernails. She glanced over and saw the girl was now wearing glasses. 'Do you have any idea how long he'll be?'

'Ice, Miss Wakefield?'

'Uh, fine, thanks.' Her toes began to hurt. 'It's just he said I'd be able to find him here and—'

'Yeah, my apologies,' the girl said with a sniff, stepping towards the couches. She handed Renata a glass. 'They said he's due in soon, but you can wait with me for the...interim. The truth is Daddy doesn't actually know I'm here.' She lowered her voice. 'It's kind of a surprise. See, he didn't want me in this film...' She paused, a hint of heartbreak passing over the young girl's face. '...which is fine, but it doesn't mean I can't come visit.' She looked down, fiddling with her fraying shorts. 'Dunno…maybe he'll, like, have a change of heart.'

Her thoughts flicked like a television changing channel. 'My mom had all your books when I was growing up, you know,' she gushed. 'Man, I read them *all*. You're what got me into literature.' She shoved aside some glossy magazines on the coffee table to reveal an Emily Brontë, placed as tactically as her unnatural vocabulary. 'I know your latest…*chef d'oeuvres* haven't been received as well as usual, but that's because they're more *literary*. Adelaide Addington, her romances. Y'know, the men she meets…' She twirled her blonde hair, showing off an elaborately tattooed ring finger. The girl's brown eyes glazed over. Renata discerned dark rings buried under the make-up. 'She's so inspiring. *You're* so inspiring, Miss Wakefield.'

The channel flicked.

'Hey, you ever thought about making a film? Just imagine…' she did her best movie trailer voiceover, '…*Starring Sandie Rye as Adelaide Addington*. I even have the blonde hair! I bet Daddy would help. Dunno, maybe he'd even—' She spotted Renata eyeing the glossy magazines pushed aside, each cover plastered with Sandie's airbrushed face. 'Miss Wakefield, I want you to know I'm more than what they make me out to be,' she said. 'I'm a grown woman, and nothing's more *imperative* to me than my career – and making my parents proud. If you ever decide to bring Adelaide Addington to life, I swear I'd do her justice.'

'You'll certainly be the first to know.' Renata stared into her cream soda. 'Maybe I should come back later.'

'Well, whatever. That's cool,' she said, scratching her nose. 'But man, I'd *love* you to stay a while longer.'

She risked a glance at Sandie, probably about the same

age as Renata when she'd been in the accident. Fifteen years she'd spent convalescing in hospital, beginning at the same point in life that this young girl was embarking upon a glamorous acting career with the support of a loving family. How far apart two lives could stray. Had Renata been raised with such love and support, where may she have ended up? A family of her own? She probably wouldn't have wound up a suicidal hermit, anyway. But behind this sculpted façade of glamour and ambition, as well as her forced impressions of intellectuality, Sandie was still just a teenage girl, maybe even as confused and lonely as Renata had been at her age. There was something bubbling beneath the surface, beneath this well-rehearsed presentation of stardom and ambition.

'Well, maybe I could wait with you,' said Renata, 'if you really don't think he'll be long.'

'Miss Wakefield,' said Sandie, hesitantly, 'did you ever worry about making your parents proud when you were my age?' So that's what was bubbling underneath the surface: *pressure*, likely placed on herself by herself. 'I mean, I don't mean to put you on the spot. It's just my mom and dad have done so much for me and I sometimes wonder if I'm, like, good enough. I just want to do right by them, y'know? Make it big so I can give back some of what they've given me – like you probably did with your parents.'

Renata squirmed in her seat. 'Well...I don't know, Sandie.' She risked another glance at the girl. 'I kept to myself when I was your age. Then I spent many years in hospital following an accident, so—'

'I didn't know that,' interrupted Sandie. 'What kind of accident?'

'It was a car crash.' Renata wrapped a loose thread from

her sweater around her finger. 'My memories of that time were left a bit fuzzy. Still, I don't remember ever writing for anyone other than myself.' She took a deep breath. 'It's great you want to make your mother and father proud, but in the end you have to do these things for yourself, because one day...' she looked away '...you might find yourself alone.'

A moment's pause settled between them. Sandie took a sip of cream soda, then set the glass down on top of an *Entertainment Weekly*, covering a grinning photo of herself. 'My parents split when I was sixteen. I dunno, I guess I went through the same stuff every kid does when that happens. It was my fault, right? Had to be my fault. At least in my head it did.' Renata watched the girl running a painted nail over the tattooed roses spiralling up her finger. 'So if it's my fault, if I screwed up my family, then it's time to find a new family, right? So, between you and me, I went off the rails a bit. Not much, just a lot of partying, trying to find that 'new family'. Never did, of course.' Her voice wavered. She looked at the floor. 'Did some stupid stuff, then realised it all comes back to your *real* family. Your blood. It hit me that, since Mom and Daddy were split, it was up to me to keep us all together. If I drifted away, so would they. Daddy never stops telling me how important I am to them, how much they love me.' Renata saw her eyes glisten with what may have been the beginnings of tears. 'It's the least I can do to make them proud, y'know?'

Sandie cleared her throat and wiped her eyes. 'God, look at me. I have *Renata Wakefield* in my trailer and all I can do is talk about myself! I'm sorry, Miss Wakefield. I'm so *imbecilic*.'

This teenager, this tanned, manicured, princess of a girl

was so far from the teenaged Renata's world, and yet she recognised so much. The details were different, but the deep-set confusion was the same. 'Families are difficult, Sandie,' she said, leaning forward. 'It sounds like you're doing great.' She took a breath. 'And...call me Renata.'

Their eyes met. Each filled the silence with a smile.

Suddenly the roar of Quentin's Harley bellowed from outside. 'That's him!' she cried, leaping from the sofa. 'I have to go surprise him!'

Sandie threw open the trailer door and leapt onto the tarmac, adjusting her glasses as she went. The fence by the entrance clattered as the man-tank stumbled out of Quentin's way, tripping into corrugated iron. The two boys in their Rye Productions t-shirts stared as Quentin stormed across the tarmac.

'SANDIE,' he yelled, marching towards the trailer. 'What the hell are you doing here? I told you not to come.'

She clasped her hands behind her back, batting her eyelashes and, perversely, pushing her chest out. Her efforts did nothing to mask her shock and disappointment at his tone. 'Daddy, I...I just wanted to see you. You know how much I miss you when—'

'ENOUGH,' roared Quentin. The watching bystanders looked away nervously. He swung round to a nearby technician. 'Is this her trailer?'

The teenager spoke for the technician, her voice hollow. 'Yes, it is. Daddy, I didn't mean to upset you.' She looked at the ground.

Quentin's eyes suddenly fell on Renata. His expression softened. He stepped towards Sandie and placed his hands on her shoulders, lowering his voice to a gentle whisper. 'You're...everything to me. I just want to protect you. I *have* to protect you.' He glanced back at Renata, and in that moment she was sure she saw a tear in his eye. 'Go,' he growled at Sandie. 'Pack your things. You're going home tonight.'

Quentin turned back to yell at the technician, his words exploding like a blown fire hydrant as he demanded to know why he hadn't been informed of Sandie's arrival.

Renata watched Quentin in disbelief before feeling something slip into her hand. 'My card,' Sandie whispered. 'Give me a shout about that part.'

'It's my charity work,' Quentin said, slipping into the blazer. 'She was meant to be taking care of it all while I was away, but she can be so stubborn.' He looked wistfully across the airfield towards Sandie's trailer. 'Gets that from me, I guess.' Renata, still shocked, looked at the ground. 'I have a warehouse full of junk – or rather, *Quentin C. Rye movie memorabilia* – that I'm planning on auctioning off for some children's hospice thing. She was meant to be dealing with it.' He tapped his cigarette. 'Think I was too harsh?'

'It's not my place to judge,' Renata said. There was a crash as a pair of technicians dropped a lighting bracket near them. 'Is there somewhere private we could talk?'

He scowled at the technicians. 'Leave us,' he snapped. The men stumbled away.

'Quentin,' she said tentatively, 'are you all right?'

Cigarette smoke rose from his mouth as he let out a long sigh. 'Sorry, Ren. Been a long week. Everything's still, well…weighing heavy, y'know? Everything that's happened because of me.'

'I told you, Quentin,' she said, 'stop blaming yourself. It's okay.'

'You hungry?' He flicked his sleeve to check his watch.

'Let me make sure Sandie's all right, then we can have that talk…over lunch?'

She scanned the ensuing chaos around them. Fresh cargo was unloaded from two trucks on the west side, while a group by the control tower continued erecting a sprawling white marquee. The disused airfield was gradually transforming into a fully functioning Hollywood production site.

'I think you have enough on,' said Renata.

'You know, Ren, I'm not just here to make a film. I'm working on a new novel.' Quentin patted his blazer. 'That notebook you keep seeing me with has its entire outline…' He stepped closer. '…and guess where I think I've left it?'

He smiled. She looked to the ground.

'That charming clock tower of yours. Let me see to my daughter then I'll pack us some sandwiches. We can see if my notebook's up there and have that chat, too.'

'My father,' she said, rubbing her wrist, 'the vicar's watching him. I should really—'

'Then go home,' Quentin cut in. 'Get Thomas fed and watered and I'll meet you later. Say seven at the tower?'

She nodded hesitantly.

'Well then,' he said, 'dinner it is.'

Her climb was more restrained this time. Two nights prior, each stone stair had burst with memories of her childhood sanctuary. Now, anxiousness slowed her steps. As she'd edged through the early twilight of the cemetery, a faint light had been visible through the tower's tall window beneath its clock face.

Quentin was waiting.

Now, as she neared the peak of her ascent, she saw candlelight illuminating the top of the stairwell. She froze before the open door, staring into the room.

He was sitting on one of the small steps by the window in front of the larger of the two overturned crates, which was now draped in a folded white tablecloth. Upon the impromptu dining table lay a covered serving dish, silver cutlery, napkins, gleaming champagne flutes, and a glowing candlestick. The candle was one of many; the perimeter of the room was lined with rows of tiny flames, soaking the walls in a warm glow. Renata stepped inside. Her childhood refuge had always been synonymous with the bitter cold, which passed freely through the glassless window built into the stone. Tonight, the combined strength of the candles affected a gentle warmth against her cheeks. He stood to pull out the smaller crate as she approached the makeshift dining table, offering her the seat like a waiter.

'Quentin, I… You didn't have to—'

'Ren,' he said, reaching into his blazer and pulling out the notebook, 'please.'

'You found it? I'm so glad.'

'Never lost it,' he said, grinning.

Tapping his foot, he opened the notebook and began scribbling. Through those horn-rimmed frames she once again saw that glimmer in his eyes. As he slipped the notebook back into his pocket, she understood the glimmer was indeed the spark of creativity, never resting nor relenting. The passion that infused his note-taking confirmed that for all she had against the genre in which he worked, she couldn't deny his devotion to his art.

'Is madam ready for the main course?' He lifted the serving dish lid to reveal two bowls of tomato and rice soup.

Renata smiled.

10

She could hardly believe the man was getting paid to write this stuff.

The ring binder given to her by Quentin was crammed with tattered fragments of lazily-constructed script, as well as the occasional excerpt of the novel on which the upcoming movie was to be based. She was shocked at the quality of the dialogue she'd been given to work on, marvelling at it having come from a professional at all. Her primary complaint was how little it said with so much; screeds of words, only a few of which carried any real meaning. She'd learnt from her mother's collection, before she'd even taken up writing, that to convey any kind of reality-based emotion in dialogue you had to strip it back to its core parts. If you could trim it like a rose, you may be left with something pure and miraculous: a character that spoke off the page.

She had no experience in scriptwriting. That her credentials in anything other than dumbed-down romantic fiction were so lacking didn't seem to bother Quentin, just as Renata wasn't bothered to be working in such a different manner than she was used to. Put simply: she needed cash, he needed…what did he need? 'A woman's touch' were his words. Having now read the material which was to constitute the emotional core of this big-budget production, she was beginning to believe the script really did need this 'woman's touch' as much as she needed the money.

The flow of trucks had thinned as the transformation of the airfield neared completion. Now, tucked away in Quentin's trailer on the north-east side away from the chaos, Renata struggled to find the words to explain the problems with the script.

'The issue isn't what you're trying to make these characters say,' she attempted, 'it's the lengths you're going to in trying to make them say it.'

He crossed his legs. Garfield socks today. 'That's an hour we've been sitting here,' he said, changing his mind to recross them. 'Can I be honest?' Her eyebrow arched. He wasn't the kind of man to need permission and she knew it. 'You lost me about fifty-nine minutes ago.'

They stared blankly at each other before erupting into laughter. The pressure in the trailer equalised with this break in tension.

Suddenly the words came to Renata. '"That's an hour we've been sitting here", that's what you just said.'

His blank expression returned.

She took a deep breath. 'That's now an hour that the two of us have been sat here in this trailer talking back and forth about the problems with the dialogue in your script,' she drawled. 'And there's your Quentin C. Rye scripted version. They both say the same thing, but the second is bloated. Your reader – or your viewer, or movie-goer, or whoever – is going to lose interest halfway through. If you're to earn their investment, you have to strip it back.'

Quentin slipped the hardbound notebook from his pocket and began taking notes, listening intently, knee bouncing.

'Not only that, but you're laying it out too neatly for your characters,' she continued. 'You have to treat them as you treat your readers: don't tell them the story, let them discover it.' He stopped scribbling and looked up. 'I mean, I didn't mean to…not that I've ever edited a script. I just think—'

'You're right,' he beamed, the pen spinning between his fingers. The Yankee twang was growing on her. 'You're right about everything. I'm stunned, Ren. I can already tell you're going to be a—'

The lights went out.

'—worthwhile investment.'

'What happened?' Renata said. 'The lights outside are down too.'

It was approaching October and the darkness had been marching earlier every evening. With the floodlights lining the airfield's perimeter suddenly cut, the site was dropped into total blackness. Renata and Quentin peered through the blinds and saw only the twinkling lights of battery-operated equipment that had been in use by production personnel.

'Power outage,' muttered Quentin. She heard plastic rustling in the darkness. 'Idiots can't even keep a damned set running. Takes them hours to get it back up. Bonbon?'

'Oh, uh…no, thank you,' she said. 'Pity though, just when we were making progress. Pick up tomorrow?'

A flame leapt from the darkness as Quentin sparked a match. 'Tomorrow? No, we have work to do. This trailer stinks anyway.' He began cramming papers into a carrier bag. 'We're going to my place.'

Renata's writing had been a peephole into something which she'd never had for herself, a distorted caricature of something unattainable. She could paint things resembling that thing they called *romance*, but that's what they remained: paintings, imitations. The caricatures never begged to be let in, and by god you better believe that door had never been opened. She'd been a spectator, safe and secluded.

Now, this man, this architect of horror, had made romantic gestures the likes of which weren't meant for her. What did he want? Surely not her, not this tired, aged wretch – not the 'Neo-Thorrach Buidseach'. Yet here was an invitation to his *little place* on the other side of town. Work: that was it. The invitation was to finish their work.

The flame died as Quentin opened the trailer door, the panicked voices of his crew audible from across the site. He turned to Renata and held out a hand.

'Let's get outta here.'

It reminded her in some ways of her cottage on that storm-battered rock in the Outer Hebrides. Lining the walls of Quentin's second-floor living room were piles of discarded books. They were lying in heaps, tattered and askew as if thrown across the room once their words had been devoured. The lounge was dotted with cardboard boxes overflowing with horror and thriller novels in seemingly brand-new condition, which she guessed were also destined for the discarded heaps once digested.

'Sorry about the state of the place,' said Quentin, draping Renata's duffle coat over the back of a leather chesterfield. 'If I'd known my people were going to be so incompetent I'd have tidied up for you.' He went to the door. 'Back in a sec, I'll grab us some drinks.'

'Quentin, we have work to do.'

'Just water,' he called back. 'Need to stay hydrated if we're going to fix this car crash of a script.'

The three-storey manor on the outskirts of Millbury Peak was by far the largest residence in town. She couldn't imagine what it could be used for during its presumably long periods of vacancy, although the dust that coated every surface hinted at the answer: nothing. She'd have to give her hands a good scrub later.

From the living room window she could see the overgrown garden, the weeds having risen long ago to reclaim the patch of land. She looked down at the gravel track leading past the house and was just able to make out his Harley leant against the wall below.

Renata turned around as Quentin's distant, muffled voice floated up the stairs. She thought of shouting down for him to repeat himself but decided against it, instead carefully stepping towards the door as she tugged nervously at the long sleeves of her woollen sweater.

As she approached the stairs leading to the ground floor hallway, response-length silences between the continuing sentences of Quentin's voice became evident. He was on the telephone.

'No, honey. I love you more than anything, you know that. Listen, Sandie, I'm not mad. Actually, screw it. I am. I explicitly told you not to come to England, and what did you do?'

Another response-length silence.

'You went completely against my wishes.'

And another.

His voice was tinged with the defiant tone of a parent resisting the pleading of their guilty child. From the snippets of conversation, it was clear Sandie had done as her father demanded and boarded the first flight back to the States. The first thing she'd done upon arriving home, apparently, was to pick up the telephone, call 'Daddy', and beg for forgiveness. Renata felt a stab of sympathy.

There'd been a time, long ago, when she'd toiled to turn Thomas Wakefield's resentment of her into favour.

How many sleepless nights had she stayed up, just a little girl, constructing that homemade crucifix to replace the glass cross she'd smashed? She'd accumulated an abundance of building materials for the project; empty cereal packets, spent toilet roll tubes, a miniature paint set, PVA glue from arts and crafts class, all stuffed at the back of her wardrobe waiting to be built into her masterpiece, her apology.

The thing had stood as tall as her (well, up to her waist at least) and had boasted a wealth of colours that would have made Joseph jealous. Who needed a Technicolour Dreamcoat when you had an original Renata Wakefield homemade crucifix?

Yeah, she'd still been able to make out the remnants of the bruise on her face. And yeah, it had hurt more than anything she'd experienced in her short life, but it had been nobody's fault but hers. That's what the girl had concluded. That glass crucifix was so big and heavy, must have been worth a fortune, and Father had doted on the thing. If she hadn't been so stupid, so careless, it wouldn't have broken and he wouldn't have had to do what he did. If only she'd taken her time going up those steps.

Choo-choo.

Well, this was going to make it all better. With Mother's permission she'd left it on the sideboard in the living room, its multicoloured tissue paper and glitter standing out like a (colourful) sore thumb in the muted, uniform lounge of the Wakefield residence.

I am very sorry, Father, the note she'd left by its side had read. *Hope you like this alot and you luv it cause I luv you alot. God bless. −Renata xx*

He'd been back late that night. Although her mother's wooden smile hadn't faltered for so much as a second whilst they'd awaited his arrival, Sylvia Wakefield's apprehension had been obvious. Renata had watched her manic cleaning, going over the same surfaces again and again, dusting imaginary dust. The girl had been good at spotting the signs of her mother's terror. Finally, the sound of the front door opening had reached them, that sound Renata knew her mother dreaded so. The woman had straightened like a meerkat, her hands flying up to check her intricately fixed head of hair as footsteps sounded from the hallway.

In the little girl's mind there had been two possible outcomes: either Father would love the gift and all would be forgiven, or she'd find her face squished once again into those cold floorboards before she got the follow-up beating she deserved. In some ways, the girl would later realise, she'd have preferred the beating to what actually happened.

Namely, nothing.

'Good evening, Father,' she'd said, her eyes flicking to the multicoloured crucifix on the dresser.

'Thomas, welcome home,' Sylvia had chirped, hands clasped neatly behind her back.

Like a raincloud obscuring the sunlight on a green pasture, the crucifix had fallen into darkness as his shadow passed over it. He'd continued on indifferently, Renata's sculpture afforded not even a glance. She'd watched, dumbstruck, as her father had walked straight past the dresser and sunk into his armchair, today's *Daily Express* rising between him and the cross.

And there it had sat for the rest of the week. He must have seen it, surely, but no comment was made. Maybe the allowing of it to sit there undisturbed should have been thanks enough, but a queasy feeling had still materialised in the little girl's tummy whenever she'd looked at the crucifix and its unread note. Eventually, Mother had gently suggested it might look pretty in Renata's bedroom instead. Despite the girl's well-performed, enthusiastic nod, Sylvia Wakefield would later find it crammed into the outside bin, the note lying crumpled by its side. Had she known its disposal to be Renata's doing? The little girl had cared not.

'I know, Sandie,' Quentin continued into the telephone, frustration creeping through his words. 'Yes, I do know that. You're the most important thing to me. You're my world, but what you did was stupid. Really stupid.'

As she tiptoed down the stairs, Renata listened to Quentin scold his daughter. *Girl's doing her best*, she thought, *give her a break*. But at least Sandie's apology was being so much as noticed.

'My love, if you stop talking for just one second I'll explain why I'm so angry.'

Renata eased herself down the steps, listening intently for creaks, pressing her hands against the walls on either side of the staircase in an attempt to somehow displace her—

…a Himalayan trek, an Everest descent…

Her feet touched down on the hall carpet, *an invisible imperfection imposed upon perfection*. She pressed her body into the alcove at the foot of the stairwell and listened. The voice from the kitchen started up again.

'I have my reasons, Sandie. Yes, I agree, she's great, but—'

The earpiece's pleading into his ear interrupted him. Renata peered round the corner and watched his breathing quicken, his chest puff.

'YOU WERE *NOT* MEANT TO GO ANYWHERE NEAR HER.'

This time, she suspected, the silence was not accompanied by a voice in his ear.

She took a step back, eyes wide, mouth dry. Whoever he was speaking about – *not me, surely can't be me* – she was sure she wasn't meant to be hearing this. Her hand found the banister, her feet the staircase.

'I'm sorry, Sandie. It's just…I have to protect you. I can't let anything happen to you, you're too important to…'

Quentin's voice faded as Renata quietly returned to the upstairs living room and perched herself on the edge of the couch.

She was clawing at the palms of her hands, the words going through her head again and again – *you were not meant to go anywhere near her you were not meant to go anywhere near her you were not* – when Quentin plodded back into the room. He kicked off his crocodile skin shoes and set down a jug of water. 'Straight vodka as ordered,' he said. 'Those stairs are a bitch. Knew I should have gone for a B&B.'

He emptied the carrier bag onto the coffee table before collapsing into the couch. Renata got up as he sat down, then stepped slowly to a framed photo of Sandie on the bureau. She had to know more.

The teenager's eyelashes fluttered out of the frame. Renata picked it up. 'She's so pretty,' she said, probing, watching for his reaction.

The breath caught in her throat as Quentin leapt from the couch and stormed towards her, snatching the frame from her hand and shoving it into the bureau. He slammed the drawer shut, then lumbered back to the couch.

Renata stood silent, mouth agape. She remembered him practically dragging Sandie from her at the film set. Was he trying to keep his darling daughter from her, or could this simply be put down to a grossly overprotective father?

you were not meant to go anywhere near her you were not meant to go—

'I'm sorry,' Quentin said, his face warming. 'I just…Ren, I worry about her, okay? Jumping on flights by herself like that. She's still just a kid, y'know?'

'And yet you had a live weapon stuck in her mouth for a movie,' said Renata. The words slipped from her mouth like soap from wet fingers. She stood frozen.

He shot a glare at her. 'Don't question my methods.' There was the hint of a tear forming in his eye. His love for the girl was uncontainable. 'She's my world. I love her more than you could know.'

She swallowed. 'I'm sure you do. What about your flammable film stock? What do you think of the men in that truck?' She threw a hand over her mouth, then watched his eyes fall to the floor. Where had that come from? 'I'm…so sorry, Quentin. I didn't mean to—'

'This isn't the first time my methods have been called into question, and it won't be the last.' He sighed as light played on the lenses of his glasses. 'The gun wasn't loaded, despite what I told everyone – her included. I could never put her in harm's way. The goddamn film stock in that truck was the real loaded gun, and it finally went off. Nearly killed two men in the process.' He lowered his head. 'Was only a matter of time, I guess.'

'Why the publicity stunts, Quentin?' She sat next to him. 'I may not be the biggest fan of your work, but I see a man overflowing with creativity. That notebook, it's hardly ever out of your hands. You bleed for your art. Isn't that enough? Can't your work speak for itself?'

His eyes locked on hers.

'Truth,' he said. 'It's all about truth, Renata.' He leant in, then motioned to the piles of books littering the room. 'These pages, these stories, every one of them is trying so damned hard to say something with nothing. What was it you said? Saying so little with so much?' His fists clenched. 'It's trash, all of it. Mine especially. Tepid fucking trash. Storytelling is the search for truth through a lie. All these stories – their books, our books, the whole goddamn lot – fiction is meant to be the vehicle in pursuit of truth, not this watered down tripe.' His eyes deepened. 'Whatever we write, Renata, it's for the *truth*.'

Her body tensed. She'd inadvertently coaxed out the core of this man's creativity, and it was explosive. They seemed to have hit upon his reason for being – besides his treasured daughter – and he was happy to elaborate.

'Those stunts were *nothing*...' His voice rose. '...NOTHING but a means by which to drag the truth from what I do.' A smile crept over his face. 'The gun: to strike *true* fear into Sandie. The nitrate film: to place the threat of fire on my actors and audiences. *True* fire.' The smile faded. 'But you're right. They're publicity stunts, nothing more. That's clear to me now. But I haven't given up. I believe I'm on the cusp of a work that's infused with the very essence of all storytelling.' A bead of sweat ran down his brow. 'Pure, inescapable *truth*. And I'm going to get there. With your help, Renata, *we're* going to get there.'

***

113

They worked into the night.

Quentin's explosive explanation of his work should have left Renata on edge, as had the baffling telephone call, but she was in awe. He'd spoken with furious passion, as if his pursuit of this 'truth' was but an inch away, yet somehow still outside his grasp. A floodgate seemed to have opened following the outpouring. The intensity with which he discussed the script was now crystalized into pure drive. No more quips, no more comedic interludes. The notebook was now permanently out, his hand scribbling constantly within its tattered pages. It seemed as if whatever he believed to be within his reach was edging closer, and he knew it.

They'd heard the tolling of the midnight bell from across the fields over an hour ago. Renata thought of the young vicar having now spent two nights in the spare room of the Wakefield house. To her surprise, it had been he who'd suggested the lengthening of his stay to give Renata the chance to put some serious time in at the film set. Either he was finally hitting it off with Thomas Wakefield, or he was trying for his scouts badge in the care of abusive old men. Scouts badge it must be.

Quentin cast the final sheet to one side and stared at the empty space where the pile of papers to be worked had been. 'There's more,' he said, 'but for now, we're done. I don't know how to thank you, Ren. You're so gifted, so talented. You're...'

He took her hand.

'...amazing.'

As the rain tapped against the window, as Quentin pulled her in by her trembling hand, as the distance between them closed, Renata imagined herself back in the clock tower. In her mind, she sat in the middle of the little stone room above the churchyard, candlelight warming her pale skin, walls glowing.

you were NOT meant to go anywhere near her

Overprotective, that's all.

She felt his breath upon her cheeks.

Even now she was a spectator. She watched from afar as Quentin edged closer and ran a finger down her arm. Suddenly, the peephole exploded, its lifelong distortion giving way to reality. Finally, the door began to open.

There must be some mistake. These were the last words to fly through her head in the moments before their lips met. *There must be some mistake, and he'll realise any moment.*

If he did, and if there was, it didn't alter the course of events. His lips sat unmoving upon hers, the warmth of his breath causing her to halt both in body and mind. Then – *so that's what it feels like* – he kissed her deeply, pressing his forehead against hers in an expression of uninhibited relief.

She felt him breathe in her scent. She felt him, already as close as he could be, try to edge through space that was not there. She felt his longing for her, and despite a fleeting attempt at restraint, she responded. She watched from afar against a backdrop of glowing stone, in her mind still hiding in that clock tower, the warmth of the candlelight causing her skin to rise in submission.

...and let the marriage bed be undefiled, for God will judge the sexually immoral and...

Guilt stabbed. She took a deep breath and pushed aside He who had pushed her aside. She was on her own now, with Quentin.

She peered through slits in her closed eyelids as she succumbed to the touch of his lips. All at once, she saw the stone of the clock tower fall away, its candles extinguishing. Her mental hideout was replaced by piles of books, dusty furniture, a discarded script, and the man who would show her how to love.

She stopped observing. Finally, Renata Wakefield arrived – here, now. She closed her eyes and sunk into the moment, and into Quentin's arms.

11

The crate tumbles down the stairwell. The girl sets the lantern against the wall and balances the smaller of the two wooden boxes on the stone steps, then descends to rescue her fallen comrade. Approaching the foot of the spiral staircase, she hears the clattering of wood on stone from above.

The second crate crashes down.

Remarkably, both are undamaged. The crates are strong. Not only have they survived their respective tumbles, but they've also endured the long walk from town and across the fields into the woods, where she stashed them until the sun went down. The girl is scrawny and weak. She dropped them more than a few times.

And her arm still hurts. Finger-shaped bruises wrap around her wrist from where Father had yanked her from the bookcase. Still, better than the fist. The books disappeared from the shelves the day after she was caught in the act, along with all those in her bedroom. Luckily, the current book she'd borrowed from Mr Harper had been in her schoolbag, but she couldn't risk her father catching her reading those oh-so-blasphemous romance stories again, so she'd set out to find a safe place to read and write and stash her books. Her excursions had led her far and wide; forests, the long grass of the surrounding fields, even an abandoned building. Whether too far from home or too likely to collapse under her feet, there was always a reason to keep looking.

Life continued throughout her searching. School, church, home: those were the three primary stages upon which the not-so-funny pantomime of her life unfolded. School, church, home. School, church, home. School, church…

Church?

Yes, that was where the answer had presented itself. It had been right on her doorstep the entire time. Well, give or take a few fields.

It was as the chattering congregation had gathered in the churchyard after Sunday service (learn the love of our Lord, then *get gossiping) that she'd seen the cat. He was black and white and he was fluffy, just how she liked them. The girl had watched him rub against the side of the church, before he'd proceeded to sample some other parts of the stone wall.* Goldilocks and the Three Bears *had popped into her head; this bowl too hot, that bowl too cold. He just couldn't find the perfect spot, poor Mr Kitty – or maybe Jazz? That's a cute name for a cat. Nearly as cute as Misty-Moo, the name she'd given the delicate little kitty she regularly found sleeping in amongst an old fleece on the seat of Father's ride-on lawnmower. Jazz's search had eventually led him around the cylindrical perimeter of the clock tower and out of sight.*

The girl had looked at her mother, the woman's forced smile firmly in place, holding the five-year-old Noah's hand as Mrs Caldwell shrieked in varying degrees at the particular aspects of the boy's face she found most ADORABLE. Then at her father, solemnly nodding as Mr Oakley the pharmacist had congratulated him on another fine service, another fine service indeed. The girl decided the coast was clear and went after Jazz.

She followed the stone wall which eventually jutted out, marking the border between the church and the clock tower. She arched her neck and gazed up the tower, a runway of stone stretching into the sky. At the end of the runway lay the great clock embedded into its surface, its cryptic Roman numerals glimmering in the sun. She imagined running along the stony road and jumping onto the clock. What would happen? Well, that would depend on whether or not she could clear the narrow window.

Window? She'd never noticed any window before. Wonder what's inside?

She followed Jazz's trail around the back of the tower and found him scratching something in the stone. The sun was high, but not high enough to penetrate this dark corner. Shadows bathed the kitty's new haunt, rendering the thing he was scratching barely visible. Jazz spotted her as she approached – he knew he'd been rumbled – and darted off like a cat out of Hell. She edged closer, peering through the shadows at the focus of his attention. It was a shoulder-high wooden hatch built into the stone. Whether or not she knew it at the time, her search was over.

That had been enough for one day. She'd take a detour after school on Wednesday to investigate properly. Father would be in town late so there would be no danger of him catching her arriving home later than usual, or in the midst of her exploration as he left church. That would be the only potential danger of this great discovery: her father's church next door. That wasn't to say she wasn't allowed to play in the neighbouring fields, and, judging by the planks of wood boarding up the main entrance of the tower, no one but her would be climbing its stone steps any time soon.

Come Wednesday, following this further investigation, she would find a small hole in the hatch, big enough for a child's finger, which would allow her to pry the wooden panel open. Inside, at the top of a stone staircase, she'll find the room in which she'll dive deeper into her reading and writing than she ever thought possible. The neighbouring fields were so overgrown that she could lie in wait out of sight as long as she needed before running across the churchyard (plenty of gravestones to use as cover if she spotted anyone) and in through her secret hatch. All this sneaking was, of course, based on the assumption that her visits would take place during the daytime. If she could continue her silent mastery of the staircase at the house, and acquire the means for some portable light (a lantern, perhaps), there could potentially be entire nights of reading and writing awaiting her.

The room is perfect, or at least it will be once the makeshift writing desk Mr Harper kindly gave her has been dragged up this stupid staircase.

Finally, as she overcomes the last step with both her wooden friends by her side, the room presents itself. The space had been crammed with rotting furniture and all sorts of rubble, but, having picked the most strategically suitable night, she'd simply thrown it all out of the tall stone window onto the grass below, then shifted it into the neighbouring woods. The room is mostly bare now, and she takes considerable pleasure in dragging the crates – writing desk and chair, that is – into her new study, high above the world.

The girl lights the lantern with a pack of matches taken from the kitchen and sets it upon the larger of the two crates, which she positions with great pride in the centre of the room. She also places writing materials from her rucksack on her new desk, then takes a seat on the smaller crate. She gazes at the stone walls glowing in the candlelight.

This'll do.

She tried writing tonight but the sight of the blank paper was too much. The infinite possibilities of that empty canvas drove her so crazy she ended up snapping her last pencil. Starting these things is always a nightmare. She kicks the broken pencil across the floor.

Today is her thirteenth birthday. Despite this, she could

have left for the clock tower much earlier and no one would have noticed. She shares her birthday with Noah, rendering her parents and guests utterly preoccupied. He was given – amongst much else – a seaside bucket and spade, shiny, metal, and red. Just the colour he wanted. They even had it engraved, if you can believe that. He loves digging for worms, the idiot. He's going to be a scientist, apparently.

Her birthday present was a pocket Bible laid ceremonially outside her bedroom door and, later, a bin bag filled with crumpled wrapping paper. 'Lenata,' the child had bubbled, his incapacity for Rs boiling her blood, 'I found some mole lapping papah you can put in the lubbish, Lenata.'

The speech impediment was real, in so far as it was a permanent fixture of his speaking voice. However, the accentuation of her mispronounced name was, she was sure, deliberately emphasised. He knew it annoyed her. She could see it in the grin through which he sneered the word.

'Lenata,' he'd whine at every available opportunity. 'Lenaaaah-tah.'

In a funny sort of way she owed him everything. Since his arrival the atmosphere in the house had settled. Her mother's bruises had ceased their constant renewal, and the girl was largely ignored – treatment she would gladly choose over the alternative.

She did miss the bond she'd shared with her mother. Although never vocalised, it had often felt as if they were just two friends stuck in the wrong place at the wrong time. Her last memory of any meaningful time spent with Sylvia Wakefield was, of all things, an improvised driving lesson. It had to happen whilst Thomas was out of town since, her mother had explained, his finding out she was being taught a 'man's skill' would have ended regrettably.

Was there anything unusual about a little girl's heavily

pregnant mother teaching her to drive in secret? Sure, but the urgency of the lesson didn't need spelt out. From the late-night shouting, the girl knew of the responsibility resting upon the shoulders of their unborn child; more than anything in the world, Thomas Wakefield wanted a son. Certainly not another failed attempt, as he considered the girl. He wanted a damned SON. An ultrasound was out of the question (blasphemous as he considered them) so it was a matter of waiting for nature to reveal whether or not Sylvia had failed her husband once again – and for the final time, the woman feared. The rage that swelled from his every pore at the mention of another girl filled Sylvia with the belief Thomas may be capable of anything in the event of such a failure, a belief strong enough to warrant the extreme measure of providing her daughter with an emergency escape.

Thankfully, it hadn't been needed. Noah had arrived – a boy, praise be – and, although the girl saw the little weasel for what he really was, she understood that she really did owe him everything. Yes, the atmosphere in the house had calmed, but more importantly he had been the driving force in her pursuit of writing.

Noah was a wonder child in the eyes of his parents. The abounding praise for the boy was always juxtaposed with regular vocalisations of her father's contempt for Renata. ('There's something wrong with that girl. She's never been right. Do you see now why I wanted a boy?') It was this incessant scorn ('You're a leech on this family, child. A parasite.') that had pushed her reading even further, not only as an attempt to correct her 'inferior intellect', but also as an escape.

An emergency escape, just like the driving lessons.

The writing had spawned naturally from her obsessive reading, and it was all because of that little worm of a brother. The girl, now sitting at her makeshift writing desk in front of a blank sheet of paper, wonders if the stupid worms he'll dig up with his new spade will recognise him as one of their own. The girl giggles at the thought.

One day, months from now, she'll find fear in a place she thought there was none: the pages of a book. Then the giggling will stop.

Soon, sitting in this clock tower, the girl will be changed forever.

Every day after school the girl stops at Harper's Books, where she's welcomed like royalty.

'Ah, young Wakefield! Make way for the good lady!' Mr Harper would announce. Despite her embarrassment, she was as yet unable to restrain a grin at this display, and so the announcements would continue. The presence of any other customers would have amplified the girl's embarrassment. Luckily, there were few.

The deal was that the girl could borrow any books that caught her eye, so long as they were returned in perfect condition. It was, of course, mostly the romance section that won her attention, which would lead her through the pages of Jane Austen, Emily Brontë, E. M. Forster, and, having completed the classics, onto the contemporary work of Natasha Peters, Rosemary Rogers, and Kathleen E. Woodiwiss. Although she hungered mostly for stories of love, she'd make occasional forays to the adventure or even crime and mystery sections, these excursions becoming increasingly frequent once she'd worked through the romance section several times over.

The light, playful tone Mr Harper presented masked his awe at the rate with which the vicar's daughter was tearing through the shelves of his shop. True to her word, the books were returned as she'd found them. Not that the books were good as new to begin with. Following the death of his wife, Mr Harper had made an obsession of reading. He'd acquired boxes of novels from every dealer in the surrounding area, and having read them all, opened the shop as a means of passing the books onto anyone that would benefit. He'd even had wooden crates made up for customers to borrow, with the words HARPER S BOOKS stencilled on their sides. They'd need them for the stacks of books they'd be buying. He and his wife were – bloody hell, 'he', just 'he' now – financially comfortable following the lucrative combination of relentless saving and no children. He didn't need the shop to live, but he did need to pass on the books. Why? Well, not every question needs an answer.

Mr Harper was not a religious man – a rarity in this town. He stopped attending service after his wife passed, much to the disapproval of the townsfolk. ('MEANING! You need MEANING in your life!' Mrs Lazenby had implored. 'Don't you want to know what it's all ABOUT, Mr Harper?') He remembered enough about Mr Wakefield, however, to fear the vicar's discovery that he'd supplied his daughter, Renata, with 'blasphemous' works such as Sense and Sensibility or Great Expectations. But what he saw in the girl's eyes upon completion of a book was the same thing he'd seen in the mirror in the midst of his grieving, deep in the solace these infinite pages had afforded him: peace. And as Mrs Lazenby had rattled on about that profound MEANING he was missing, and about the REASON for being here, as well as the REASON for his wife being DEAD in the DIRT, one thought remained in Mr Harper's mind: not every question needs an answer, dammit.

So he'd inadvertently accumulated a shop's worth of books, opened said shop full of books, and was now effectively running a free library only a few 'customers' made use of. And all the while those ludicrous crates sat gathering dust in the storeroom.

The girl had figured some of this out for herself, and some of it he'd shared with her. She sensed, to the degree with which a girl her age could, his gestures of kindness were not fully altruistic; she knew he was getting something from letting her borrow any book she liked. His payment was company.

She also knew, better than he did, what her father would do if he knew of the books she had unlimited access to. What she didn't know was what he would have done had he caught her with one of the books from the alcove, that mysterious, forbidden alcove. Namely because she didn't know what was in there.

'Anything, young Wakefield!' Mr Harper would bellow, a face like sunlight. 'Ever hear the story of Aladdin? Well this,' he'd said, sweeping his hands across the shelves, 'is your cave, and I'm your genie!'

The girl had glanced at the back of the shop towards the alcove. Clouds suddenly obscured the sunlight of the man's face. Yes, he knew about her father alright. His wife had been well connected and she'd shared with him just about every rumour in Millbury Peak. There was even a chance he knew Renata's father better than most. Maybe, just maybe, there were reasons he'd stopped attending service besides his loss of faith. Yes indeed, he knew of the man, and he knew just how angry a copy of Pride and Prejudice might make him, let alone something from the alcove. Oh yeah, he knew the rumours, and for once he believed them.

'You will NOT go near those books, Miss Wakefield,' he'd said through the clouds. 'Not one of them. Do I make myself clear?'

The alcove had then been stripped. This dark pocket of the shop was now bare, and over the following months nothing but dust would grace their shelves. For a time, consumed by her lust for the rest of the shop, the girl forgot about the forbidden area. The stories lining these walls seemed infinite. Whilst these endless pages were available to her, she would never need another book.

Until she did.

'Man the deck, me hearty!' said Mr Harper one day as he limped on an imaginary peg leg towards the shop door. 'Need to find us some pirate's grub, I do!'

As Mr Harper headed down the street, leaving the girl flicking through a Gustave Flaubert novel she'd read twice already, she found her eyes drifting to the bare shelves of the alcove. He'd never left her alone before now, and the unexplored territory called to her. What were these accursed texts that could land her in more trouble than anything else in the shop?

She replaced the Flaubert and crept towards the empty alcove, keeping an eye on the shop window for any sign of Mr Harper. The shelves were indeed bare, but the alcove was not completely empty.

The whistling that suddenly approached the shop was, to the girl, an air raid siren. Without a moment to even look at the cover of the battered paperback she'd spotted hiding on the floor under a shelf in the alcove, she'd rammed it into her coat pocket and rushed to a neighbouring shelving unit, pretending to be engrossed in a Madeleine L'Engle fantasy. Mr Harper stepped through the front door carrying cups of soup and hot rolls, none the wiser.

And now, back in the safety of her clock tower, there's an intruder. She knows it's there, waiting patiently in her coat. Already she's been here for hours; the night has drawn in and a biting wind is piercing through the little stone room like a spear. She should be in bed. They all think she's in bed, but she's here, finally ready to confront the demon that's been awaiting her all evening. Heart racing, she reaches into her coat.

Under the lantern's light the book is unassuming. Tame, even. The classics she'd worked through were bibles, thick as logs with pages thinner than air. This thing is slender, its cover illustration laughably cheap. She whispers its title:

HORROR HIGHWAY
QUENTIN C. RYE

She giggles at the cover and its name. It's like throwing a white sheet over a kitten and hoping people will run screaming from the ghost. Just a cheap paperback, *she thinks.* Can't fool me. *She giggles again.*

For the final time, she giggles.

She believes, after the tomes she's conquered, she can digest the book by quickly skimming through its pages. She begins to flick.

A little boy is told to slip the tip of a sharpened blade into his baby sister's soft skull in order to save the lives of his parents. He complies.

A man chokes through shattered teeth, their jagged tips sticking from his raw gums like tiny fangs. He is fed his own genitals.

Through blood and tears a woman screams as she is raped in a shadowy alley to an audience of cheering hobos.

The girl's tears dot the pages. She can't stop flicking. Why can't she stop flicking?

Eyelids removed, tiny games of noughts and crosses carved into corneas with a drawing pin; holes drilled under fingernails and down the length of each digit, bleach funnelled into the fleshy shafts; broken glass sandpapered into skin, broken glass, all over, sandpapered, skin, over and over and over and—

Pages roll by. Death, torture, and pain wash over her.

Then she finds it.

A flaming pickup truck tears through a lone woman standing in the middle of the road, her emerald green dress flapping madly in the wind as metal rips her from the asphalt. She's tossed, her contorted body flying up and over the vehicle through billowing flames. The fire catches upon her dress. The flaming truck speeds into the distance while the woman lands on the road and lies crumpled, paralysed as the burning green fabric melts into her flesh.

Eyes stung by tears, the girl throws the book across the stone-walled room and backs away. It lands amongst a pile of dirt and rubble. The demon rests. It has done its work.

There it shall lie for thirty years.

There it shall await Renata Wakefield.

12

Renata picked up the ringing telephone and carried it into the hall on its long cable. She closed the living room door, sat on a step at the bottom of the staircase, and answered.

'Hey, Renata? It's Sandie!'

'Sandie…uh, hello,' she said nervously, searching for the words. 'What can I do for you?'

'Nothing, just calling for a chat.'

'From…America?' Renata paused. 'I've not thought any more about the Adelaide Addington movie, you know.'

'Oh, no sweat. I really just wanted to apologise *profusely* for how Daddy carried on at the film set, shouting at me like that. He doesn't usually do that. That happening in front of you was *so* embarrassing. Guess he's under a lot of pressure at the moment with this new film.' The sound of a knife on a chopping board came through the line. 'I'm on the hands-free. You hear me *satisfactorily*?'

'Fine, yes.'

'I really enjoyed talking to you when we met. Won't be, like, a regular thing or anything, I promise. I won't start stalking you – I've had my fair share of that.'

'I don't mind, Sandie,' said Renata, 'but I'm a little concerned your father doesn't want us speaking. I wouldn't want to cause an upset.'

The girl giggled. 'There's a lot Daddy doesn't know about me, Renata. One more thing won't hurt.'

'Sandie, have you any idea why your father wouldn't

want us talking? He seems rather adamant about it.'

'It's weird, isn't it? I mean, he's always been real protective over me, but this is just dumb. Sometimes I think he loves me too much for his own good, the goofball that he is.' The chopping stopped. 'He does seem pissed at me, though. I dunno if I've done something wrong, besides talking to you, of course. But why he wouldn't want us chatting, I got no idea. Guess I need to think of a way to make it up to him. Maybe I could get rid of some of the…*miscellany* he wants to sell to raise money for his charities.'

The flicking television channels of Sandie's mind cycled through various other disparate topics, wedging in those oh-so-impressive words wherever she could. Finally, the conversation drew to a close amongst further promises of Sandie being first in line for the Adelaide Addington part, should it ever materialise. Renata hung up the receiver even more perplexed about Quentin's behaviour. So Sandie also found his keeping them apart strange. What kind of harming influence could Renata possibly have on the young girl?

She carried the telephone back into the living room, replaced it on the sideboard, and stepped to the bookcase. She had work to do.

'He's a rat,' spat Thomas. 'His type are vermin, ungodly. Keep working for him and pray the Lord's forgiveness finds you.'

Her advance from Quentin was extravagant, too extravagant, but he'd had it no other way. She pulled a folder from the dusty shelf and reached to the back to run a finger over the envelope of cash stashed behind the books. Yes, it was still real. A few more of these and she could secure her father's care, maybe even clear her debts.

She moved a few thick religious texts in front of the envelope, along with Thomas's mammoth bible, and returned to the couch.

The fire lit up the peeling wallpaper and patches of mould around the room. Furniture draped in musty sheets, framed pictures of loved ones now gone, ornaments of which only the ghosts in the pictures knew the significance: these were the kinds of artefacts dotting the mausoleum.

Above the raging fire loomed the flood. She'd considered taking the painting down but it held a weight carried over from her childhood. It was a living thing, an organism, and never had she so much as dared to touch it. Best leave it where it was.

The folder held the remaining script to be reworked. Renata had saved the hardest part for last; this bundle, they'd agreed, needed to be completely rewritten. Since her night with Quentin, from which her skin still rose at the thought, there seemed to be a hint of inspiration returning. She had to put down a lot of ink before tiny globules of true creative juice found their way through the nib of her pen to the paper, but they *were* there. She just had to persist. For Quentin, she had to persist.

Thomas swiped a moth from his face. 'A rat and a Jew,' he snarled, interrupting her train of thought. 'All those Hollywood types are Jews. They've wrecked their country with their death movies.' His blank eyes rolled in their sockets. The dishevelled mongrel by his side let out a gargled moan. '*Death movies*, that's what they are. That's where your blood money's coming from, girl.'

Her pen remained poised as he raved on. Lately, her father's hateful spiels were provoking in her something more akin to anger than fear. Anger at his ignorance, or at the terror under which she'd lived as a little girl? Could it be anger at his treatment of her mother? Rage can become to a writer the catalyst of their craft, but not this writer.

Not yet.

The anger paralysed her, as if her very thoughts had been injected with the blind old man's medication. Tonight his rambling was infuriating her. There was a cork jammed in the bottle of her abilities. Nothing came.

'And now they come to this town with their cheap thrills and actress whores and…'

Still nothing.

'…they soil this once great country with their filth. *Blasphemy*, it's nothing short of…'

A moth landed on the blank page.

'…a slap in the face of God. Let the will of their Creator strike them down. Let me tell you, girl…'

The insect stood frozen.

'…for these heathens, for all of us…'

It would be so easy.

'…in the name of the Father…'

She reached for it.

'…the flood is coming.'

Its brown abdomen crushed between her fingers.

As if his visionless eyes had seen, Thomas fell silent. Samson twitched. The question of what made her do it didn't present itself as she wiped the pulp on her skirt. She was too taken by the bubbling over of her mind, too taken by the pen that suddenly and furiously began filling the page. Aside from the crackling fire, the only sound in the room was the scratching of pen on paper.

She wrote.

***

Thomas's spiels resumed in fits and bursts. And yet, as this sudden and almighty inspiration flooded from the pen, his words passed around her like water bypassing a rock.

She reached the end of the final page of script after three hours of the pen's pouring, then sat back to look at her jagged scrawls. It wasn't until she turned back to the first page that she was reminded of what had sparked this torrent of activity. At the top of the page, above the first words of her maniacally scratched work, lay soaked into the paper a tiny wet spot: the dying juices of a moth. She looked at her fingers in horror – more dying juice – and raced to the sink in the kitchen.

Her father, having succumbed to a quivering half-sleep, choked back to life. 'Girl,' he shouted through to her, his words a froth of confusion, 'what…where's the…get the…'

She shut off the tap and returned to Thomas, slowly drying her hands. She fixed her gaze on the man's eyes. They were as misty as the fields.

'He's not coming back, is he?' she said. His unseeing stare clamped around her as that ragged fingernail began its incessant tapping and scratching on the arm of his chair. 'I need to know, Father. If Noah isn't around then I have to deal with your care myself.'

'A pig.'

She looked blankly. 'Father?'

'She never stopped believing you'd come back,' he croaked.

Renata felt a mass in her chest, an empty solidity rising to her throat as the face of Sylvia Wakefield materialised in her mind.

Midnight, midnight; it's your turn…

Suddenly the water battered the rock. She felt the

133

familiar stab of nervous fingernails in her scabby palms. Tears begged to be born in her eyes.

'I knew you were gone,' he trembled, 'just like your brother. And when I made efforts – oh, such efforts – to…*convince* her, she squealed—'

He smiled.

'—like a pig.'

So out the front door and through fog-drenched fields she ran. She wasn't meant to be here. The beam would have held, it would have taken her weight. By now, her neck should have been snapped. It would have held. There was nothing keeping her here, only some ancient promise made to a dead woman. There was nothing keeping her anywhere.

Except Quentin.

Tears fell to the fields speeding under her trailing skirt. For a time, the thickening mist rendered both the Wakefield house and the town ahead invisible. Like a sailor lost at sea, she registered a momentary loss of orientation, during which all sense of direction seemed to dissolve. She ran through space, a white, smoky space. The misty vacuum was a microcosm, her life miniaturised. The walls of fog became the cottage on Neo-Thorrach where she'd hidden herself, the passing grass the stream of dim-witted words she'd churned out endlessly for a dim-witted readership. She clenched her eyes shut as she ran; maybe the fog and the grass could be something else? Maybe they could be white, endless corridors? Pure, simple, everything in its place. No disorder, no disaster.

She opened her eyes and saw the town materialising from the abyss ahead. Millbury Peak still had her.

Quentin's rented manor finally came into view. She made a beeline for the Georgian building, scrambling down its driveway and thumping on the front door. She suddenly wondered where she'd go if there was no answer. The clock tower, no doubt. It would be freezing tonight, but she couldn't go back to Father. He wasn't a moth she could extinguish with two fingers. He was a thread of fear running from her childhood to this very moment, except the fear was changing. She was still a cowering child waiting for the shouting to stop, but the child was angry. She wondered if this rage had replaced the fear, but no, she was still afraid of Thomas Wakefield, of Millbury Peak, of everyone she met.

But there was hope. Somewhere alongside the fear and the anger and whatever else boiled inside of her there was another man, the thought of whom convinced her she could be alright – maybe even *normal*. This man made her feel like a human being, as opposed to an imposter in a world belonging to everyone but her.

Quentin opened the door.

Part of her felt ridiculous collapsing into his arms, like a hopeless, romance-saves-all cliché from one of her budget potboilers. Another part felt as she had when their lips had met, when his forehead had pressed into hers in that expression of unadulterated relief; as she had when his hand slid under the fabric of her skirt, his warmth meeting hers; as when she'd lay beneath him, her mind swimming in a blend of anxious terror (*there must be some mistake*) and complete trust. She felt as she had when watching herself give to him her very being, just as she'd watched her countless literary creations do over the years. She felt as she had that night when her body ceased its subliminal resistance and, for the first time, received a man.

His tightening arms said everything his lips didn't. She burrowed into the thick fabric of his turtleneck. She felt the voiceless whispering of his embrace assure her it was okay, that she was safe. She looked into those horn-rimmed frames, the evening chill tickling her tear-stained cheeks.

'Quentin, I don't want to be alone anymore.'

13

The girl is now sixteen years old, the boy six.

Her birthday is today, as is his.

She sits on her bed. The room is bare, save for a small dresser and wardrobe. Her identity lies not in this room, but another across the fields, high above a cemetery. A secret room. She will go there now.

Moments ago, she realised the papers, her seven chapters, were not where she thought she'd left them the previous night. Her eyes widen in panic. She must have set them down in that damned larder when returning the soup flask.

Downstairs: a cheer for every gift her brother tears open. No cheers from the kitchen, meaning the coast is clear to the larder. She checks her room one last time for the papers. All she finds is that old diary. Its opening pages are sparse, dotted with the occasional account of daily life. Reliving each day became painful, so the entries grew fewer. Many pages are left blank until suddenly, halfway through, the pages fill. She discovers storytelling.

Whooping from downstairs. A woman shrieks. Screams of laughter from another.

The girl is finished with the diary. She now writes on the crisp, yellow writing paper Mr Harper gives her. Scrawled upon a pile of these sheets, the missing sheets, are the first seven chapters to her best story yet. Adelaide Addington is finally speaking off the page. Those pages. For weeks she's toiled over her creation, the pages a mess of corrections and amendments, but within this code only she could decipher lies the first thing of which the girl has ever felt proud. If the papers have been found, and she's wrong in her belief that no one could decipher them, then things will get bad. Father will get bad.

The diary's served its purpose – for now. She stuffs it into the back of the dresser drawer. It will lie here for decades, until it is reclaimed to serve an unthinkable purpose.

She grabs her rucksack and slips out of the bedroom door, then slinks downstairs. The whooping in the dining room – the 'special occasion room' – has been replaced by chattering. The front door is open, but she won't use it. Mother and Mr O'Connell are locked in deep conversation on the porch, a glass of scotch swirling in his hand. She'd never make it past them. She'll use the back door.

The girl sneaks through the impeccably clean living room as the grandfather clock continues its unrelenting ticking. The latest of Father's precious hounds, the latest Samson, glares at her as if she's committing some terrible sin, the knowledge of which it cannot share. She glances nervously at the flood painting.

'Whale is it?' Noah says, red curls hanging over blank eyes. He stands in the doorway, expressionless. 'Whale's my plesent, Lenata?'

She backs through the kitchen door, fists clenched. Get the papers and get out, *she tells herself.*

The larder door towers over her. She tugs on its cast iron pull handle, the cold from inside rushing over her as the heavy door swings opens. She finds herself unable to enter. It's the same every time, her legs refusing to carry her into her former prison cell. She thinks of those two days six years ago in the pitch-black without food or water, soiling herself, no concept of time. But that was then, this is now.

Choo-choo.

She takes a deep breath and steps over the threshold,

walking hurriedly to the far end where the flask sits. She looks back. In the entrance stands Noah.

The short, flimsy specimen stares at her. His dirty red hair falls around his face; dirty, like the mud he spends his days digging up. In his hands are that stupid bucket and spade. Unknown to the girl, this spade will come to serve another purpose in weeks to come.

An unthinkable purpose.

The siblings stare at one another for a moment, frozen in silence. The boy's mouth twitches. She tries to speak but cannot. Her eyes beg him to reconsider what she knows is inevitable. Not again. Please, please, please not again not again not—

The door slams.

Like father like son.

The larder light is left on, unlike last time, but this only means she's able to watch the shelf-lined walls close in around her closing in closing in like the back of those bin lorries she sometimes sees gobbling up all the rubbish except she's the rubbish and she can't believe this is happening again and I need to get out closing in I can't take this not again closing in closing in please someone anyone I can't—

Rage and terror and panic bubble up inside her like a shaken Cola bottle, before melting into the searing realisation that her precious papers are not in the pantry. They must be elsewhere in the house, sitting in wait of prying eyes. Father's eyes.

She spots four drill holes in the floor, drilled six years ago exactly wide enough for a chair.

She screams.

Time folds in on itself and dissolves to nothing as her hellborn wails fill the larder and, for however long they go on for, become her universe. The chattering of the guests would have masked her cries had the thick door not soundproofed her cell. Her screaming finally ceases, if only from exhaustion. Tears soak her cheeks. She stumbles back from the locked entrance, edging fearfully around the four drill holes, and falls into a corner where she wraps her body into a tight ball on the floor. She imagines Noah giggling outside, that machine gun snigger he saves for such occasions.

'Ee-ee-eeee!'

Her crypt is cold and unforgiving, but she is not alone. One of those stupid moths sits on the floor under a shelf. Is it dead? Hopefully. She hates those damned things, always eating through her clothes and flapping in her face just when she's about to fall sleep. She hates them. She hates her brother, too. She hates this house and everything in it.

Is it dead? Maybe she wishes it was.

She reaches.

The door opens.

'Rennie, what are you doing in here?' her mother asks, tired eyes scanning the shelves for a platter of party food. 'Come on, out you come.'

'Why Lenata do that, Mummy?' says the boy. His vacuous eyes lock on the girl. 'Silly Lenata.'

The girl scrambles to her feet and follows her mother out of the larder, glancing back at the moth. The sound of a motor approaches from outside, accompanied by cheering.

'It's time, children!' says their mother, smile locked in position. 'Come, hurry! It's time!' She picks up Noah – way too big to be picked up – and, balancing the platter in her other hand, struggles through the house.

Wiping her eyes, the girl steps into the empty living room and looks through the window. She sees the guests ushering Thomas Wakefield to the dark blue Ford Cortina awaiting him, a giant red ribbon tied around the width and length of *the vehicle. Its bow ripples in the breeze.*

'It's from us all!' cries Mrs Moncrieff. 'For all you've done for the town!'

'Thank you, Vicar!' calls Mr Cooper.

'God bless you!'

'You deserve it, Mr Wakefield!'

Thomas turns to the crowd, his red hair glistening in the afternoon sun. 'It's my son, Noah, you should be thanking. He's made me what I am.' The boy grins through a mud-streaked face. 'And where, may I ask, is his car? It's his birthday, after all.'

The girl watches from the window as frenzied laughter erupts. She returns to the kitchen, where her eyes fall on Samson's food bowl. The dog's canned breakfast still lies within, brown stripes crosshatching the syrupy mush. Her mother's orange fabric scissors sit on the floor by the bowl's side, their blades lined with Samson's breakfast. She looks back to the bowl.

The brown stripes are her papers, cut into ribbons and prodded into the rancid swill.

The shaken Cola bottle of rage bubbles up once again.

At the sight of her work degraded and vulgarised, something closes within her. The girl will write again – she will make a living as an author – but her facility for true *inspiration shall remain in that bowl of festering meat until the diary reawakens, until the nightmares cease forever, until the spade fulfils its final purpose.*

An unthinkable purpose.

She stares at the bowl in disbelief. From behind her, sniggering. She turns to see the boy standing in the doorway, unable to contain himself.

'Ee-ee-eeee!'

She thinks of the moth in the larder. How easy it would

have been to—

'Noah, my little munchkin! There you are!'

'Ee-ee-eeee!'

It would have taken only two fingers.

'There's more presents! The guests are waiting!'

'Ee-ee-eeee!'

Easy, so very easy.

'Up we go!' The woman once again heaves the boy into her arms and returns to the chattering guests. The girl watches the back of her mother's damned immaculate hair as she walks away. For a moment, she wishes the bruises would return. When there were bruises, there were words. Now that the worm is here, now that the late-night shouting has ended, ever since rosy pink replaced black and blue, her mother is just another distant presence, another pair of eyes to forget the girl's existence.

The boy looks back over his mummy's shoulder, his glare locking onto the girl. His eyes cut through her.

Like knives.

He smiles.

She grabs her rucksack and runs for the back door. She must get out. She must get to the only place she knows is safe.

No one notices.

No one follows.

No one cares.

'Ee-ee-eeee!'

She runs.

14

The flames fell from above, an ocean of fire whose defiance of gravity finally tired. Black oil gushed from her hands. The road beneath the car ripped then exploded.

The dreams were getting worse.

Their details used to fall away from her upon waking like sand in an hourglass, but you can't dream the same dream for nearly thirty years without eventually piecing it together. By now she could remember the jigsaw of her dreams vividly; the red spade, the speeding car, the country roads, and her oily hands were all clear to her. What was unclear was whether the jumbled puzzle related to her accident or the cover of that damned book. Or neither. Or both.

Then there were the stabbing pains, the same pains she was so intimately accustomed to from her waking world. Yet in the dreams, thirteen stabs. Always thirteen stabs.

Only one jet-black hand, dripping with tar, gripped the wheel this time. The other reached for the sole occupant of the passenger seat: the red spade. Noah's red spade.

Burning fields sailed past the car, her father's Ford Cortina. She felt its chassis tremble then fall away. Despite its crumbling, the car somehow raged on. And all the while: *One... Five... Nine...* The stabbing pains continued with their usual, terrible regularity.

That vague yellow shape rose before her in the mist, remaining in place irrespective of her speed, beckoning her into its fold.

Ten

The wheel broke from the dashboard and flew from her oily hands into a fireball behind her. The spade remained in her black grasp.

Eleven

The last remaining remnant of the car went spinning into the sky, a Catherine wheel of flames. Somehow her body's trajectory continued. She flew towards the spectre. It raised its face, but not enough. Never enough.

Twelve

Her fist tightened around the handle of the spade.

Thirteen

She awoke.

The flames transposed into the warmth of Quentin's sleeping body. She slipped out of bed and rubbed the sides of her head, massaging out the car, the spade, her black dream-hands, and the stabbing pains. She'd told no one of the dreams, only having mentioned to Quentin in passing that she had recurring nightmares. Maybe she'd be able to share the details with him. Maybe the dreams could go away.

She checked his discarded watch. Nearly 6 a.m. The mist outside had the faint glow of dawn. Birdsong dotted the morning silence. The echoes of the stabbing in her head still resonated. She reached for her satchel, her fingers begging for the comforting feel of coiled hemp, until she remembered: she'd left it at home, and with it the noose. She'd found a new comfort.

She looked at Quentin's sleeping face.

In the weeks since they'd met, he'd had given Renata a gift completely unfamiliar to her: something to lose. Could there really be the hope of a normal life for her? She'd spent years writing of an emotion forever foreign. Now, it seemed, love had finally risen off the page to meet her. An image flashed before her of a house like this where they could live out their remaining years. *Love* and *sharing* and *trust* and *romance* still seemed disconnected and alien, but a part of her believed these things could be as real as she allowed them to be.

She slipped into Quentin's dressing gown. Her duffle coat lay over a chair. Although she couldn't match his gift to her, there was a modest something for him in its pocket. This, their second night together, had been as magical as their first. 'Magical': that's the word in all her books, right?

'Quentin, I don't want to be alone anymore,' she'd told him from within his embrace.

His fingers had melted into hers. 'Ren, I want you to tell me something. I need you to tell me something.'

'Anything.'

His eyes had poured into hers. 'Do you love me?' She'd felt his hands squeeze around her own before she allowed her eyes to dart away.

'Quentin, I…' He pulled her closer. 'Yes, I do.'

She'd been relieved when he'd smiled. He hadn't backed off, he hadn't panicked, he hadn't laughed at her misinterpretation of events. Maybe there hadn't been a mistake after all. Maybe he felt the same.

He'd pulled her into the house and wrapped her in a woollen blanket. They'd gone upstairs. He'd sat her on the bed, then, pulling the notepad from a drawer, sat scribbling opposite her.

She'd watched, bewildered at his timing.

Just as her curled toes started to hurt, the scribbling had stopped. He'd turned an apologetic expression to her and stepped to the bed, a smile spread over his face as he'd lay her down on the cool sheets. She'd never seen this smile, never seen him this happy. Finally, he'd breathed in her ear, 'I love you too, Ren.'

Their first time, just a few nights prior, they'd been like two threads intertwining. The second, more desperate expressions of yearning had reigned. Renata had clung to those broad shoulders as he'd taken her with such urgency, such hunger. In his touch she'd felt that unbelievable truth they'd shared on the doorstep: they were in love.

Renata pulled the dressing gown tight and walked to her coat, stepping over his crumped brown corduroys. In its pocket lay the Zippo lighter she'd had the locksmith engrave:

ONE TRUTH: OURS.
THANK YOU, QUENTIN.

The gift said what she couldn't. She believed she'd finally come to understand his obsessional pursuit, this *truth* for which his work strived. Maybe, whether they knew it or not, everyone was in search of some truth – even her. Maybe Quentin was just more aware of it than others. And maybe, just maybe, he'd been looking in the wrong place. Maybe both their searches were over. Maybe their love was the only truth they needed. *One truth: ours.*

Whatever. All she knew was that she had to thank him for making her feel like a real person. She stepped towards the coat, then stopped. The chair over which it was draped sat against a walnut chest of drawers. In one of those drawers, she knew, was Quentin's notebook.

There was no deliberation. It was immediately clear she was going to look inside. The stiff leather notebook's confidentiality had been obvious. He'd stashed it in the drawer with such secrecy, not even realising she'd spied him in the dresser mirror. The more stealth with which he operated, the more endearing and intriguing the notebook became to Renata. What insight may its fabled pages offer into her love's mind? Her interest was piqued past the point of no return.

Besides, it couldn't hurt. Quentin's passion was fascinating. She'd witnessed his intensity during their writing sessions, as well as between the bed sheets. Just a few weeks ago he'd been nothing more than the face on a book display, but the events of those few weeks had done nothing but arouse her curiosity. She wanted to see what he saw. She wanted to see the thoughts of an untameably creative mind.

She looked at Quentin through the morning glow. He lay facing away from her, snoring lightly. As she eased open the drawer, she was suddenly reminded of her night-time navigations down that creaky staircase. Luckily, this wood didn't creak. She peered inside.

It was empty except for some bulk wrapped in a dirty rag. Not notebook shaped, that was for sure. Upon reassessing the drawer's depth, she found there was space behind the object. She reached deeper. Her hand fell on an envelope.

It had an international postage stamp on it, was adorned with hand-drawn love hearts, and was unsealed. Should she? As with the question of whether she *should* peek inside Quentin's notebook, these considerations didn't enter into her mind. She slipped the letter out of the envelope and quietly unfolded the paper.

Sandie. Always Sandie. The more Renata learnt about Quentin's adoration of his daughter, the more enamoured she became with him. Was it the contrast between a mind capable of such horrors, yet such love? Yes, the curly words written in pink ink were Sandie's, but words such as these could only be written to the most loving of fathers.

Frantic retellings of the most menial news from back home; proposed plans for days out together upon their reunion; demands for him to recall *that time you got custard all over your face at dinner and we ended up having that food fight and Mom just watched on, like, literally freaking out*: the love bubbling out of the letter warmed the damaged heart inside Renata that, not so long ago, she believed could only remain forever cold.

Every passing day with Quentin was convincing her further that, after a life without love, this was her time.

She replaced the letter back in the envelope, peering over her shoulder to make sure the slumbering form of Quentin was still asleep, then replaced it at the back of the drawer.

Her hand brushed against cold leather.

The notebook.

Couldn't hurt.

She lifted it out of the drawer, feeling the weight in her hands. In the wrinkles of its heavy leather cover she could feel the hours invested within. She removed its elastic closure then stood marvelling at the closed notebook, this hub of a creative mind ready to be opened. He'd told her it was the heart of his new novel's development; that in these pages were the pilings of all his thoughts and ideas for the project. In the notebook was the core of this grand, truth-infused horror opus on which he was working.

She cracked open the cover and skimmed through its heavyweight pages.

It was filled with notes on her.

Step by step accounts of their interactions, from their

meeting at the airport right through to the previous night; observations and precise detailing of her reactions to the truck explosion, the surprise dinner in the clock tower, their time spent working on the scripts; an exacting narration of her confession of love. Even her awkward waiting on the edge of the bed as he'd finished writing the previous evening. Everything. It was all there. Every nuance of her character, every nervous little habit, spelt out on paper amongst a network of arrows and highlighter ink, underlined sentences and circled sections.

The notebook was her.

She jumped as Quentin awoke with a yawn. For a second she thought she was going to drop the thing, its hardbound thump on the floor surely enough to alert him, but somehow she managed to replace the elastic ribbon and slip it back into the drawer.

The shape under the covers shifted. 'What you doing up?'

'Just, uh…' She reached for a glass of water on the chest. '…sorry, just getting a drink.'

'Mine's a scotch on the rocks,' he chimed with that New England cadence. He swung his legs out of the bed then walked towards her, naked, his bare feet padding across the panelled floor. He took the glass from her and downed its contents, before reaching for her hands. 'Ren, you don't know this yet, but today's a big day for you.'

The notebook's pull on her was stronger than ever. What did it mean? Was this a romantic gesture? A novel about her? But *everything* was in there. What could he possibly do with such obsessive detailing, with this *character study*? She stared at him.

'Real big day,' he continued. 'Bigger than you know. I got something to show you, something wonderful.' He pulled her into his nude frame. 'But I need you to tell me again. I need to know it's true, Ren.'

Her lips were dry, locked shut. She ripped them open. 'I...love you, Quentin.'

He grinned. After dressing, he fastened his watch, checking the time as he did so, and stepped over to the chest of drawers. He pulled out the notebook and the wrapped rag sitting next to it. 'Good enough for me! Let's go.'

The morning was still and silent as they walked through empty streets towards the airfield. They said little. Renata struggled to keep up, feeling like a dog on a leash as she trailed behind Quentin's hurried strides.

He wrote as they walked.

No one was stationed at the entrance. He lifted the barrier and stood to one side, nodding for Renata to go first as he fidgeted with the pen between his fingers. She looked out at the abandoned marquees, trailers, and rigging that dotted the tarmac expanse. Then, in the centre of the airfield, the aircraft hangar. A smile widened on Quentin's face. He pointed a finger to the enormous structure. Was he trembling? 'Lead the way, Ren.'

The hangar rose through the mist as they approached, Quentin now following her like an excited child. She'd been told the metal building, which had surrendered to several decades of rust, had been housing the centrepiece of the production, a set of such importance that entry was strictly limited. A huge section of the half-cylinder's front facing was retractable to allow access by aircraft, with NO ENTRY signs covering the colossal door. It was open just enough for them to enter. She stopped at the entrance and looked back at him.

'Please,' he said, motioning to the gap, 'it's time to take our work to the next level.' Hesitantly, she ducked under the hangar door. 'I told you, Ren,' he said, his words infused with anticipation, 'it's a big day for you. For us both.'

The space was so expansive she felt like she'd traded one outside for another. A man-made sky curved over them, the sounds of fluttering birds audible from above. The morning chill had been biting but, somehow, the cold in this metal temple was all-consuming.

Their walk across the concrete plain felt like an eternity. Finally, they reached the far end of the hangar, where a vast projection screen sprawled across the metal wall like an impromptu cinema. Directly in front of the screen was a raised platform, upon which a large sheet of tarpaulin lay draped over something. Something big.

'Quentin, what is this?' she asked. 'What are we doing here?'

'You've worked hard on those scripts,' he announced, a thespian to his audience. The words echoed through the chamber. 'You really brought those love scenes to life, you know.' He stopped by the platform and turned to face her, the knives of his eyes finally materialising behind their horn-rimmed frames. He tapped his foot maniacally. 'But the romance is over, Renata.'

He held the wrapped up rag in one hand, a corner of the tarp in the other. Keeping his gaze fixed upon her, he yanked the tarp off in one grand sweep. Upon the raised platform, facing the projection screen, was a car – a dark blue Ford Cortina. Quentin pulled from his pocket a small remote control and pointed it behind and above her. She heard mechanical whirring as the screen awoke, streaks of shadow and broken image struggling to life. Then, in a blast of light, the movie started to roll.

It was a dark country road.

'As you know,' he declared, 'in *Horror Highway* it was a woman in a green dress mowed down.' He glanced proudly at the projection screen as a yellow shape appeared on the rolling road, then flicked his gaze back to the white-faced Renata. 'I hope you don't mind, but I've used a little poetic licence to make this a touch more...personal.'

She watched hypnotised from the tail end of the Cortina, which, from her position, gave the rough illusion of its speeding along the projected road. The shape became clearer.

He unravelled the rag.

The walls of the hangar melted away. She entered a trance, enslaved by the image before her, until all that remained was the speeding car, the road, and that shape in the distance, the ghost which forever loomed just out of reach. A bead of sweat traced down the length of her back. Her knuckles whitened around an invisible wheel.

'Midnight, midnight...' he called from the darkness, his words seeped in ecstasy. To Quentin C. Rye, a biblical event was unfolding, a cosmic cycle completing. His universe was this hangar, Renata his Eve. The shape took form on the screen. Sweat stung the scabs in her palms.

'...it's your turn...'

It was the shape of a child, yellow raincoat hanging off its puny frame. Quentin dropped the rag and revealed a small red spade. He crouched and smashed it off the ground, those mad eyes drinking in every nuance of her being.

One

Pain burst in her brain like never before.

Two

He cracked the spade off the concrete.

Three

She counted the blows as her brain swelled with a profound agony.

Four

'Please, stop!'

Five

'...clock strikes twelve...'

Six

His words were infused with orgasmic pleasure.

Seven

She lost balance and fell to her knees.

Eight

Her bladder let go.

Nine

'...burn...'

Ten

'...burn...'

Eleven

'...burn.'

Twelve

The shape, an image of a figure superimposed upon the speeding road, finally took form.

Noah.

Thirteen

Blackness took her.

15

'Look after your brother, Rennie.' Her parents huddle around their son, patting down a spring of curls here, smoothing a crease in his jumper there. He is a prize trophy and, tonight, the girl is that trophy's minder. 'Get him to bed by eight o'clock and make sure he's warm,' her mother continues, smile wooden as ever, hair a sculpture of perfection. 'You know where the extra blankets are if he needs them. And I want this place as clean and tidy as we left it when we come back.'

Her father crouches by the boy. His tremors are getting worse. 'If you need anything, son, you tell her.'

'Me and Lenata have fun!' squeals the child. The woman's eyes shine with adoration. The man's lips curve in a rare smile.

The cool summer's night is perfect for a stroll into town with Samson – a stroll which, seven years ago, before the boy's arrival, the girl couldn't have imagined occurring any more than her father's acceptance of the new church. That's what's happening tonight, a meeting at the town hall for everyone to vent their rage at the modern facility due to replace the church across the fields. 'It's a tragedy,' Mr Lawson, a physician from Millbury Peak Community Hospital, had declared after service two Sundays prior. To everyone's amazement, even Mr Crawford's wife, the mousy librarian (forever 'Mr Crawford's wife', never 'Mrs Crawford') had, for the first time in history, spoken up, denouncing the decommissioning of the old church as sacrilege and – yes, indeed – 'a tragedy'. The school's head teacher had expressed his disapproval by way of a series of *grunts, while Mrs Cunningham wept her agreement that the act could be called nothing less than – you guessed it – 'a tragedy of the highest order'.*

And so tonight was the night for strategizing the fighting of this gross injustice. Their efforts would fly in the face of a decision already made like a bluebottle in the face of a train. The old church would rot, cursed to serve only two purposes: its clock tower would continue to toll the noon and midnight hours, and its cemetery would continue to swallow the town's dead. Nevertheless, tonight they would gather while the precious Wakefield boy would be left in the care of the not-so-precious Wakefield girl.

Tonight, true tragedy will reshape the Wakefield family.

The girl watches from the living room window as her parents set off, her father stopping to buff the navy paintwork of the Ford Cortina lined up to perfection in the driveway. She feels a gaze from behind like a ghost's embrace. She turns to Noah.

He points through the open door of the kitchen to the bucket and spade. 'Wolms,' he says.

'No worms,' the girl replies. 'No digging tonight. You're staying in.'

The boy lowers his hand. To her relief, he shuffles over to an abandoned toy fire engine and begins rolling it back and forth on the carpet by the fireplace.

An hour passes. The girl sets her pencil down and rises from the chair, walking to her bedroom window. The summer's evening has turned to night. Her eyes follow the country roads that outline each of the surrounding fields. In the distance, the church. By the church, her clock tower. Everywhere else, an endless patchwork of fields.

She descends the staircase and looks into the living room.

The boy is gone.

'Noah?'

No sound, no sign.

She returns upstairs and opens his bedroom door, cartoon bears and elephants chuckling in her face.

The boy is gone.

She runs back downstairs and swings open the dining room door: the boy is gone. Even the closet under the stairs: the boy is gone. Back to the living room: the boy is gone. The kitchen: the bucket and spade are gone.

Wolms.

Damn it.

For a moment, her mind's eye is filled with the face of her father discovering his daughter's allowing of Noah to go into the fields to play at night. 'Lenata let me. Lenata said I could go, Daddy.' She can hear it now. 'I was scaled, Daddy. It was so scaly. Lenata said I could go, Daddy.'

Damn him.

She opens the back door into the empty garden.

Gone.

She steps into the night and looks out over the low-cut hedge across a sea of grass, the narrow country roads intersecting as they trace the perimeter of each field. He could have ended up in any of them in the hour since she last saw him. She would never be able to get round the fields fast enough to find the boy before her parents returned, and he knows it. The boy knows it. He knows she doesn't have time to find him. He knows their father will hold her responsible. He knows she knows.

Hatred floods her veins.

Suddenly her mind's eye turns from the future to the past, to the driving lessons.

Unbelieving of what her mind is telling her body to do, she walks across the living room and into the hall. On a hook by the front door are the keys to the Cortina. She takes them.

It's dangerous, no question. Aside from wrapping the thing around a tree, as little as a scratch would be enough to push her father into a whole new realm of rage. She steps outside and looks at the car.

It's covered in scratches.

They etch like roadmaps over the doors, the bonnet, the fenders, even the windows. It's like an autopsy, metal and glass veins exposed to the cool summer air. She can see what happened as if it's happening right now: the boy running around the car, scraping the spade across its paintwork, giggling that machine gun giggle.

'Ee-ee-eeee!'

However this plays out, it won't be in her favour. Could she draw attention to the scrape marks in the spade as proof of the boy's guilt?

No, the girl used the spade to set him up.

Could she hide in her room, feign ignorance, and lay the act of vandalism, as well as his wandering into the night, upon him?

No, their little cherub would never do that.

Could she follow through with her original plan, use the car to find the boy, return him, and deal 'only' with the repercussions of the scratches? Damage limitation. The roads would be dry. The car wouldn't get dirtied. There'd be no evidence of its outing into the night, only the scratches. Who knows, maybe they would believe her? She may survive the vandalism enquiry. A missing Noah she would not.

She clenches her fist around the keys and stares at the gleaming Ford Cortina, her father's pride and joy.

Damn it.

***

She's jostled as the car hits a pothole. She yanks the wheel to straighten the vehicle, watching the road for alignment. Keeping a steady speed ('ABC: accelerator, brake, clutch, Rennie.') she rolls the Ford along the track ('Mirror, signal, manoeuvre, Rennie.') while squinting out the side windows for any sign of her brother.

Moonlight blankets the swaying grass. Trees tremble in the distance. The night is quivering in apprehension. She skids the car to a halt as she spots something in a rippling pasture. Just a scarecrow. She eases the vehicle back into motion.

She hears rain pattering on the roof; tapping, as if her father's incessantly tapping finger had been multiplied into an army of drumming digits sent to taunt her. She prays this sudden summer downpour will delay his return, not hasten it. Soon, the rain becomes bullets firing through the headlights. She turns left at an intersection between fields, cringing as a puddle splashes onto the side of the car.

The Cortina gains speed as she presses the tip of her outstretched foot into the accelerator. The wheel feels as heavy as a manhole cover, the car cumbersome, but the seventeen-year-old maintains control. She has lots of ground to cover. She can handle this thing. She presses harder.

It occurs to her that, since the brat was wanting to dig for worms with that stupid bucket and spade, he'd probably be hunkered down in the mud out of her line of sight. She should have locked him in the larder like he did to her.

Her eyes drift from the fields back to the hailstorm of bullets shooting strips through the beams of the headlights. Strips, like cut up paper in a dog bowl.

Damn him.

The intersections fly past as she presses harder. Through the rain she imagines her father's eyes, his feelings towards her spelt out in their glare like chalk on a blackboard. He never wanted a girl. He never wanted her.

Faster.

More eyes join her father's, the eyes of her mother, teachers, family friends, churchgoers. Every pair of eyes in this damned town.

Eyes like knives.

She sees the clock tower, her sanctuary. Or is it her prison? Why should she be banished to a cold, stone chamber? She sees the bruises around her mother's practised smile. She sees her father's fist. She sees that godforsaken house – the boy's heaven, the girl's hell.

Faster.

The fields become a speeding haze of grey. The rain's angle of descent twists until horizontal, as if the car were flying into the sky.

Then the shape.

In years to come, her subconscious will embellish the dreams with details inaccurate to the fact; there is no fire, no brimstone, no flames from the sky or the breaking apart of the car, and the red spade does not lie on the passenger seat. The shape in the road, however, will be the same. A part of her psyche will bury the whole episode; another part will exhume it.

It hovers in the distance, that bright yellow spectre, bullets of rain flying from its outline towards the approaching Cortina. Indeed, for a short time it remains a constant size. There was time, but the opportunity to slam the breaks came and went. The girl's eyes narrow. Her knuckles whiten around the wheel. A book called Horror Highway *leaps into her mind, in which a pickup truck tore through someone standing in the middle of a road.*

Easy. Oh, so easy.

The headlights grab the yellow shape and stretch it to fill the windscreen. It cracks off the glass and disappears over the roof. The shape is gone.

The rain twists back to a vertical descent as the girl brings the car to a halt. The sound of the engine's idling purr is accompanied by the rain's tapping on the roof. She stares out the windscreen, fists still locked around the wheel. At this point the girl's thoughts are a jumble, more like that of a baby's; simple images and concepts are predominant in the mental narrative trying to form.

She knows she hit something.

She knows it was wearing a yellow raincoat.

She knows it was holding a bucket and spade.

She gazes through the windscreen at the two beams of light shining from the car. Her hands peel from the wheel and push open the door. She steps out. Rain soaks her face and trickles underneath the collar of her jacket. Her eyes follow the headlights until she suddenly becomes aware of something behind her, something in the car's wake. The girl turns and walks the length of the vehicle, running her fingers dreamily along the scratches in the paintwork. The scene is painted red by the idling car's tail lights. The shape is still in the middle of the road, except now it's on the ground in a puddle of rain.

She goes to it.

The shape still has a head, two arms, and two legs – that remains unchanged – except one of said legs is now bent at the knee to a perfect right angle...forwards, not back. Something protrudes from the torn skin where the leg bends, something cleaned by the rain to what may usually be, when not lit by these strange red lights, a brilliant white. She's somewhat intrigued by how little blood the thing seems to have shed. Then she sees the blood.

Guess that puddle wasn't rain after all.

'Daddy gonna be mad at Lenata,' it splutters. 'Lenata

gonna get it.'

Funny, it doesn't even weep.

The girl picks up the spade by its side. Time to dig for wolms. Lips quivering, the thing looks up at its sister as she holds the spade high into the rain.

It shakes its head.

'Lenata?'

She swings.

One

It wails.

Steel tears down upon the shape.

Two

Another scream.

Three

A crunch as it ploughs into the exposed bone. The resulting pain is too profound to merit a scream, only a choking whimper as it twitches on the ground.

Four

Its outstretched hand gets mangled.

Five

Details begin to resonate in the girl's mind: curly hair, gaps in its baby teeth, the raincoat, all cast in that ominous red of the watching tail lights. She knows this shape. She knows this seven-year-old. The spade freezes over her head.

He opens his mouth to either beg or scream, she'll never know which. Blood from the back of his throat gurgles then explodes from his lips like a burst water balloon, dripping down his chin and polka-dotting the raincoat. The girl stares at his twitching eyelids, both repulsed and fascinated. The suggestion of vomit pushes up from her stomach, and yet at the same time she is elated, watching from high above in the storm. The adrenaline turns her veins into electricity, the spade her conductor. The suggestion in her stomach recedes.

She finds herself once again thinking of that moth in the larder. How easy it would have been to—

Another burst water balloon from his mouth. The polka dots are running now. Her brother's bloodshot baby-blues are bulbous, begging, reaching for his sister's humanity. His quivering, upside-down clown mouth of despair gapes wider, revealing chattering milk teeth, the tiny crevasses in-between threaded with blood. Maybe we all have a little flood in us, Mother *had said.* Something about strength, about being strong. Was this what she'd meant?

Noah gazes into the eyes of the flood, into infinity, into Renata Wakefield.

She swings.

Six

Water ricochets off steel.

Seven

Blood flows.

Eight

Knuckles white around the wheel.

Nine

Foot pressed into the pedal.

Ten

Splintering bone.

Eleven

The spade slices through soft skull.

Twelve

She massacres the thing, and with it her father, mother, teachers, church goers, family friends, the house, the creaky staircase, the clock tower, the fields and the night and the town and everything in it. She drives them all into the wet gravel. Weak. Her whole life, weak. Not now. In this moment she is strong.

She holds the spade in front of her, her own shadow

shielding it from the red glow of the still-idling car's tail lights. The boy's blood weeps from the steel, blood cast jet-black from the moonlight, sappy oil issuing forth over hands that will remain forever unclean. She raises the spade back into the sky, then delivers it home.

Thirteen

Renata awoke.

16

Grant unto us, Almighty God, in all time of sore distress, the comfort of the forgiveness of our sins.

Something was different. She recalled none of the usual pain throughout the dream. It had felt real, like a memory pulling itself together after an eternity. Her parents leaving them in the house alone, Noah running into the fields, driving her father's car through the night in search of the boy, the yellow raincoat stretching to fill the windscreen…

In time of darkness give us blessed hope, in time of sickness of body give us quiet courage; and when the—

No, no more praying.

Her mind groped for order in the confusion. The last thing she remembered before the black, before the dream swallowed her, had been…Quentin? He was the vortex of a tornado around which the chaos of her memories spiralled. He'd taken her to…the film set. The aircraft hangar. There had been…a car?

A Ford Cortina.

The spade. Thirteen times he'd smashed it into the concrete. Thirteen, just like the dreams. And Noah, the boy's image superimposed over the road projected on the screen.

Midnight, midnight…

Towns like Millbury Peak weren't meant to harbour such insanity, such madness. Why had she come back? *Why*? Honouring a promise made when she was just a damned girl. What had she been *thinking*? It had only

164

landed her here, wherever here was, with this pain in the back of her hand... What *was* that?

No, she wouldn't have come back if she'd known what had been in store for her. Why had she come back, and why had she stayed? Those were the questions she kept asking herself, weren't they? Was it really honouring that promise, or was it something else? Maybe the answer lay in another question: why had *Mother* stayed?

Fear.

Nothing's more important than family. That was the official line, the words drilled into her during every Sunday school class. But she'd come to see that this grand importance of family was all relative. They'd lived under a reign of terror in that house, every day being presented new levels of tension and dread. Was her mother's endurance of that hell, in itself, why Renata had stayed with her father this long? Maybe she'd remained because her mother had remained. She could tell herself that she was honouring the promise, or even staying to see Sylvia's killer brought to justice. But no matter how dark this endless black was, it was still able to light the simple truth that she'd left her island, forced herself to dive back into the world, postponed her plans of suicide, remained through all this madness with the tyrant that was Thomas Wakefield, all for the same reason Sylvia had kept on keeping on through those years: fear.

On the other hand, meeting a girl like Sandie Rye, you could believe those words from Sunday school. She'd painted a picture of such love, and it was easy to see that family really was the most important thing to Sandie and her parents Quentin what had he done what why who he'd *lied about everything what HOW COULD*

But none of that mattered anymore, because Renata

was dead.

Darkness engulfed her. Were her eyes open or closed? She could not tell. The endless black was indifferent to such trivialities. She probably had no eyes, no hands, no body – only a dim awareness of this barren purgatory where she was destined to float for eternity. Except she did have hands, or at least one. She knew this because of that damned ache, not dissimilar to when Father had dragged her into the larder. Her wrist had turned black and blue after that episode, with the bruising creeping gradually down over her hand. It had been weeks before she'd stopped worrying that it was permanently damaged. No, this pain was not dissimilar to that, but more...sharp. Upon straining with every scrap of strength she could muster, she reached her other hand over and ran her fingers down her forearm, over her wrist, and towards where the pain seemed to emanate from. She felt the skin of her hand under her fingertips as the pain drew nearer, until flesh turned to plastic as her touch met with thin tubing. With horror, she followed the tube as it ran under strips of surgical tape and met with rigid, harder plastic. She probed further as it ducked under more tape, before her finger touched lightly upon the intravenous needle lodged in her skin.

She yanked her probing hand away from the drip as the sound of a striking match leapt from the darkness. She finally managed to peel open her eyes, feeling immediate contentment upon discovering she was in the bed of a hospital room. Had she never left those white corridors, after all? Had these weeks of madness in Millbury Peak been just another nightmare? Relief swept over her, a kind of relief that, if she'd been honest with herself, she would have known was temporary. Reality was waiting; she knew this. But for these few seconds, she could be back in those corridors, those sweet, serene corridors. So white, so—

'Morning, Renata.' Quentin sat on the other side of the room, legs crossed. A cloud of cigarette smoke mushroomed between them.

Through half-shut venetian blinds a dampened sun provided the only light. She heard footsteps and chattering outside the door. A clipboard hung over the rail at the foot of her bed, the back of which was headed with the words MILLBURY PEAK COMMUNITY HOSPITAL. No, not the right hospital. Not *her* hospital. Back to reality. She looked at the drip in the back of her hand, then at the pale blue hospital gown as it rose and fell, rose and fell over her chest, faster and faster with her quickening breath. More smoke inflated around the figure in the shadows. Her heart raced. Her teeth clenched. She waited for the smoke alarm to go off.

'Two days,' he said as he recrossed his legs, his corduroys riding up his socks. Mickey was back.

Renata tried to open her dried out lips but failed.

'You've been out two days,' he continued. 'I've been right here the whole time. How's that for lover's dedication?'

She ran a bone-dry tongue along the inside of her lips, unsealing them. She tried to speak but found the words caught on thorns in her throat. Quentin came closer and held a glass of water to her mouth. She gulped greedily, the thorns melting under the flow of liquid. She bit down on the inside of her cheek. *Where was that smoke alarm? Go off, please. Go off.*

'How do—' She choked on the words, then cleared her throat. She stared at the man through tramlines of sunlight in the smoke. 'How...do you know what I dream?' She spotted the room's pristine sink in the corner, a bar of fresh soap sitting ready to go at the base of the gleaming silver tap. She thought again of the smoke alarm.

Go off, damn you. Go off go off go off go off go—

'Dream? Don't make me laugh. I told you, dreams are just piss in the wind. I don't know what you dream.' Quentin returned to the chair. Strips of light smeared across the lenses of his glasses as he leant through the smoke, smiling. He was spinning a pen between his fingers. 'I know what you *did*.'

There it was, the stabbing pain in her brain, back to make up for lost time. She ground her teeth against the spasm of agony. 'I…don't know…what you're—'

'*Thirteen* times?' Quentin jeered. 'The autopsy showed *thirteen* blows to that poor kid. Honestly, I'm not sure even I could have come up with that shit.' He flicked ash from his cigarette onto the floor. 'You should write horror.'

'The dreams, I…don't understand. I don't—'

'I still remember the day your pop called,' he interrupted, wiping his glasses on his turtleneck. 'Imagine: a budding young author being told his debut novel had driven a seventeen-year-old girl to murder. Good old Thomas was pretty pissed off, understandably. My book was, he said, *blasphemous, unholy, a work of Satan.* Blah, blah, blah. You see, although after your little joyride you were out for the count – "vegetative state of unresponsive wakefulness", they called it – you were still able to mumble two little words.' His smile stretched. '*Horror Highway.* I'm told that's all you said for years of your downtime. Over and over again.' He stubbed out his cigarette. '*Vegetative state of unresponsive wakefulness* – know how I remembered those words, Renata? Because in all those years following that phone call, all those years I disobeyed your dear old daddy and kept churning out my blasphemous, unholy works, I began to see my readership as just that: *vegetative.*'

His eyes pierced her own. She spotted that glimmer again, that twinkle of creative energy, except now she saw it for what it really was. He leant forward.

'If they'd been awake, *truly* awake, they wouldn't have demanded that same tripe year after year, that same old psycho with a kitchen knife. You get me, I know you do. You see, us writers are all the same. We start out with something new, but it's only new for a while. Before long we're jumping through hoops for those…those *bastards.*' He rose from the chair and began pacing the room. '*Tone it down,* they say. Then *ramp it up. Can't you make it more like your last one?* I told you, Renata, fiction is the vehicle in pursuit of truth. How can you pursue the truth if you never get to say anything *new?*'

He rose his hands in apology like a lecturer realising he'd lost his class. 'Sorry, sorry, sorry. This must be a lot to take in. I told you it was going to be a big day for you.' The chair screeched like fingernails on a blackboard as he dragged it to her bedside. 'Nothing's changed, my darling. I want you to know that.' He sat and took her hand, smiling encouragingly. 'You're still helping me in my work, in my pursuit of truth. I'm sorry if I had to *edit* the truth a little to get you to play along.'

Her muscles felt atrophied. It took all her strength to pull her hand from his. 'I…don't know what you're trying to tell me, Quentin. I don't know what you're trying to do. You come into my life playing these games just when my mother's died and—'

Her stomach dropped.

'You…didn't.'

His hand rustled in his pocket.

'Kola Kube?'

She stared.

Quentin turned and walked to the window, flinging a sweet into his mouth. He peered between the slats of the blinds. His tone turned solemn. 'When your dad called, he told me everything that happened. Every detail, from the colour of the spade to how many blows they found on the boy's body. Every detail, Renata.' A hint of joy squeezed through his words. 'Every beautiful detail.' He turned back to her, that grin creeping through. Evidently, this was too much fun. 'Mr Daddy Wakefield had friends in all the right places, not least our dear old buddy Detective O'Connell and his chief inspector. The whole thing was kept as quiet as possible so as to save him and his beloved town's reputation. The car was scrapped without a trace, Noah was buried in secret under a blank stone – even the autopsy was carried out on the down-low. Grisly motherfucker wanted all the details.' Quentin spoke with expertise. There was that lecturer again, except without the apologetic tone. He knew his class was captivated. 'Most importantly, he got rid of you.'

Her eyes remained fixed on him, jaw limp.

'Yeah, word spread of you and your brother requiring permanent care. "Always such a fragile girl." In reality, he just wanted to put as many hundreds of miles between him and his beautiful son's murderer as possible. Of course, you were still in your – come on, you know the words!' He grinned at the silent Renata. '– *vegetative state of unresponsive wakefulness*, and so were none the wiser. They shipped you off to some nuthouse up north and forgot about you, kiddo. Put it all behind them.' His lips quivered with excitement. 'But I didn't.'

He stood at the foot of her bed, fragmented sunbeams pointing over his shoulders like accusing fingers through the smoke. 'I *never* forgot about you. It took some detective work; Daddy really covered his tracks, but I followed your progress.' He stroked his chin. 'Fifteen years in Manse Copse Psychiatric Institution in the north of Scotland: nine in a specialised unit set up just for you, six in the rehabilitation complex to gear you up for release. You were observed every step of the way, for their benefit more than yours. So they could...wait for it...*study ya!* You were an *oddity*, baby! A seventeen-year-old country bumpkin driven to random slaughter who sits drooling the same two words year after year? *Horror Highway, Horror Highway, Horror Highway...* Sure made tracking your progress easier. They kept calling my agent to find out why this nut was babbling the name of my book. Well, I was a good boy, Renata. I only observed from afar. Didn't interfere in the little Wakefield girl's recovery. After your first few years in the loony bin, your unresponsive state was replaced by an extreme dissociative psychogenic amnesia...translated: you forgot the whole fucking lot! Mind just blanked it all so you could get up and about again. Fascinated the doctors, from what I hear. Once up and about, you were an antisocial little freak, apparently; just sat scribbling in your room quite the thing, happy as Larry. They decided the only way for you to live a normal life was to feed the amnesia, let you believe some *accident* had put you in hospital. You ate that shit right up and carried on your scribbling. Then you popped off my radar. Was she dead? Was she back to normal? Was she out there caving in little boys' skulls again? I eventually learnt they'd figured the only way to keep you believing this shit was to officially release you. After all, your body was fit as a fiddle. So they fling you onto an island in the middle of nowhere where nothing could trigger your memory or tip you off your tightrope of mental blockage – yeah, the rock was their idea, not yours. But how could they afford that? How could *she* afford that? I found my answer on the cover of a cheap paperback in an airport newsagent…'

'Stop, please stop. I don't *understand*, I don't—'

'THERE SHE IS,' Quentin yelled. 'THERE SHE IS, her name on the cover of a goddamn *book*, no less! Yeah, it looks like shit, but still, she's *writing?*' He slapped his cheeks in mock disbelief. 'It takes a man to cry, Renata, and let me tell you I *wept* at that steaming bowl of irony served to me that day. *What a wonderful world!*'

His grin wavered. Suddenly he turned his back to her, slicking back his greying hair and straightening his tweed blazer. He cleared his throat and turned to face her again, expression composed. 'All my life I've hunted the truth. Novel after novel I aimed for a note never before struck. My obsession cost me my marriage – basically, she didn't know what the fuck I was talking about. *Truth* this, *truth* that. Maybe you don't either, maybe no one can but me. Regardless, I kept searching. I kept dangling that hook but all I could drag up was the same old rotten stories, same old recycled trash. And yet they all kept gobbling it up like the hungry fucks they are. I knew, though. I knew I was getting nowhere.'

He smiled down at her proudly, a scientist regarding his prize specimen. 'I told you, Renata. I *never* forgot you. And one day it became clear, so clear. Matter can never be created nor destroyed, just recycled. Life, death, birth: it's all just the same shit refashioned. How can you create truth out of nothing? I needed a vehicle for the fiction, just as the fiction was the vehicle of truth. It needed to be forged in reality, in *true* horror. It came so quick, so clear, as if gifted from above: *you* were the answer.'

'Did you KILL HER?' Renata yelled, jolting in the bed. '*My mother, did you*—'

Quentin's fists thrust into the pillow on either side of her head as his face flew towards hers. 'I *burnt* her, baby!'

She froze.

'I *burnt* that bitch like a witch! Your little detective buddy's been telling you porkies. There *was* no note left at the crime scene. I carved that *Midnight, Midnight* rhyme right into her wrinkly old flesh while she lay on that altar. Oh, I promise she was awake for it all. Had to carve 'it again after the fire, of course. Words were all charred and shit, really quite—'

Renata went for his throat. The drip yanked from her hand and left a trail of blood down the stiff bed covers. Far off in the distance she heard the stitching of her gown tear. '*Damn you!* You didn't *know* her or what she'd been through or—'

Quentin drove his fist into her stomach. Her body stiffened like a board then went limp, deflated. 'But how else was I gonna get you home, huh? It got you back to this shithole of a town *and* started you on the path to flipping out again. Two birds, one stone, babe. Work smarter, not harder.' He gave her a quick double thumbs up. 'Barbeque Mamma Wakefield to get you home,' he said, stroking his chin, 'carve that rhyme into her to get me involved, then find ways to get you close to me. By the way, you did a fine job at comforting me after that *tragic* explosion outside your house, and all your hard work on the script really is appreciated, even though I deliberately made it crappy. All ways to get us close.' He leant down to whisper in her ear. 'Tell me, Ren. You do still love me, don't you?'

'I'll…kill you.'

Quentin applauded mockingly. 'Yes! We have a winner!'

After lighting a fresh cigarette, he reached into his blazer and proudly presented the notepad, the character study on Renata. He licked a finger and began flicking through its pages. 'I got me the whole shebang right here, all the little details. Your crazy little tics, all those idiosyncrasies that hint at your madness, tell-tale signs you know nothing about. But I do. All the plot points that have led to this moment, every word from your mouth, every twitch and jitter leading inevitably to your unhinging: I have it *all*. My book won't be a carbon copy, obviously, but I'll have enough to create something *truly* meaningful. It's just a waiting game now, Renata, darling. A risky waiting game, I'll admit. After all, you're a killer. You'll come after me, and when you do, who knows what shit you'll try and pull?' He blew smoke into her face. 'I can't *wait* to find out. I'll be ready. The risk, the *danger*: it's an essential ingredient in this grand search. Or maybe it'll be dear Daddy Wakefield to get the spade treatment next, huh? No matter, I'll be sticking around to see where this goes from a safe distance. I've been following you for a long time, put a lot of money and effort into you, and it's time for this little investment to pay off. I can't *wait* to see how you flip out. Just make sure it's good. I want this book to sell.'

'I don't believe it,' she said, fingers curled, nails gouging the palms of each hand. Blood crept from her fists. 'None of it.'

'You don't need to. I've already broken one of your rules. What was it…?' He flicked through the black notebook. 'Ah, here. "Don't tell them the story, let them discover it." Well, I've told you enough. It's time for you to discover the rest for yourself.' He reached under the bed and pulled out the red spade, then placed it ceremonially on the nightstand. 'Don't believe me, please. I beg you, don't take my word for it. Discover the truth for yourself.' He looked at the spade. 'Funny,' he said, 'that your mother should be buried so close to such a little unmarked stone.'

The door swung open.

'What is this, cigarette smoke?' barked the bulldog of a nurse as she grabbed the Marlboro from Quentin's mouth. Renata cringed as the woman threw the smoking stub into that sparkling sink in the corner. 'This is a hospital, *sir*,' she said as she climbed a chair and began fiddling with the ceiling-mounted disc. 'Bloody smoke alarms don't even work. Right, get out of here. Go on, or I'll call security.'

Quentin winked at Renata as he dropped the nine-volt Duracell into the bin. He went to the door.

'Discover the truth for yourself.' His eyes flicked to the spade. 'It all comes back to the truth.'

17

'Wake up.'

The cold air stung as her mind struggled into consciousness. The voice growled again.

'Miss Wakefield?'

The hospital bed felt hard, like stone.

'It's okay, it's just me.'

She struggled to sit up. The figure that knelt by her side began coughing. She desperately tried to focus on the shape's outline, marked by the sun pouring through a tall window. She strained against the glaring light, finally realising where she was.

The clock tower.

She felt the hospital gown under her duffle coat and the dull ache in her feet, then remembered her barefoot trudge along the Millbury Peak backroads and across the fields. Funny, all these years fantasising about being back in hospital only to end up escaping one. But what were those jaundiced eyes and that tatty raincoat doing here? What was *he* doing in her clock tower?

'Detective O'Connell,' she said, rubbing the drip wound on the back of her hand.

'I told you, Miss Wakefield. It's Hector to you.'

Her joints ached from the stone. The chill bit into her face. Light filled the room. Her eyes fell on a shrivelled makeshift bouquet of lichens, dandelions, and daisies sitting by the window. Dread suddenly flooded in.

Quentin.

'I was worried about you, Miss Wakefield. No one's heard from you in days. I couldn't even get hold of Mr Rye. His crew's packed up shop and left town. Ran out of money people are saying. I ended up checking with the hospital in case anything had happened to you. They said you were there two days until you just…' He paused. 'You must be wondering how I knew to look for you here.' He took a breath to calm himself, then reached for a thermal flask and poured Renata a cup of hot tea. His hands were still unsteady, sweat still beaded his forehead; alcohol withdrawal hadn't finished running its course. 'Like I said, I've known your family since you were a girl. I'm a detective, Miss Wakefield. I piece things together. Little signs popped up here and there over the years until eventually your special hiding place became obvious to me.' He handed her the steaming cup. 'I kept it to myself, of course. Didn't tell a soul.' He smiled. 'Especially not you. Wouldn't have wanted you knowing your secret hideout wasn't so secret.'

Quentin was responsible for everything he claimed to have done, he had to be, but could she really have…killed Noah? Or was it another one of his games? The detective's words glowed with as much warmth as ever, but her eyes were now open to their undercurrent of deceit. This man knew exactly where Noah was. Quentin hadn't lied about that.

'Now, Miss Wakefield, you must tell me what happened to you. Why were you in—'

'What do you know of my brother?' she interrupted.

The man suddenly became an art lover, Renata the exhibit. He scrutinised her, his yellowed eyes drinking in anything her straight face betrayed. She stared back, screaming inside. *You KNOW. Whatever happened to Noah,*

177

whether or not Quentin's telling the truth, you KNOW.

'I told you, I'll arrange for the care of your father. You don't need to stay any longer. Millbury Peak isn't good for you, it's—'

'Why?'

'Miss Wakefield,' he began, 'the detonator recovered from the site of the truck explosion, it's been analysed further. Firstly, I've been told a device such as this had to have been paired with a relatively low powered explosive, not of a high enough amplitude to cause such a blast.'

You KNOW.

Out came the toothpick.

'Secondly, the detonator's broadcasting capability was meagre. The explosive couldn't have been detonated from further away than the convoy itself.'

Whatever happened to Noah, you KNOW.

'These facts point to the person responsible for the explosion not only knowing there was an explosive substance in the truck to augment the strength of the blast, but also that they must have been nearby.'

'I thought you were retired, Detective,' said Renata. 'Wasn't that grand gesture in aid of finding my mother's killer?'

His tooth-picking intensified.

'There's a connection between Sylvia's death and the explosion, Miss Wakefield. I can feel it.'

'Quentin,' she began, forcing calm into her words, 'you're sure he's not responsible?' She curled her toes until they hurt.

'He's no more responsible for the truck or your mother's death than I am for his god-awful books. Quentin's a good man.'

Why can't you see him for what he is? WHY? The old fool

was as blind as her father. She, too, had been blind. But stopping criminals wasn't meant to be *her* damned job. Her toes cracked. 'You still haven't answered my question.' She locked eyes with Hector. 'What do you know of my brother?'

Hector winced as the pick pierced gum. 'I know nothing, Miss Wakefield. I'm sorry, but I have to go.' She clenched her teeth behind pressed lips. He made for the door, then stopped. He popped the broken spring release of his pocket watch cover with the toothpick, then stood staring at its face for a moment. 'Promise me one thing: think about what I said, about leaving. This town, it has nothing for you.' He looked at her hospital gown. 'Whatever happened to you should be warning enough. You have a life, a career. All you'll find here is pain. I don't want that for you.' There was no deception in his pleas for her to leave. In those tainted eyes she saw clear desperation. 'Leave Millbury Peak.'

Detective O'Connell's heavy footsteps faded down the spiral staircase. She lifted one of the upturned crates. The red spade Quentin had left on her hospital bedside table lay underneath. It was clean, obviously new. He must have bought as close a replica to the real thing as he could. How could he know so much? What was his endgame?

She looked out of the narrow window in the stone.

The mist was beginning to clear.

18

Her breath became clouds of icy condensation as she entered the house. The air was rancid, as if drawn from the lungs of roadkill. Renata closed the front door against lashing rain.

A dense mustiness hung over the living room. Cold, white moonlight emanated from the windows. The wasted form of her cassocked father awaited her in the armchair, the epicentre of the room's stenches. The bouquet of smells was its own creature, the sum of its parts beyond dissection. Urine, faeces, vomit: these may all have played a part on the vile stage of the elderly vicar's abandonment, yet this repugnant collaboration defied definition. The room, too, had become a beast in its own right; Thomas's gaunt form sat nestled in its bosom, these two monsters' disparate grotesqueries finally as one. The walls of mould and rotting floorboards were as much the flesh of Thomas Wakefield as the unidentified brown soup running out from under his cassock and down his leg was the house's lifeblood.

She folded her arms against the shape under her duffle coat, keeping it in place against the hospital gown.

It weighed heavy, so heavy.

'Good evening, Renata,' he spoke from the shadows, vapour lurching from his lips into the stagnant air. 'Nice of you to join me.'

Stepping over the wheezing shape of Samson by Thomas's feet, she went to the long-dead fireplace and began throwing scrunched up newspaper and kindling into the grate. She reached for a matchbox upon the mantelpiece, but found it to be empty. She remembered the lighter still in her pocket.

ONE TRUTH: OURS. THANK YOU, QUENTIN.

Lightning flashed as pain scorched her brain.

she loved him would have done anything for him she—

The lightning subsided.

'You seem to spend your life leaving, girl.'

Her father's voice registered but made no impact. His mutterings were meant to be loaded with the weight of a sledgehammer, every word a planetary event. Now, nothing.

Love: ripped from her. Life: a lie. Truth: denied. And Noah, could she really have…? She was the tool of a psychopath who was fuelling her unhinging, nothing more than the means for the completion of his grand work. Now, as every truth of her life crumbled, as the farce of her existence became clear, Thomas's words lost their weight and floated like ash from the grate.

'Answer when your father addresses you.'

The dried softwood birthed flame. Renata clicked the lighter shut as she stared into the dancing fire, a burning ballet of infinite permutations. She added more logs. The weight under her coat grew.

'You must be cold,' she said into the flames. The fire recoiled as if the lost weight of her father's words was reborn in her own. The crackling of the firewood filled the silence. 'Where's Ramsay?' she asked. She could feel Thomas's fragility behind her, that frail frame ready to shatter.

'*Where's Ramsay?*' his voice echoed mockingly, followed by a snort. '*Where's Sylvia? Where's Renata?* What does it matter? I told you, girl, this family is forsaken.' His voice steadied. 'Soon, the Lord shall pluck me from this cursed darkness and cast me into the void with all the—'

'And Noah? Are you ready to speak of him, Father?'

'The boy!' spat Thomas. 'Again with the boy! Let me tell you all you need to know about him. He left, as you did. But while you were scribbling pornographic sacrilege, he was *unable* to be with us. He was *taken* from us, he—'

'Tell me who took him,' Renata said, struggling to her feet. The unbearable weight under her coat continued to grow.

'Taken from us, as the waters of the flood took the mistakes of the Almighty, that *beautiful* deluge. Except the boy wasn't a mistake. No, child. *You* were the mistake.'

She stood over him, her shadow engulfing his lank form.

'*You* were never meant to be,' he growled. She unfastened her duffle as he spoke and reached for the weight. 'It is evident to me in my final days—'

She pulled out the spade. Lightning lit her pale blue gown. Slowly she raised the red steel over her head.

'—that it was the seed of Satan that grew inside your mother, the spoils of which yielded none other than *you*, an unclean—' He paused to swallow, doing nothing to appease the tiny pendulums of saliva swinging from his lips. Dried, rust-tinted spittle hung tight to his underbite, quivering maniacally as he continued. '—The Whore of Babylon reborn, infecting by way of the page—'

A whimper came from the floor as she stepped on Samson. She looked down at the dog.

'—*and there came one of the seven angels which had the seven vials, and talked with me, saying unto me, Come hither; I will show unto thee the judgment of the great whore that sitteth upon many waters—*'

Its half-closed eyes looked up at her with dull concern as the spade remained poised above in her shaking hands. This mongrel specimen, this Samson and every Samson before it, had earned more looks of adoration from her father than she could ever have dreamt of receiving. Where was her love? Where was her look of adoration? She met its gaze, foot still on its leg, steel frozen in mid-air. The spade begged to be driven into the raving skeleton of Thomas Wakefield. She fought it, forcing her attention to the creature below. She pressed her foot harder into its leg. The grey mutt moaned, quivering in chorus with the demented old man.

'*—and I saw the woman drunken with the blood of the saints—*'

Brittle dog-bone cracked.

'*—and with the blood of the martyrs—*'

She fought the spade's pull as sweat ran from her hands and down her wrists. She battled the will of the steel, elemental and unrelenting, struggling to keep it from driving down into her father. She focussed her attention on the moaning Samson, moving her foot up the canine's body to its head. She grimaced as every muscle fought the strength of the spade.

'*—the beast that thou sawest was, and is not; and shall ascend out of the bottomless pit, and go into perdition—*'

She thought of that woodland clearing all those years ago…she couldn't do it then and she couldn't do it now, she couldn't do it then and she couldn't do it now, *she couldn't do it then and*

'*—and they that dwell on the earth shall wonder, whose names were not written in the book of life from the foundation of the world, when they behold the beast that was, and is not,* *and yet—'*

Samson's skull became the pedal.

'*—with whom the kings of the earth have committed unbonded copulation—*'

All she had to do was push the car a little further through the fog, that was all. Then the shape would become clear. Everything would become clear. She pressed the pedal harder against the carpet. A dull, outward gulp marked the expulsion of the hound's eyes from their sockets. Its feeble struggling ended.

'*—and the inhabitants of the earth have been made drunk—*'

A dying retch from below. The final Samson wheezed its final breath, then stilled.

'*—with the wine of her fornication.*'

The fire's crackling echoed in her ears. The grandfather clock watched on impartially, a silent monolith. Her shoe lay flat on the grimy carpet, cranial discharge encircling its sole. Lightning burst across the room, momentarily illuminating the rusted name tag on the dog's collar, then its expelled eyes as they sunk into bloody mush. She lowered the spade.

'You want to know the truth about Noah?' he said, his blind gaze oblivious to the porridge of gore at his feet. 'Your mother didn't believe you deserved the truth. She wanted to protect you from it.' He stuck his chin up at her. 'But I'm beginning to think you deserve it. What do you think, girl? Do you *deserve* the truth?'

Renata turned from him, lifting her foot from the crater of Samson's skull, then walked to the door.

'Speak, girl.'

FOR RYE

She stopped at the sideboard mirror, fixing the kirby grips in her hair, before looking down at the spade in her hand.

'I know where to find the truth.'

19

The clock tower flashed, a pillar of light, then fell back into darkness. Weeds groped underfoot, rendering her shoes as waterlogged as her coat. The soaked hospital gown clung tight while her duffle flapped madly in the storm. The churchyard was a swamp out of which headstones leant drunkenly at every angle, its undergrowth reaching from below for sunlight that was not there. Rain battered the immutable scene, the graveyard as stoic as cliffs enduring the tide. She hunched forward and pushed through the storm, spade in hand.

Soon it would all be over.

As the truths gifted to her had stripped the weight from her father's words, so had it dissolved her concern for him. Why had it been there at all? To honour her mother and the promise? No, it had been born of fear, she saw that now. Fear of a crippled old man. No matter, discovering for herself the reality of Quentin's words was the only thing of importance now. Oblivion awaited, but she couldn't meet it without knowing. Then she would end herself.

Renata's eyes fixed on her mother's grave, then moved to the diminutive white headstone by its side. She'd barely registered it previously, but the unmarked pebble of a thing now seemed indisputably linked to Sylvia Wakefield's. If there was any truth to Quentin's words, if the dreams were in fact remnants of an act committed a lifetime ago, buried deeper than the dead, this stone held the answer. He was right about one thing: she had to discover the truth on her own. No more lies, no more deceit. Could she really do this? She placed a hand against the slab and, for a moment, heard that laugh in the howling gale.

Ee-ee-eeee!

She knelt and planted the blade of the metal spade in the soaked soil. Whether or not the answers lay here, there would be no coming back from this. Not that she wanted to, or that the rope would let her. One final confirmation of the truth, then the noose would have its way.

She drove the spade.

The wet ground succumbed as she'd expected. Her tool met quicksand-like dirt, swallowing the steel. Lightning lit an audience of stone. Thunder rumbled over wailing wind. Her soaked coat weighed heavy, pulling her to the earth. The thin, pale blue cotton of her gown became a second skin, sealed with rain to her feeble body. She thrust the spade into sodden mud, her grunts barely audible through the screaming storm. The tower, her childhood friend, gazed down disapprovingly. She glared back at it. *What would you have me do?* The clock face stared, a vast eye wide in disbelief.

She felt the spade's quality in its weight; he'd made sure this replica was extra sturdy and robust, reinforced for your corpse-digging pleasure. Still, the child-sized tool was making her task long and arduous, like tunnelling with a toothpick, and she eventually went to search the base chamber of the clock tower for a more effective implement. Sure enough, a full-sized shovel sat propped against the wall. She ran a finger along its edge, finding it to be almost razor sharp. This thing was brand new and prepped for the task at hand. She had a feeling she knew who'd left it here.

Returning to the site of her work, she found the mound of dirt by her side to grow with a greater pace under the influence of the new shovel. The pit deepened around her.

Hours passed. The pile, turned to mud by the pummelling rain, began slithering back into the hole. She threw her aching arms into the mound and pushed it back, screaming. She tried to shove aside the panic of her hair constantly coming undone from its mass of clips, running her hands over it, smearing it down with rain after every thrust so the water would keep it in place. Thunder bellowed far off in a world from which every plunge of the shovel was a step away. Her first step had been long ago on a road not far from here. Now, one plunge at a time, she would take her final steps.

She thrust.

The mound grew large, the pit deep.

She wiped away the hair.

KEEP DIGGING, the inscription on the boy's spade had read.

Thrust.

KEEP DIGGING.

Wipe.

Now he was the worm, she the excavator. The walls of mud rose around her.

Show yourself, worm.

The moon drifted as the night wore on. Renata worked frantically in the deepening grave. Her blade began to blunt, blisters burst on her hands, cramp cracked in her arms, but still the shovel-loads of mud flew out of the pit. She was a woman possessed. The light at the end of the tunnel was somewhere in this grave.

Then, with the first distant hints of dawn, she struck something hard.

Vibrations rang up the shovel and through her arms, stopping her dead. Mahogany peered through a letterbox in the mud where the steel had made contact. The rain fell around the tiny window and worked the dirt back over as if trying to cover up a dirty secret. She fell to her knees and scraped the mud with the edge of the shovel. Steel grated against wood until the dark coffin lay bare before her.

It was small.

She dropped the shovel and began scratching at the walls of dirt until two small footholds formed on either side of the box, allowing her to step off the lid. She stood over the coffin, legs and arms akimbo as if mid-star jump, looking down at her treasure chest. Feet still anchored on either side, she bent over and curled her fingers around the lid, feeling for a gap in its edges. She sliced her long fingernails through the embedded dirt until the rim of the lid made itself known. She tugged at the mahogany, eyes clenched against the driving rain.

Nothing.

She heaved again, desperately ignoring the agony of her torn hands and, worse, the hair hanging over her face, but the lid didn't move. Whether by the passing of decades or a deliberate effort before burial, the wood was sealed. She threw the shovel from the pit and reached out for the smaller spade, lightning exploding over her chasm, rain pouring down its walls in black waterfalls. She wedged the steel of the child-sized implement under the rim and began working the lid.

The coffin creaked in protest until its cover finally snapped free. She raised the panel, groaning at its weight as she straightened her legs and leant it against the rear wall of the pit. She stood with her back to the open box, eyes closed, panting for breath, running her bloody hands over her hair again and again and again. Lightning flickered, a lightbulb expiring, then a dying growl of thunder from across the fields as the rain calmed. The storm stepped back.

Then the smell hit her.

She sprayed vomit over the upturned panel, steadying herself against the glutinous walls. The stench was somehow physical, making itself known even as she held her breath, tangling around her like a net. She spat the taste from her mouth. It was time.

She turned around.

Its hands lay clasped. Dinky shoes pointed to the sky. The suit was in superb condition. A box of liquefied human would have yielded no answers. Luckily, this was something else.

Two pots of black fluid marked hollow, bubbling eye sockets. In place of a nose was a tunnel boring through the centre of its face. Gleaming baby teeth, cleaned to a shine by the rain, huddled behind what used to be seven-year-old lips. Poking out from the tiny open mouth was undertaker's thread, dancing in the wind, its mouth-shutting duties now as expired as the lips they once bound.

And still, after all these years, those damned red curls.

Renata spotted something wriggling behind its curtain of teeth and dropped the spade. It clattered against steel. She looked down and saw it lying on top of another small spade, also red, also child-sized. She peered down at the engraving on its face:

TO OUR DEAREST NOAH: KEEP DIGGING.

It was him. Her eyes passed from its desiccated hands to the tiny mouth. There was more she needed to see.

Noah looked almost mummified, skin tight and leathered. Millbury Peak's frosty seasons had no doubt played a part in the cadaver's relative preservation, the cold earth having prevented the liquefying she'd half-anticipated. The skull itself, despite the ruined lips and mouth, still held in near perfect form. This was to be the fruit of her labours.

She knelt, knees planted on either side of the blank vessel that had been her brother. The rain, now calmed to a steady drizzle, had rinsed off a little of Noah's hair, as well as some of the scum encrusted upon the skull, but not enough.

It had to be cleaned completely.

She held out her trembling hands and reached for her brother's face, his head propped up on a small cushion. The rain renewed its efforts, prompting an eye socket to overflow and weep its thick treacle lazily down into the almost-smiling mouth. The leathery, stiff face looked up at her, empty eyes pleading as they had that fateful night.

The crispy curls snapped in her fingers as she began crudely massaging its dried-out hair, the smooth scalp eventually lying bare beneath her hands. She switched relentlessly from gnawing on her lips to gritting her teeth. Gnawing on lips, gritting her teeth. Back and forth, to and fro. Gnawing, gritting. Gritting, gnawing.

Her fingers, still tangled with a few strands, continued kneading the scum-laden skull until bony white finally emerged through the film of decomposition. She peered closer through the low light at intricate streaks of pink across the pale scalp.

She worked the skull harder, further revealing the

pastiche of plastic, rosy-coloured blotches. Running a scum-coated finger over the patterns, she discerned a world map of white oceans and pink landmasses, the very blueprint of the boy's end. She reached for the spade, not the replica but *the* spade, and lined its blade against the plastic markings in the bone.

It fit.

The embalmer had done a fine job. Noah's skull had been patched up and smoothed to perfection. With his curls, there would have been no evidence of the cranial trauma the seven-year-old had suffered. Tonight, the repair job was horrendously visible. She went round the hardened plastic stuffing with the spade head, lining it up to each crack. This had indeed been the instrument of his demise.

Quentin had spoken the truth.

Lightning flashed, but this time in her head.

Pain seared, the usual pain, except it didn't die. She threw her hands to the sides of her head against rain-plastered hair, teeth clamped. Distantly, she realised this was the end. A brain aneurysm perhaps, or some kind of seizure. Images began falling through the rain.

She looked to the sky, clasping her head through the blinding light of agony.

Through the storm she saw the boy in the road. She felt the accelerator underfoot as her fists tightened around the wheel, then an impact against the bonnet, the yellow raincoat disappearing over the roof. She felt the car skid to a halt, and, in the immensity of the tempest, saw the twisted shape of her brother flat on the gravel. She saw the spade slicing down upon the boy; the red steel before her appear to melt as moonlit, jet-black blood trickled from its blade, covering her hands like tar; the child lying in the middle of the road, dead. She battered her fists against the walls of the pit and screamed into the merciless sky as razors tore through her brain, and with it the memory of that night.

She felt.

She remembered.

The pain subsided.

She fell back, her mud-coated gown ripping as she landed. The creature's legs snapped like twigs under her weight. She stared into the black. It was no longer a dream, nor a fantasy engineered by some psychopath to push her over the edge. It was as real as the smell of death in this abyss, the grave of the brother she'd butchered.

It flooded back, the memories of that ruinous night unfolding like time-lapsed flowers in bloom: the blood splattered yellow raincoat; collapsing next to Noah's body under the car's tail lights; looking up at her weeping father; then, finally, the white walls of the institution, where her lips had formed those same words over and over, year after year.

Horror Highway, Horror Highway, Horror Highway…

And now he'd won. He'd compelled her into unbarring the gates of her psyche, then let the truth do its work. He'd get the inspiration for his story, and be loved for it.

The doors were unlocked, the floodgates opened. In this pit of death, huddled with the monstrous remains of her baby brother, the truth finally found her.

20

A stinging chill hit Renata as she stepped into the house, out of the storm still tearing across the dawn sky. Onto her tattered gown she wiped the blood and scum from her ruined hands, then smeared her hair back. Not a strand out of place. She went to the lounge.

The atmosphere was heavy. Tension pulled the room tight, a narrowing vacuum. Thomas still sat in his armchair, embers glowing faintly in the lifeless grate before him. Had that abhorrent collage of smells subsided, or were her senses just numbed? The brown paste had completed its journey down her father's leg, and was now sunk into the carpet by his feet – but that was irrelevant; inconsequential, just like every other detail. She could do without smell, without sight, or touch, or taste, or any of it. All that mattered were the memories, now so clear, so true.

She went to him.

A quilt lay over the old man's lap. His hollowed cheeks puffed clouds to the sound of teeth chattering in time with his tapping finger. She pulled Noah's spade from under her dripping coat.

'Come to finish your dirty work?' he said.

Renata stared at him, her hand tightening around the handle. He cocked his head then pulled off the quilt. The pulverised dog lay draped over his lap. He ran a shivering hand over its tangled coat, cranial matter gathering between his fingers as they jittered through Samson's caved-in skull.

'You going to put down your own father, like a *dog*?' The steel trembled in her hand. 'That your plan, whore? We both know you have it in you.'

Her glare tore into his unseeing eyes. She raised the spade. He swept the smashed hound from his lap then clenched the arms of the chair, his ragged nails digging into frayed fabric.

'DO IT.'

The spade remained poised above her once again. A burst of lightning flashed across her pale blue gown. Her body tightened, face trembling with manic intensity. The pattering of rain punctuated the silence. The scene froze.

She laid it on his lap.

His eyebrows twitched. Bony hands groped the object. Blank eyes swam in their sockets like fish in their bowls. He ran his fingers over the handle, then the head, then its inscription. His tremors quickened.

'*Beast*,' he breathed. 'In the girl the *beast* lives.'

She knelt at his feet. 'You knew where he was,' she said.

'He was taken from us,' spat Thomas, 'by *you*.'

'You did much to protect me, Father,' Renata said, rubbing her wrist. 'What I did…you kept it quiet, sent me away. But it was too little too late. By then you'd already made me what I am.' She took his hand. 'The truth is, you were only ever protecting yourself. You turned your only daughter into a monster, and in doing so, *you* killed your son.'

He wrenched her close. 'My only mistake,' he said, 'was holding back on your beatings. My Noah was more than you could ever have been. More than your heathen mother, too.' Her grip on his hand tightened. 'Yes,' he sneered, 'he was so much more than that battered, bruised harlot.' His hollow eyes penetrated her flesh. His leathered lips smiled. 'She got what she deserved. I told you, this family is forsaken. The fire that claimed her is coming for you, too. For the Wakefields, flames are reserved. *Forsaken* is our blood…as were the years your mother suffered at my hands once you were gone. Believe me, child, when I say the wench lived her final years precisely as you knew her…' He yanked her into his rotting breath. '…bruised and battered.'

Her eyes narrowed.

'Tell me you *see*, child.'

She pounced.

Renata's torn hands clamped around the old man's throat, constricting with the strength of a boa's death grip. The skin of his neck was loose, seemingly disconnected from the withered muscles beneath. His hands flew to her wrists, tightening so feebly she could barely discern whether they clawed in protest or merely held on through the inevitable.

The man wheezed his last, agonised words.

'And the…great drah-drah…'

His ragged fingernail began tapping and scraping an elaborate sequence against her wrist as her fingers interlocked around the yellowed clerical collar. He choked his final sermon in agonal fits as she crushed his neck.

'…drah-dragon was…thrown down…that ancient *serpent*, who is…is…' His blind eyes rolled back in their sockets. '…called the *Devil* and…and *Satan*…'

She shook his limp body by the throat, his head flopping idly. 'You did this!' she yelled. 'You brought this on us!'

'…the…the deceiver of…the…world…'

Blood coughed onto her cheek. The vice of her grip tightened.

'…and he…*Say-Say-Satan*…'

Tightened.

'…was thrown down to the…'

There was a snap.

The skeletal frame jerked. Renata released the broken neck, its head slumping back into the chair.

Thomas's eyes groggily opened. 'The hex…*hexa*—'

The old man's words turned to gargles. A delicate line of blood traced the wrinkled trenches of his chin as fierce spasms shook his body. She reached forward and squeezed her thumb and forefinger over his nose, the palm of her other hand pressing firmly over his mouth. 'This was you, it was all you,' she said, then whispered in his ear, 'Tell me *you* see.'

The time between spasms stretched. The tapping and scratching of his finger against her wrist slowed. Gradually the jolts became fewer, finally diminishing into mere twitches. There was one final, weak tap, before his hand dropped limply into his lap. The rain's pattering ceased. Thomas Wakefield's passing was marked by a silence of absolute solidity.

Then, without warning, the wave rose within Renata. It was warm, as if the dead logs of the fire were reborn inside her. It was all-encompassing.

It was the wave of inspiration.

Words bubbled within her. What words? She did not yet know. They were there, this she knew, and that was enough. Words buried, waiting to be exhumed, just like the worm she'd unearthed – but magnificent.

So magnificent.

She placed her hands on either side of her father's face and pulled him close.

'Father, I forgive you.'

21

She stood before the lifeless fireplace, rope in hand. The painting towered above the mantelpiece. Faces screamed through the spiralling flood, some succumbing to the oceanic claws, others fighting for higher ground. She imagined the waves as fire, reaching to claim its victims. *For the Wakefields, flames are reserved,* the corpse in the chair still seemed to moan. *Forsaken is our blood.*

Her hand tightened around the noose.

It was time.

Renata looked to the stained ceiling and saw no anchorage for the rope. Her search of the rest of the house for beams had yielded no results. There was a decrepit attic, but its rotting ceiling was too low. Door handles? No, she didn't want to do it that way. She needed height. She could let nothing go wrong.

She thought of the clock tower, but frowned at the image of tainting her childhood friend. Finally she decided she would head back out into the dawn, the storm finally abated, and cross the fields to the trees beyond where a tall oak would facilitate her end.

She took one last look at the stiff shape of her father. Holding up her own long nails for comparison, she glanced at his talons still dug into the arms of the chair. She curled her fingers and stabbed her palms. Like daughter like dad.

Renata turned to walk towards the door, then stopped at the bookcase which had once housed her mother's romance novels. It was these shelves that had birthed her love of reading, with countless nights spent sneaking downstairs to secretly pick a book once the shouting had subsided. Then, one morning, she'd found the bookcase empty, the black and blue of her mother's smiling face renewed. She'd never seen the books again, never knew where they'd ended up, but she knew their removal had been the work of her father, his disapproval of that *ungodly smut* finally having had its way. Her father's religious texts, discoloured and caked in dust, now occupied the shelves on either side of a packed folder, the words *Quentin script* scrawled down its spine.

Rage swelled.

The love, the romance in the books once occupying these shelves: she'd really believed it had finally found her. She'd given Quentin her body, but so much more, too. She'd reached out, revealed herself to him, spoke not in a pale imitation of what was meant to be said, but *spoke*.

She thought of his embrace and, for a fleeting moment, felt the warmth of his naked skin. The man she'd loved was as dead as the thing in the armchair, or the boy in the grave. Worse, he'd never even existed.

She tore the folder from the shelf and flung it across the room, smashing the pot of a blackened peperomia. Soil sprayed over the carpet. She spotted the envelope of cash perched at the back of the shelf and felt tears forming in her eyes. She threw her hands against the frame of the bookcase and shook it, throttling it like her father's shrivelled neck, strangling the life out of that damned—

Something shifted behind the bookcase.

She froze.

Intrigued, she carefully pushed its weight into the wall, again feeling the disturbance. This time it was accompanied by the creaking of wood. She pressed the side of her face against the wall and peered through the narrow slot behind the bookcase, coughing on dust from the disruption.

There was a door handle.

She threw her weight against the bookcase's side, but her father's crammed tomes gave too much weight to the unit. She swung back to its face and started pulling off books, leather-bound volumes thumping to the floor, bibles thick as tree trunks piling at her feet. The envelope, having fallen to the floor, was now drowned in books. She swept her hands across the shelves until the thing was bare, then kicked the scattered texts from around the base of the bookcase and returned to its side. She pushed.

It moved.

She grunted at its weight as it slid aside, the hidden wooden door finally making itself visible. She turned the handle.

The door creaked open.

Black.

Renata reached through the doorframe, half expecting the dark void to form a solid, impassable wall. It didn't. She watched the rope still in her hand pass into the darkness. She pulled the noose back, staring at her hand as she compared the sudden change of temperature, then stepped through.

The house was bitter cold, but as she passed through the door the air became fangs, biting her skin through the still-sodden hospital gown under her open duffle coat. She stood at the top of a flight of dilapidated wooden stairs descending into the dark. The rusty light switch resisted her fingers at first, then cracked into place. There was a weak crackle as long-forgotten circuitry awoke.

Light exploded from glass tubes stretching the length of the ceiling. Renata covered her eyes as the fluorescent strips drowned the space in total white, until, as her eyes adjusted, the details of the cellar opened up before her.

Upon the rough brickwork lining the narrow chamber hung rusted pipes, tangling like snakes over creeping mildew. The mouldy space seemed to constitute part of the building's foundations, an integral part of her childhood home's anatomy, yet hidden from her all these years. The air was different; not quite rank, not quite natural, it was breathable yet somehow intrusive in her lungs, and icy cold. The mystery of the moths' nesting place was immediately solved as she looked to the alien-like clusters lining the edges of the ceiling, white and cloudy like frozen smoke. But one detail above all others won her attention.

Everywhere, books.

They were strewn across the concrete floor in tumbling piles, like the naked, tangled bodies of a wartime death pit. The books' covers lay open, arms and legs flung out, pages crumpled and spines damp. She descended the wooden stairs and knelt by the books, plucking one from the pile by its open cover.

She recognised it.

She recognised them all.

Her mother's own attempts at writing had burned in the fireplace, but Thomas's wrath had decreed mere banishment on her romance novel collection – banishment to this hidden chamber. She peered down the narrow basement. How could this have been kept from her? *Why* would it have been kept from her? Quentin had succeeded in reigniting her memory, images and words now leaping through the mist of her mind into crystal consciousness. Memories were unfolding. Now, staring into this forgotten cell, she thought back to the day they'd moved in. There had been, she now remembered, two items in place upon arrival: the painting and the bookcase.

Her father had meant for the cellar to remain hidden. Even so, there was nothing particularly of note in the tomb of light besides the books. It was a dumping ground for sinful texts, nothing more. So why hide its existence? Why not just use the cellar as a junkyard and padlock the door? Why not—

Her breath caught at the sudden realisation.

What if his hate for their little girl had spiralled deeper? What if there had been lessons needing taught under the cover of darkness? This place was Thomas Wakefield's last resort. It was a prison-in-waiting.

She looked down the cellar, her eyes following the mishmash of ancient piping, and saw the place for what it was. It had lay hidden all these years, ready to aid her father in measures too sinister to share, too dark to risk being discovered.

This cell: he'd kept it ready for her.

Her legs went weak. She reached for the rickety banister to steady herself. He'd been right all along: this family was forsaken.

She cast her eyes to the ceiling. The upstairs floorboards were visible from below, long joists running their length between muddled spaghetti-clusters of electrical wiring. A single beam stretched the width of the room. It looked strong, solid.

She could take no more truths. Quentin had what he wanted. In her unravelling she'd performed unthinkable acts in which he'd no doubt find the inspiration for his masterwork, imbued with that sacred truth he'd so long craved. She was manipulated, used, defiled. Everyone in her life had each broken a single part of her, amounting to a whole, with Quentin delivering the killing blow. At first, back on Neo-Thorrach, she had wanted to end it all in light of dwindling options: a drought of inspiration, debt, nothing and no one to live for. Now, her need for finality rose from the truth finally revealed to her. The truth of her life.

The beam stared down at her. Rusted nails pointed accusingly from its splintered surface. She gripped the noose.

At the far end, beneath a knot of heavily rusted tubing and by a rotting wooden hatch, lay a decaying desk partially covered by a grimy sheet. From this she dragged one of two chairs, which she positioned beneath the central beam on a strangely shaped slab of concrete. She stepped up onto the chair and threw one end of the rope over the beam, looping it round and tying it securely.

Finally, time to rest.

it'll hold it'll hold it'll hold

Damn Father.

Renata lowered the noose over her head, the scratchy hemp pulling loose a strand of hair.

Damn Quentin.

She fixed the rogue strand, cursing herself for doing so, then tightened the coarse rope around her neck.

Damn them all.

She kicked.

There was a crack, but not the crack she'd intended. It came from above as the beam buckled against adjoining struts, leaving her hanging some inches lower than she'd intended.

it didn't hold it didn't hold it didn't hold

The snap of her neck was prevented by an unclean

drop as she stumbled off the chair, which clattered back against the concrete. She was barely aware of her hands flying to the noose locked around her throat, and watched from afar as these alien fingers clawed at the rope. She wanted to die; apparently, her hands did not. As she watched this distant, dying struggle, she thought of just one thing.

Rye.

How dare he use her like a puppet then cast her aside, strings knotted and twisted beyond repair. Only one string now remained, and her neck was collapsing under its grip.

She kicked and clawed.

How dare he interrupt her private, long-awaited end with these horrors, dragging her back to this hellhole to be used as an instrument of his ego.

Her eyes bulged from their sockets. Veins swelled in her head and neck. The rope gouged deeper. The bricks of the walls swam around her as the glaring light of the fluorescent strips began to fade. The beam buckled again.

How dare he.

Vaguely, she felt the overturned chair against the tips of her feet as the cellar closed in, light giving way to darkness. She closed her eyes.

Damn him.

The starved rope's teeth sunk deeper.

Damn Rye.

Suddenly, from the darkness of her dying mind, it dawned on her. It emerged from the black and hit her like that fist all those years ago, except this was different. All the horrors of her life shrank before it, cowering from its terrible totality. It was the final key to the last door of her subconscious. It was the one simple, absolute truth. One and only one.

Rye had to suffer.

Her eyes shot open.

She tore at the rope, not in an automatic effort of self-preservation, but in a battle of pure, crystallised purpose. Her toes fought to balance on the overturned chair, a grotesque ballet dance. A hint of ghostly blue fell over her face as her neck crushed, but still she clung to consciousness like fingers on a cliff edge.

One truth: Rye had to suffer.

…ONE TRUTH…

Suddenly, her hand left the rope and dived into her coat pocket.

ONE…

She fumbled desperately.

…TRUTH.

She switched pockets.

ONE TRUTH…

Deeper, deeper her hand plunged.

…OURS.

Her fingers met brass, the Zippo's engraving vaguely familiar under her touch.

THANK YOU, QUENTIN.

She pulled the engraved lighter from her pocket and flipped it open, every twitching, aching muscle begging for unconsciousness. Like a driver falling asleep at the wheel, her mind battled her body's demands. The lifelong victim within shrank to nothing as something else rose, something invigorated, something with no interest in dying this day.

Something vengeful.

Again and again she flicked the flint until a flame finally sparked into life. She held it to the rope above as she battled to keep her toes on the chair. Her body began submitting to the noose. The warmth of letting go rose within her. Gravity hugged her arm and pulled.

Still she held up the lighter.

Through fading vision Renata watched the burning rope in the distance, strings of black smoke rising from the small flame. Her head slumped forward. Her drowning awareness bobbed up and down on the surface of her failing consciousness, struggling to stay afloat in the blackening abyss. She had work to do, she couldn't die, not now, not like this, she had work to—

Her arms fell. She lost the chair. The lighter clapped against the concrete thousands of miles away.

The rope snapped.

Thank you, Quentin.

The floor flew towards her, the thousand-mile distance closing in an instant. She didn't register the impact, only the tidal wave of air crashing through her throat as the noose loosened. Her windpipe exploded open. With tingling fingers she removed the rope. Light poured in as she devoured the cold air. She reached for the lighter by her side and turned its engraving to face her.

ONE TRUTH: OURS. THANK YOU, QUENTIN.

Her scream filled the cellar as she threw the Zippo across the chamber. She fell onto her back and stared at the ceiling as her ruined hospital gown inflated and deflated like a balloon over her gasping chest. Inflated and deflated, inflated and—

A shape fluttered past the severed rope, circling it twice before scrambling across the ceiling to the far end of the narrow space. The feeling of realignment with her body's respiratory processes was euphoric. She felt the overcompensation of blood in her head return to her extremities and watched her world fall into focus, and with it the fluttering moth. The frantic insect descended from the ceiling towards the desk from which she'd dragged the chair. It landed on the dirty sheet and strutted along the covering. Renata watched, suddenly realising something lay beneath.

She steadied her breathing then struggled to her knees, before crawling to the desk and hauling herself up. The moth froze in cautious observation then fluttered away. She pulled the sheet from the desk, coughing at the dust. Her throat settled. She opened her eyes. On the desk lay her mother's typewriter.

Renata's only recollection of the machine was when she found her mother pecking at the keys in the empty lounge in the dead of night. It soon disappeared forever, apparently relegated to the same purgatory as her collection of romance novels. Here it had been all along, waiting to be discovered.

It was of a similar design to her own, a solid metal brute with functionality modelled after the IBM Selectrics of the sixties and seventies, interchangeable typing elements allowing for emboldened or italicised type, amongst others. Renata's eyes moved up the keys to the carriage, where a single, aged sheet remained loaded. Her eyes pulled the print into focus:

```
I know these words will never reach you,
Rennie. I write this in a cellar I didn't
know existed until a few days ago. Your
father's upstairs, finally in the throes
of infirmity. He requires constant care
now. I've been forbidden to contact you
and I know I won't, no matter how badly I
want to.

I wish I could tell you how sorry I am.
```

```
You deserved so much better. What
happened wasn't your fault - this is
still your home, and we're still your
family. You once promised that you'd be
there for your father if anything
happened to me. As I get older, as I
approach the end of my life, I find
myself praying every day that you don't
remember that promise.

I've been told it's best to leave you
alone, and I think I believe that. You've
found peace away from the truth. I pray
you never come back here, and that your
peace remains.

I know these words will never reach you,
but you remain in my heart.

I love you, Rennie.
```

Pain. It erupted in her brain, deeper than ever before. She fell to the ground.

As she writhed in agony, as her mother's words from beyond the grave spiralled around her head, she thought of how she'd been dragged back to this damned place by that psychopath. She should have held onto her peace. She should have stayed away, ignored the promise, ended herself sooner. If only *he* could feel this pain, if only *Rye* could beg for mercy, if only *his* very lifeblood could burn in his veins and—

Her back arched. Another scream filled the cellar as her body contorted on the concrete. She was tearing at her skull when something else, something besides the agony, exploded into her mind. Renata suddenly saw what she had to do. She saw what she had to write.

A...novel?

At this vision the pain backed off, a leviathan doubting itself, then smashed back in.

This idea, this *book*, was replaced by Rye's daughter, Sandie, that vacant blonde he cherished so. She was a moth, just a little moth, like the one in the larder. Maybe if she lit a flame the moth would—

Again, the leviathan of pain reared back, surrendering ground.

Just a little flame. That's all that would be needed for the moth to return, then—

The pain began falling from her in great waves, gathering itself in her hands as the plan formulated in her mind. She wrapped her fingers around the pain, owned it. It belonged to her, now hers to do with as she pleased.

She would gift to Rye the agony he'd gifted to her. She would do it in his own language, the only language he understood: the language of written horror. From these very hands, such unclean hands, she would issue a flood upon Rye.

Her eyes lit up.

Yes, she would write a book.

Her eyes rose to the typewriter, sitting so majestically above her. She struggled to her knees, trembling with excitement, then smeared her wild hair out of her face and tore the sheet from the carriage. From a box underneath the desk, she withdrew fresh paper and a new ribbon, then ripped the cellophane packaging with her teeth and quickly fitted the ink module and paper into loading mechanisms she recognised from her old Adler. She lay her fingers on the keys.

D

The ribbon hadn't dried.

e

The hammers still fell.

a

It was meant to be.

r

She needed help writing the book. All she had to do was light a flame and the pretty little moth would come flying to her. She would punish Rye where he could be hurt most: his love for his daughter. Was she capable of such a thing? Her fingers hit a few more keys. Renata's end would come soon enough, but first she had to return the pain. She stared at the paper.

Dear Ms Rye,

22

Battered.

Beaten.

Brutalised.

But not today.

The island of Neo-Thorrach is an abused spouse, stoic and determined. It takes what it believes it must and raises not a qualm. The North Atlantic cuts it no slack, pounding its worn cliffs and outcrops, kicking up the gritty sand of its grey beaches, continually harassing the dead land which sprouts nothing of note – its only form of rebellion. Yes, an abused wife, just like...

No point thinking about that today.

The winds have calmed, you see. Although it's still freezing, the rain has dried up and the skies have cleared. This serenity is the rarest of occurrences, so there's no point thinking about all that today. Better to enjoy the break in the storm. That perpetual, never-ending storm.

The woman, the 'Neo-Thorrach Buidseach' as the Gaelic children of the neighbouring islands have named her – the 'Infertile Witch' – pulls her duffle hood over her head and wraps the scarf around her face, eyes squinting through the biting chill. She trudges up a worn incline, the same incline she's trudged a thousand times before, for over this craggy gradient lie the cliffs. How much of her time on this island has been spent pacing these cliff edges? Yes, it clears her mind, and yes the sound of the waves detonating against the rocks below seem to help her mentally arrange whichever writing project is currently taking form in her head, but there's something else the cliffs provide. Something she can't quite put her finger on. There's a comfort in those dead, perilous edges. Something about the power of possibility in your hands, the possibility of plunging into non-existence without a moment's notice.

Today, she treads the jutting lips not to ponder her work, but to reach the island's sorry excuse for a pier at its northern point. Whoever first attempted to settle on this rock, whoever threw that pier together, didn't seem to hang around long enough to add much else; the pier, its rotting wooden bothy across the thicket, and of course her cottage are about the only structures she's found on the diminutive isle. There were a few other modest constructions, but she's since stripped them for fuel. She has to take all she can get.

But the island's enough for her. Its uninviting qualities were exactly what made it so inviting to her in the first place. For the first time in her life, she's found somewhere she can be truly alone. Well, not quite the first time. Sometimes, late at night when she doesn't want to sleep, when she can't face the dreams of the car and the road and the flames, she wades through the mists of her mind. She sits in front of the crackling fireplace, trying to form a mental image of that room of stone from all those years ago, that chamber at the top of the clock tower. She sometimes smiles at the irony of having traded one stone chamber for another.

But that was a different life. This island is now her clock tower, and the only intrusion on her seclusion she has to worry about are her publisher's courier and the private deliveries, both of which use the bothy by the pier as a drop-off point for her supplies and correspondence on set dates, aiding in her solitude.

The small wooden hut emerges in the distance. She stops to pour soapy water from a flask over her hands, rubs them into a lather, rinses them with un-soaped water, then presses on. You have to keep your hands clean in a place like this. She looks out at the surrounding islands as she marches through the undergrowth. Thin streaks of land smear the horizon, far enough away to look like mistakes on an oil painting, close enough to shoot a shudder up her spine at the thought of the eyes, those agonising knife-eyes just a short maritime leap away. She tears her gaze away to survey the skies for any sign of storm clouds. The weather looks promising, but here on Neo-Thorrach that can change in a meteorological instant. Still, today is courier day, not delivery day, and so all she can expect to have to carry back to the cottage is correspondence from Highacre House Publishing (maybe they've edited her new manuscript) and possibly more warnings from her accountant. Next week will require a few trips with her handcart to carry the delivery of supplies back from the pier. Oh, but she must remember the clock is ticking on the generator's engine isolators and fuel valves, and she still needs to see about getting someone out to replace the filter housings of the water purifier, not to mention—

You don't have the income for this anymore.

She pushes aside the words from her accountant's last letter as she steps over a dried up rivulet and hastens her pace towards the rocky beach. Her boots crunch on the gravel and shale as she makes her way past the disintegrating pier and approaches the hut, its door swinging freely in the gathering gale.

She slips inside and, as usual, finds no change in temperature. Nevertheless, she values this brief moment of shelter from what is becoming a stinging wind, and usually takes a moment before making her way back to—

She spots the parcel.

Sitting next to an A4 board-backed envelope from her publisher is a long, thin package wrapped in red and green paper, adorned with images of mistletoe and snowmen. She looks at the postal mark on the envelope and, for one of the few times in her ten years on the island, realises it's nearly Christmas.

She reaches for the scribbled note by the parcel, in which the courier explains he came via a neighbouring island where some resident children begged him to bring this Christmas present to the lady on Neo-Thorrach. Warmth begins to rise in her chest as she picks up the package, until it quickly sinks back down as she examines its shape and weight. She rips the mistletoe and snowmen from around the gift. She rises to her feet, staring at the witch's broomstick in her hands.

The door creaks and clatters in the wind.

Tonight, the fire rages.

She resets the clasp in her hair, fixes an extra clip, then coaxes the logs in the grate with the iron poker. The Aga stove usually gives off enough heat to warm the room, the same room she almost exclusively sticks to, but a little extra is needed some nights. However, fuel is running low; they didn't name the island after the Gaelic word for 'infertile' for nothing. She's positively scraped the barren rock of all it can offer, burning its scraps of peat and flotsam, as well as the few sources of wood she's located. Extra fuel has always been filled out in her deliveries, a ready supply of paraffin for the Tilley lamps and coal for the Aga regularly included amongst the chicken feed and petrol for the generator. However, it's been an expensive business, and as the accountant likes to keep reminding her: You don't have the income for this anymore.

She likes to think of herself as self-sufficient, but having canisters of petrol and bags of coal shipped out is hardly living off the land. She mostly needs the generator to run the purifier, *but if she can make further use of the constant rain then she can probably manage to make the switch to sediment filtering and distillation of seawater, thereby doing away with the generator and its petrol requirements. But that still leaves the Aga fuel, and if she doesn't invest in some more livestock soon then her diet of tinned and dried foods is probably going to give her scurvy or something. This place isn't meant for living. Life isn't meant to be a battle for fuel. She knows she should get on the grid, even some place in the countryside would do. But the knives, the eyes…always the eyes.*

The flames in the grate renew, rising and twisting before her. Once, there had been another fire in another house in another world. The amnesia from the crash

not a crash it wasn't a crash

had stripped the teenager not only of the incident itself, but of much to have come before. The memories of her life had returned slowly, drip fed during her fifteen years in care,

not normal not a normal hospital

the dread of the Wakefield residence emerging back into view with every passing year.

She'd shared none of the bad memories with her doctors, and the fact that nothing of the crash whatsoever had come back to her hadn't worried them in the slightest. They may even have seemed relieved. She'd told them she was so pleased to finally remember her mother and father and brother and her life in Millbury Peak, but in reality had spent countless sleepless nights lying awake, clawing at the palms of her hands, agonising over the reawakening memories of her childhood. In truth, that disastrous night had remained utterly black, like the silhouette of a mountain against the backdrop of a starry sky.

black hands black dripping from my hands black
The bottomless void of that night persisted in its darkness

in all the decades since, with the doctors telling her it may even be better that way. Better not to disturb something your psyche obviously wants left alone, they'd said. So she did just that. She left it alone.

The evening had brought with it the beginnings of a snowstorm that would last through the remainder of the week and right into New Year. Seems like she'd made it back to the cottage just in time. She looks out at the burgeoning storm. If it's nearly Christmas, that means it'll soon be her tenth anniversary on Neo-Thorrach. Fifteen years in hospital

too long too long for just a crash

and ten on this bleak rock. That's twenty-five years away from her family. It still shocks her to think of them never having visited while she was in care, yet she also feels they did her a favour. She had no longer needed a clock tower to escape from the tyrant that was Thomas Wakefield, instead having had free reign in her very own section of the hospital

isolated segregated studying you they're studying you

She could read in her room, explore the grounds

supervised

or just pace the long, white corridors,

they're empty just me whole section to myself why

one of her favourite pastimes. And when she'd started writing again, well, then she'd churned out her first novel, posted copies of the manuscript to literary agents, and eventually found representation, leading to her publication. Would any of that have happened in that house with that family? She suspected not.

Noah will be in his thirties by now

the spade the spade something about the spade

probably have his own family, maybe moved away and will no doubt visit Mother and Father at every opportunity. Always the perfect son.

Her initial years in care were hazy

Horror Highway Horror Highway Horror Highway

but once she'd began recovering, her years in the

mad house

hospital had been the happiest years of

pedal

her

spade

life.

blood

Pain. Searing, blinding pain. She closes her eyes and rubs the sides of her head, trying to visualise those pure, pristine corridors. Damn headaches.

She prods the fire, causing a burst of heat, then settles down at her writing desk to read the letter from her publisher. Usually, these A4 envelopes contain revised versions of her manuscripts, amended and edited for her review with handwritten notes in the margins. Her Adler typewriter produces faint type no matter how fresh the ribbon, and it's always a joy to see her manuscript professionally reproduced by her editor, clear and crisp. What this envelope contains, however, causes her to freeze in shock.

They'd returned her manuscript, faded and unedited. The accompanying letter reads:

Dear Ms Wakefield,

Thank you for the submission of your latest novel, *Love in High Places*. Following our latest correspondence, I trust you understand that sales of your recent efforts have been dwindling. Although you have one final book in your current contract with Highacre House Publishing, I hope you'll appreciate that

due to all costs associated with
production, marketing, and distribution
of your novel, we have to ensure the work
you provide is of a high enough calibre.

If I may be so blunt, Ms Wakefield, this
submission is not on par with your usual
output. I've said it before and I'll keep
saying it: I strongly suggest you come to
London so we can properly discuss your
future with this publishing house, and so
our editors can advise you and set you
off on the right track to producing a
quality product. They can help you
conceptualise new instalments in your
Adelaide Addington series that will live
up to your previous efforts and shift
units.

I look forward to hearing back from you,
hopefully with a proposed date for you to
come to our offices so we can all work
together on this. Failing that, please
send a revised version of your
manuscript, or a new submission.

Have a very merry Christmas.

Damian Abbott
Highacre House Publishing

She lowers the letter and stares at the typewriter. If only he knew how reluctant the words of this manuscript had been to materialise on the page. It was no longer a case of lowering her fingers to the keys and letting the stories spill out. No, something had changed. And while the rust in her creativity had taken hold, the generator had started playing up, the purifier had been breaking down, the latch on that damned front door needed fixed once and for all, and her bank balance, for the first time, stopped resembling the available funds of one who must bear the costs of living alone on an uninhabited island.

Living on an island: it sounds fancier than it is. She certainly doesn't own it or anything. Being the sole inhabitant of a tiny, desolate islet in the Outer Hebrides boils down to a lot of learning and a lot of work. Above all, she's found it comes down mostly to fuel. But she doesn't want to think about the fuel situation right now.

She'd poured a substantial amount of her savings from the three novels, published while still in hospital, into structural repairs of the two-hundred-year-old cottage, meaning the building now stands mixed with brand-new beams running every which way over the ancient stone and across the ceilings. Much had needed to be taken into consideration for the outfitting of the run-down little abode into a practical living space, not to mention some serious renovation work on the dilapidated outhouse at the back. Before long, the cottage was filled with everything she needed for this new life of reclusion. She was a citizen of 'Comhairle nan Eilean Siar' of the Outer Hebrides island chain, so her accountant told her. But all she really cared about was the typewriter sitting on the desk by the window at which she planned to live out her days in solitary bliss.

It never occurred to her that people might stop reading her books.

So now she doesn't know what to do. Writing is the sole method by which she can live on this island undisturbed and alone. She can't face the real world, she can't face anything but this rock. She thinks of her mother and that sweet, encouraging smile of hers, and for the first time in years craves the squeeze of her hand. Exhaustion from the uncertainty and worry sweeps over her. She could do with a good sleep tonight.

No dreams of fire and brimstone. But she knows there will be.

Every night the fire rages.

The front door, which opens straight into the lounge-cum-kitchen, blasts open as the broken latch clatters to the stone floor. Within seconds snow is thrashing around the room. She jumps to her feet and grabs some rope from a crate by the window, then feeds it through the broken hatch's fixtures on the door and its frame. She pulls the rope tight so as to secure it shut, then stands with her back against the door, fists clenched, nails digging into the palms of her hands as her precious heat slips out of the house. She clamps her eyes shut. What's she going to do? It's writing or nothing at all, that's the simple truth. Writing or nothing. If she can't write, then she can't—

She opens her eyes. Her gaze rises to the ceiling. A beam runs its length.

Writing or nothing.

She slowly unties the rope from around the latch. The door swings open, slamming violently against the wall. The blizzard explodes inside, snow spiralling around the woman's delicate figure. She wraps the rope into a coil and cradles it in her arms, her eyes alternating between the hemp against her bosom and the beam above.

Writing or nothing.

She will live on the island for a further three years, during which time she'll attempt, and fail, to salvage the rejected manuscript, as well as producing another, more dead end than the last.

Tonight, the seed has been planted. The beam is strong, solid. It would hold. Maybe death – the ultimate solitude – has been calling to her since the first day she walked along those ragged cliff edges. She doesn't need a rope or a beam to end herself, this she knows. If she really needs out, the cliffs could do the rope's job with far less effort. But a body torn apart on rough, razor rocks at the foot of a cliff would be a messy thing. No, the rope could provide a clean snap. Tidy and contained. Pure, simple, everything in its place.

No disorder. No disaster.

And once she's made up her mind, once the rope is knotted and noosed and ready to go, her courier will leave a letter for her in the little wooden hut by the pier, a letter from a detective in a town called Millbury Peak. If anything or anyone could draw her back to the real world, it would be Sylvia Wakefield. Or, more specifically, the death of Sylvia Wakefield, and a promise made a lifetime ago.

But now the woman, slender and unassuming, will stand in the doorway of a centuries-old cottage, the blizzard of a lonely white Christmas blasting around her. Her eyes are now locked on the beam above, her hand gently stroking the noose in her arms. The rope will stay with her until her return to Millbury Peak, where in a secret cellar she will defeat it. The rope will break under a meagre flame, as another flame is reborn inside her. And with the snap of hemp will come the breaking of the woman she once was, and the emergence of something else begging for release, and release it shall have.

Tonight, the fire rages.

Every night the fire rages.

23

Winter came. The nights drew further into the day. The skies over Millbury Peak had continued to pour as gales persisted in blowing the rainfall to extreme angles. But today, the day of the auction, the wind and rain subsided.

A cane clicked up the pavement towards the town hall. The woman approached the pillared building, its stone columns quite out of place in the quaint country town. There was a lot out of place in this town.

Her dark glasses pointed in the direction of the sweeping cane in her gloved hand. She stopped at the foot of the steps leading to the entrance.

'Miss Wakefield, what…' The voice trailed off as its owner gawked at the tinted lenses and cane. 'What happened to you, Miss Wakefield?'

Renata stared, eyes obscured. 'Early onset glaucoma, Sandie. Doctors told me to wear these until my treatment. Don't worry about little old me. I can still see a bit.' She placed a weak hand on the girl's arm, under which a bulky Dostoevsky screamed for attention. 'And I told you, it's Renata.'

She watched pity fall across Sandie's face, the kind of pity one would usually reserve for a lame animal. The girl was vulnerable, sensitive, Renata knew this. It was still easy to see, however, with or without sight, the ivory tower from which Sandie looked down upon the world; unreachable, protected. Lifelong privilege had fooled her into a false sense of invulnerability, and the sight of a lesser mortal only strengthened this sense of superiority. Renata suspected that to this girl, those less fortunate were nothing more than the exhibits of a Victorian freak show, there to either make her feel better about herself, or be used to show off her own brand of self-gratifying compassion. Yet from behind her father's old cataract glasses, Renata discerned innocent fragility beneath Sandie's superficiality. There was a little girl under the make-up, wanting nothing more than to please her father. Renata knew because she'd once been the same little girl.

Sandie adjusted her own glasses – a fashion accessory more than anything, Renata suspected – then hugged her. 'You *wholly* don't deserve this, Renata,' she spoke in her ear. 'You poor thing. You and me are gonna stick together, okay?'

It had been so simple: she'd used the information on the business card the girl had slipped her to acquire her address. She'd received a reply to her letter within a week; the moth just couldn't wait to fly back to the flame. Renata had only needed to express her desire to appease Quentin's guilt at the harm caused by the truck explosion, wondering whether Sandie could think of anything they could do for him – perhaps together. Naturally, she'd also asked they keep their correspondence a secret. Unrestrained enthusiasm had gushed from the patterned pink paper of Sandie's reply at the suggestion of collaborating to this end. Perhaps they could raise money for the victims?

This was the opening she'd needed. Sandie eventually tired of waiting for the written replies, taking once again to the telephone. Renata had eased from Sandie the archive of memorabilia she'd previously mentioned, stuff hoarded from his films he intended to someday auction for charity.

They could raise money for those *poor men*, as well as spend time together – perhaps even discuss the casting of Sandie in any future movie adaptations of Renata's books.

Sandie had said Daddy, for some reason, was having her stay with relatives in Phoenix, who'd left her alone in their city penthouse once they'd absconded to Vegas on a gambling trip. She could slip away to Millbury Peak unnoticed and surprise her father with this charitable gesture. Would he be angry at Sandie again? Possibly. Did she have to prove to him that she was *her own woman*, capable of her own enterprises and ambitions? Definitely.

Why he'd ditched her with some aunt and uncle that she barely knew, she could not say. She'd explained that her father had always been manic in his love for her, but that her scolding at the film set, then her banishment to Phoenix, were both, like, *so* out of character. But Renata knew exactly why Sandie had been sent away: he was hiding his precious daughter while he waited on his lab rat to unhinge. Nevertheless, the flame had been lit and the little moth had come a-fluttering back. And now, barely a month after her first letter, here stood Sandie Rye, hugging this poor, supposedly blind old woman.

So simple.

'I was so happy when I got your first letter in the mail! Just as well the housekeeper forwarded it onto me from Daddy's house. Nearly rumbled, huh?' She giggled, scratching her nose. 'I really enjoy...*conversing* with you, Renata. I'm just freaking out that we'll get to spend more time together. We're going to have so much fun.'

Renata forced a smile as she looked her up and down. As before, skimpy cut-offs clung tight around Sandie's butt. This time they were pink, matching the strappy top which sat just high enough to shamelessly tease the contours of the teenager's midriff. Her appearance was as calculated as Renata's cane and dark glasses. There was still a pseudo-intellectual within the girl begging to be taken seriously, but it had no chance against the beautiful blonde bimbo.

Sandie's industriousness was undeniable. She'd assembled a trusted crew – trusted enough to keep their project under wraps – who now busied themselves inside the town hall with preparations for the charity auction. Renata had emphasised the need to keep the event secret so Sandie would be able to surprise her father only *after* its success, therefore invitations had been restricted to contacts reliable enough to keep quiet.

'What you got in there?' asked Sandie, her manicured nails and tattooed finger reaching for the Millbury Hardware bag in Renata's hand.

She stuffed the carrier into her duffle coat pocket, then adjusted the beige scarf around her neck. 'Nothing. Let's go inside.'

Sandie led Renata into the town hall, proudly carrying her Dostoevsky like a handbag. Leather couches lined the lobby, occupied by attendees awaiting the event's commencement. Besides the couches, an illustrated map of Millbury Peak and a bank of telephones were the lobby's only furnishings. Renata guessed the last event to be held here had been as long ago as her childhood, and even then she remembered nothing of the town hall. Life had now been injected into the place, with suited officials hurrying through the waiting area, seeing to last minute preparations as the time approached to open the main auditorium's doors.

'Miss Rye,' said one such official, shoving past Renata

to get to Sandie. 'It's a pleasure to have you here. I've been informed of the discretion you've requested regarding today's proceedings, and I'd like to assure you that—'

'Sir,' Sandie interjected, 'care to watch where you're going? In case you hadn't noticed, my friend is visually impaired and I *wouldn't* like to see you knock her on her ass.'

The suited gentleman spotted Renata's cane and dark glasses, then turned back to Sandie. 'Miss, I'm terribly sorry. I didn't mean to—'

'When's it starting?' she asked, batting her eyelashes. 'Wouldn't keep us ladies waiting, would you?'

'Please, Miss Rye,' he gushed, 'if you follow me I'll show you to your seats before we open the doors.'

Renata was led by Sandie through the tall doors of the auditorium. She had to stop herself looking up at the great domed ceiling and decorated walls, instead maintaining her supposed lack of sight by focussing on the path her cane tapped out. They were shown to the front row and seated right below the podium. They heard another official announce to the lobby that the event was commencing, and guests soon filled the auditorium to just over half capacity. The auctioneer, a round, grey-haired man, stepped onto the stage and towards the podium. To facilitate remote bidding, a trio of officials manned telephones at a desk to the side of the stage.

'Ladies and gentleman,' the man at the podium began, 'thank you for being here, and our deepest gratitude to everyone who made this event possible. As you're all undoubtedly aware, today is the orchestration of a very special young woman.' He looked at Sandie. 'I'd like to add, having worked with her father in various charitable events such as this, I regard Mr Quentin C. Rye as one of the most generous, noble individuals I've had the pleasure of working with. Is there anything you'd like to say before we begin, Miss Rye?'

Sandie leapt up.

'It's *so* cool to be back in Millbury Peak,' she said, entering performance mode. 'What we raise today will go to the *valiant* victims of that *lamentable* accident involving Daddy's production crew. They're messed up pretty bad, so I'm really hoping this'll get them, like, plastic surgery, or something. Anyway, there's someone else that deserves a mention.' She motioned to Renata as if unveiling a prize pig. 'My friend, Miss Renata Wakefield. I couldn't have done it without you!' Sandie's perfect white teeth spread into a beaming grin. Her crop top slid higher up her stomach as she stretched her arms excitedly. 'Give it up for *Renata Wakefield!*'

There was ripple of hesitant applause.

'Right, yes. Indeed. Thank you, Miss Rye,' said the auctioneer as Sandie took her seat. 'Let us begin.'

Amongst the items up for auction was a replica of the emerald green dress from the cover of *Horror Highway*. Renata flinched at the sight of it. There was also the typewriter Rye had used to write his first novels, the gun he'd controversially had 'loaded' and stuck in his daughter's mouth on set ('Daddy's a *nut!*' she'd said when an attendee in the lobby inquired as to her feelings on this), and unreleased nitrate film stock from his archives, locked in flame-retardant crates. Renata had overheard chatter indicating there were mixed feelings towards the nitrate film's inclusion. Aside from the endless safety checks that had been required, the auction was raising money for an incident caused by nitrate film. *Not in good taste*, she'd heard over and over again, as if the lobby had been filled with one-trick parrots. *Not in good taste at all*. Nevertheless, Sandie insisted the film go on sale, at the very least to rid her father of the stuff responsible for his guilt.

That terrible, terrible guilt.

Damn him.

'Up first we have an early seventies, German-built Olympia SGE 50M typewriter, used by the man himself to write such early classics as *Slaughter in Crimson Manor*, *Zalikha*, and the very first Quentin C. Rye novel, *Horror Highway*.'

Renata's fists clenched.

'Besides the important role it's played in the horror legacy of Mr Rye, the model itself is somewhat of a rarity, having been in production for only a few years and—'

It was bulky. It looked heavy. It would do.

'Five hundred,' a voice barked from somewhere in the audience.

'Five hundred! Do we have any advances on five hundred?'

Renata raised her hand timidly. 'One thousand.'

All eyes turned to her.

'Goodness! An exceedingly generous offer,' said the man at the podium.

Chatter sizzled through the room. 'Renata,' Sandie whispered, 'check you!'

'One thousand three hundred,' the voice contended.

'Three…thousand,' she stammered, tugging on a sleeve. A chorus of gasps went up from the audience.

'Three thousand…that's three thousand pounds! Do we have any advances on this handsome sum? Anyone?'

Silence descended as the eyes of the audience glanced around for further drama.

'Going once! Going twice!'

Sandie grabbed Renata's arm in excitement.

'*Sold* to the lady in the front row!'

Applause filled the hall.

'What a remarkable opening to proceedings! A contribution of mammoth proportions, an absolute...'

Renata turned to Sandie. 'Excuse me, I'll be right back,' she whispered, adjusting her scarf.

Her cane tapped down the aisle as the man at the podium introduced the next item. She stepped into the lobby and stood behind a stone pillar, removing the scarf to rub at the raw red ring around her neck. She redid a couple of pins in her hair, then made her way to the bank of telephones.

'Good afternoon. You're through to the Millbury Peak Rye Charity Auction.'

'Oh, hello. Yes,' Renata said. 'I'd like to place a bid, please.'

The typewriter did its duty. Having lost interest in carrying around the Dostoevsky, abandoning it at the hall, Sandie wrestled the bulk of the typewriter under its protective covering up the high street, its weight like a gale slowing her progress.

'Can't we just grab a cab, Renata?'

She watched the girl's legs buckle. The machine was tiring her. Good.

'We're not far now,' Renata said, her cane patting the pavement. 'Besides, I thought you wanted us to spend more time together?' They stopped at a pedestrian crossing and waited for the signal to change. The road was empty. 'It's so kind of you to help a useless old lady like me.' Her dark glasses pointed straight ahead. 'You'll have to stay for a cup of tea, Sandie.'

The girl leant the typewriter's weight against a lamp post. 'I'd love to!' she panted. 'But not much further, right?'

Renata turned to the teenager, her eyes piercing through tinted lenses. 'We're close,' she said. 'Very close.'

The footpath out of town led them between the fields towards the Wakefield house. The weather remained dry until Renata had shown the girl into the now-immaculate lounge, when the patter of rain against the sparkling windows made itself known. The clean-up of the vile house had taken days, during which she'd been careful not to skimp on the bleach and bottled ammonia. A pristine house meant the overpowering smells of chemical cleaners didn't seem out of place, and these chemical scents kept that other stench at bay. She glanced at her father's still-stained armchair, then at the bookcase.

'Oh my, I knew that awful rain wouldn't hold off long,' chirped Renata, spraying air freshener in a zigzag above them. 'No matter. At least we have an excuse to talk, just us.'

Sandie set the typewriter down on a polished walnut table by the living room window, sighing with relief. She rubbed her arms. Fragile little moth.

'Cool,' she said, 'maybe we can talk about your books. I'm serious, they'd *so* work as films. Just imagine, Adelaide Addington on the big screen!' She batted her eyelashes. 'All you'd need would be the perfect actress to pull it off.'

'Oh, there'll be time to discuss everything, Sandie,' said Renata. 'Please, take a seat while I make some tea.' She stepped into the kitchen and filled the kettle.

'Splash some cold water in mine, would you?' Sandie

called from the living room. 'I'm *so* impatient. I'll just burn my mouth if it's too hot.' She glanced quizzically at Renata's dark glasses and cane. 'Wouldn't you…like me to make them?'

Renata lifted the kettle before it began steaming and filled two mugs. 'No,' she called, 'I can manage, thank you. Stay where you are.'

'You can manage to clean too, by the looks of things,' Sandie said, coughing on the stink of cleaning fluids. 'The place is pristine. Kinda cold, though. This how you like it?'

Renata took a packet of Dexlatine from the drawer and pushed six pills into a bowl.

'No worries,' Sandie said, 'I've worked on some freezing sets. I'm, like, *inordinately* professional when it comes to…'

Another three pills fell from the blister pack. Renata ground them.

'I just think the character needs someone who, y'know, gets her. Like, what I'm thinking is…'

She dropped the powder into the mug on which a cartoon worm grinned maniacally.

'Someone with *passion* for Adelaide. I mean, I just think she's so, like, *unfettered* to the conventions and unchallenged tropes of modern—'

'Tea's ready.'

Renata set down the tray and sat next to the teenager. Sandie adjusted her glasses and glanced around at the shining wooden surfaces and impeccably fresh décor. 'So you live here on your own?'

'It's my father's house,' said Renata, positioning the mugs and a plate of biscuits in front of them. 'He's taken ill and is resting upstairs. He's asked for no visitors, but I'm sure we can make an exception for stardom.'

Sandie flicked her hair and smiled that practised smile. 'You're so *sweet*, Renata.' She edged away from the biscuits. 'None of those for me, though. Low-carb cleanse,' she said. Then, peering into the mugs guiltily, 'But...well, maybe some sugar in the tea wouldn't kill me?'

Renata returned to the kitchen.

She couldn't know for certain whether the Dexlatine would have the desired effect. Ideally, such a high dose would freeze the girl's muscles as it did her father's, but quicker. There was, of course, every chance it would simply knock her out – or kill her. She could work with all these eventualities, but she hoped for Sandie's survival.

Drink up, little moth.

She returned with the sugar and spooned a shallow heap into the mug. The cartoon worm grinned as she took a seat. 'How many, Sandie?'

The girl wiped her mouth. 'Oh, sorry, Renata. I just remembered something about this model who, like, took sugar in her tea and it went straight to her thighs and...'

Renata stared at the empty, non-drugged mug.

'...one of my fitness instructors says, well, I forget now, but...'

She placed the sugar on the coffee table and stood.

'...I mean, he's cool and everything, it's just...'

She stepped to the table by the window.

'...I'm, like, *so* pleased with my figure at the moment and...'

She gritted her teeth at the typewriter's weight.

'God, check me going on about myself again. Listen, I wanted to thank you for something...'

She approached the back of the couch and heaved the machine above Sandie's head.

'...for, well, being my friend. Not everyone's as

genuine to me as you are, and it's really cool. You're like a big sister to me. Always keeping me straight and giving me advice and inspiring me. So, y'know…thanks, Renata.' The girl turned around.

Their eyes met.

The moment hung.

'Renata?'

The typewriter dropped.

24

Patterned cornices lapped like waves against a ceiling that refused to fall into focus. She turned her head and saw blurred shapes rolling past, then lay back and let the carpet continue its massage of her neck. It was a fairly comfortable situation to have found herself in, except for the screaming headache. As for how she'd gotten here? Not a clue.

Then the stairs.

Each step scraped from her buttocks right up her back, thumping her head before falling away behind her. That wasn't what she needed, not with this headache. She faintly imagined the set of stairs to be a jaggy-peaked mountain range. She giggled at the absurdity.

Light hit her, so much she wondered if she was heading outside. Of course she was, that's where mountains live! She giggled again.

She suddenly remembered the typewriter.

The giggling stopped.

Then the smell hit her.

It pervaded every pore. The stench covered her from head to toe like an upturned swill bucket, leaping down her throat, up her nose, even stinging her eyes. She retched.

The room into which she was dragged was like a vacuum of cold, the kind of cold she imagined you'd feel walking onto the surface of the moon butt naked. Actually, it wasn't so much the air was cold, more that there was no air, whatever left in its place cruel and hostile.

The final jagged peak passed beneath her, giving way to an exquisitely solid surface. Its icy touch shocked every inch of her exposed skin, of which there was plenty. Focus dripped gradually back. Her eyes squinted at the sun, which in this place was shaped like a long, thin sausage. She struggled to make out a shape rolling past in the sky.

It was a severed rope.

The further she was dragged into the room, the deeper the stink dove down her throat. She felt its fury in her lungs. She coughed and choked.

Two gloved hands heaved her off the ground, which was a shame; it hadn't been as comfy as her bed, but with such a sore head she was probably better down there. She was dumped in a chair. There was a rustling as the same hands to have dragged her pulled something from a Millbury Hardware bag.

A thin, black snake wrapped around her wrist, fastening it to the arm of the chair. Before long, the snake's friends joined him, wrapping themselves around her other wrist and ankles.

Her vision finally sharpened, her thoughts cleared.

She looked at the snakes: cable ties.

Renata, glasses and cane discarded, watched fear fall over Sandie as the reality of her situation hit home. The girl writhed against the ties, her eyes darting around the cellar like a trapped animal. Her feeble excuse for clothing betrayed every detail of her dread: the skin of her arms contracted into goose pimples, she flexed every muscle defensively, her neat cleavage heaved in panicked respiration. Renata looked the girl over. She was an illustration of beauty, more a representation than a living thing; from the flawlessly manicured nails to the assiduously applied make-up, she was an imitation. The contours of her body were toned to perfection, a figure into which hours of sculpting had been poured. The teenager's every inch was engineered with meticulous care. She was a dictionary definition, nothing more, but the wannabe intellectual had always vied to be let out, to be taken seriously. No amount of books under her arm could make this wish a reality. Renata removed Sandie's glasses and peered through them. As she suspected, just plain glass. They dropped to the floor.

Sandie's choking turned to rasps as the lubricant of her throat dried. She wheezed and spluttered, mascara running down her cheeks. 'Please,' she said, 'what is this? Renata, you—'

The woman raised a hand, silencing the girl. She pulled a tub of Vicks from her pocket and held Sandie's head in place as she applied the gel under her nose. The menthol began to numb her nasal passages. The choking eased.

'I wasn't born this way,' Renata said, dabbing the Vicks under her own nose. 'I was made.' Sandie watched in horror as she removed the leather gloves from her hands, still ruined from the physical trauma of her brother's exhumation, and wiped leaking scabs onto her pleated skirt. She knelt upon the hexagonal slab on which Sandie's chair was positioned and whispered into the girl's weeping eyes. 'I can't feel what you feel. I can't feel what any of you feel. Your love, your pain – none of it. I understand that now.' She placed a hand on Sandie's tear-stained cheek. 'But what *you* feel, my dear, is still of use to me.'

'I don't understand,' Sandie said, watching her rise and walk to the door. 'Renata, please. Whatever this is, we can—'

The hand raised again, then moved to the light switch. The fluorescent bulbs flickered off.

'Take some time to settle in,' Renata said through the darkness. She stepped out of the cellar.

The door slammed.

The blackness embracing Sandie robbed her of all spatial awareness. The length and height of the cellar, the distance between the roughly brick walls, the position of the door through which the woman had left: it all disappeared. She floated in space. Disorientation dominated her every sense.

Panic remained.

A solid rectangle of light formed at the opposite end of the cellar, throwing the girl's world back into perspective. The door opened with a struggling creak. Her sense of time had warped so perversely that it may have been days she'd been sat here. Hunger gnawed at her insides and a desperate thirst, at odds with the violent need to urinate, moaned within. With senses so shaken, as well as the deprivation of her body's natural requirements, the rectangle took on an almost angelic form. It was like a vision, a heavenly apparition from which possibility poured:

The cops! Daddy!

The room was soaked in a terrible glare as light exploded from the ceiling. Wrists still bound to the chair, all the girl could do was squeeze her eyes shut, but it was no use. The brightness corrupted every molecule in the cellar, passing through her clenched eyelids effortlessly. She recoiled at the sudden barrage of light, gripping the arms of the chair.

Slowly the blaze of light became bearable. She unpeeled an eyelid and saw a figure in the doorway. Not the cops, nor Daddy, but Renata, her face straightened into the same expression of sombre duty as it had been the hours, days, months, or years since she'd left her. The woman descended with a tray, kicking some of the piled, damp books on the floor aside as she approached Sandie.

'Please,' the girl croaked. The words were sandpaper in her throat. 'I need water, food...the bathroom. Renata...I'm begging you.'

The tray came into focus. Half a baguette sat on the plate, ham and salad spilling out its sides. From the sight alone she could taste the pepper on the tomatoes and the dressing glistening on the lettuce. An ice cube bobbed in the glass of water by its side. Renata knelt by Sandie and carefully held the baguette to the girl's mouth. Scepticism was swept away by bodily need; she snapped like a turtle, clamping her jaws around the crusty bread. Renata regarded her deeply. She tipped the glass delicately against the youth's lips. The water drained in seconds.

'I need to pee,' said Sandie, sitting back with a sigh. Renata gazed into her eyes, allowing an unfilled silence to linger. 'What do you *want?*' the girl demanded.

She stepped to the desk behind Sandie's chair and set the tray down, then spoke to the back of the teenager's head. 'I meant to ask, what hand do you write with?'

Sandie twisted round, but Renata remained out of sight. 'What? Why are you—'

A small, silk-bound diary fell on her lap. 'I was hoping you'd write a journal for me, Sandie.'

'I...I don't understand, Renata,' she stammered, head shaking. 'I just want to—'

'Actually, it was mine long ago,' Renata continued. 'I'd have been about your age. In its pages I recorded my days, but in those days there was no comfort.' She stepped in front of Sandie. 'Fiction became my comfort. The entries became less about my life and more about the lives I invented, but what I wrote is of no significance.' She placed a finger under the girl's chin. 'You see, all that matters now is what you'll write.' Tears traced Sandie's cheeks. 'Now, sorry to keep asking, but what hand do you write with?'

'Left,' she whimpered.

Renata produced her mother's orange-handled fabric scissors, blades like garden shears, and snipped the cable tie of Sandie's left wrist. Renata opened the diary on the girl's lap, dropped a pen on the blank page, then stepped back.

'Please, write.'

She's told me to write in this diary and to tell whoever reads it to ignore the dates. I dunno what else to write except my name is Sandie Rye, aged 19, daughter of Quentin C. Rye. I'm confused and scared but my captor is treating me well and she should know I'll cooperate any way she wants and my parents are very important people and they'll give her anything she

241

The pen dropped as the closed blades of the scissors stabbed through the side of Sandie's knee, lodging behind bone. Her brain scrambled to process the sudden wall of agony, a roar of pain exploding from her mouth before the pen hit the concrete. In her head, the scream seemed somehow detached, lingering abstractly in the distance before finally rushing in as if through an opened airlock. The girl became a vessel of suffering, anguish incarnate. Her wailing dominated the small, narrow space. Faintly, the midnight tolls of the clock tower could be heard filling the fields.

Renata held the closed blades in place behind Sandie's kneecap, whilst also holding the girl's free hand against the arm of the chair. The teenager looked down at the orange handles fastened to the side of her knee, then vomited, undigested baguette bursting over Renata's shoulder. Urine merged with the current of blood streaming down her legs.

'You fucking *PSYCHO*,' screamed Sandie. 'What do you *WANT*?! I'll fucking—' She gagged before she could finish the sentence, her body convulsing into a rage of spasms.

'Such furious fluttering,' whispered Renata. 'Fear not, little moth. I, too, struggle with the first word.' She leant in, ignoring the girl's lashing free hand, and clenched both handles of the still-impaled blades, one in each fist.

'What do I want? I'm sorry, dear child, but I want you to try harder.'

She heaved the scissors apart.

help me please whoever reads this it hurts my leg she stabbed me its I dont know why please

what the fuck do you want me to write everything keeps going black and

I keep passing out but she wakes me and makes me write I dont know what to say shes fucking insane whoever reads this my name is Sandie Rye please God help me someone anyone please

25

Her mother, now dead, burnt alive by *him*, had slinked around the house like a guilty dog. Even as a child the terror under which Sylvia Wakefield lived was obvious to Renata. The real shock had been the contrast between life under Thomas's rule and who Sylvia became when he left on ministerial duties, when her father would take the Ford Cortina to Stonemount, or south of the Crove to smaller parishes such as Claybeck or Tull Pyke. Sometimes, with a couple of days to themselves, the real Sylvia Wakefield could finally surface as if emerging from hibernation. Mother and daughter would bake all day, laughter and song filling the kitchen as clouds of flour led to Samson's inevitable sneezing. As Renata grew older, it became obvious these times were acts of reversion, a kind of ritualistic regression for her mother from her current life back to childhood. *She needs this*, she would think as balls of dough flew across the kitchen. *This is like the exhaust pipe of Father's car, letting it all out. She needs this.*

Upon his return, her mother's exuberance would instantly dissolve. The front door's slam would mark the lowering of her gaze and the falling of her smile back into calculated composure.

Yet there was another time, just one, when the real Sylvia Wakefield emerged, but not to laugh and sing and throw dough balls. She'd opened in another way, a deeper way, courtesy of this black beast of a machine which now sat before Renata some thirty years later in a basement she never knew existed.

Now that the burst dam of her subconscious let every memory flow free, she vividly recalled the dread of descending the staircase in the middle of the night, every step threatening to scream its treacherous creak through the walls to her father. She remembered one particular descent, successful – until she'd opened the lounge door to find someone there.

Luckily it had been the right someone.

Her mother had looked up from the typewriter with the same terror Renata felt descending the stairs: the terror of being *found out*. That horror quickly dissolved into a smile reserved only for her, but another moment stuck in her mind from that night, the briefest second before her mother looked up in dread. It was an enduring memory, and there was only one way she'd ever have been able to describe it.

Arts and crafts class. Two years prior. Christmas. 'Make a Santa,' Mr Feldman mumbled as he sank into the chair behind his desk, a newspaper rising in front of his face. Every manner of sculpture was produced that afternoon, mostly as far from the intended Santa as possible. Renata had driven her tiny hands into the bucket labelled PLASTICINE – RED a little too late, and they came back with nothing. Same with the WHITE bucket. The putty was in everyone's hands but hers. Scraping several empty buckets, she'd managed to gather just enough Plasticine to warrant an attempt at the given brief, albeit in a sickly yellowish-green.

The image of that day's creation re-emerged the night she witnessed her mother slumped over the typewriter. The Plasticine figure had meant to be standing upright, but upon returning from lunch break she'd found a Daliesque creature drooping forward, perhaps from the overhead heating, or the knock of another child. Or, more likely, simply from Renata's lack of innate engineering ability.

Every iota of the yellowish-green Santa seemed to be pulled forwards and down; even the carefully sculpted fingers stretched towards some invisible treasure. Its head, top-heavy and insufficiently supported, bent as if in search of a lost contact lens. Its whole being was both pushed and pulled down, and it was with this push and pull Renata witnessed for that brief moment her mother falling into the typewriter. There was the side of her mother under tyrannical rule, there was that exhaust pipe of childhood regression, and then there was this.

Purpose.

She saw the woman's index fingers stabbing the keys like crazed woodpeckers. She saw the chair slid so far back in accumulated tension that her behind barely remained seated. She saw eyes reaching out from their sockets as if handing the contents of her head straight over to the paper. Her mother, like gravity-stricken Plasticine, had fallen further and further into the keys, diving into the typewriter.

Renata had stared in awe. At the machine her mother was strong. A tornado could have swept the house away and those fingers would have kept on pecking, oblivious. It possessed her, and she possessed it.

But now she was dead, burnt alive by *him*. And tonight, in this basement with this brutalised girl, it possessed Renata.

Whatever her mother hammered out that night, and others like it, would never be read. Romance stories, she guessed, in the same vein as the books banished to this place. That banishment, however, had proven too tame for her mother's writings, which ended up in the fireplace during one of her father's particularly vicious rampages. No, her mother's legacy at the hands of this typewriter wasn't to be in her writings, but in Renata's vision of her that night, lost in the machine's spell.

As Renata had told the little moth, she really did struggle with the first word. She knew what she wanted to say, of course. The noose had squeezed that from her. As she'd hung, the sudden, shattering understanding of *what must be done* had exploded from her. She knew exactly how this story was to play out.

She thought of this strange career she'd forged, nothing more than manipulation on a professional level. Through the same recycled plots and cheap language she'd led along the mindless cattle of her readership. Their troughs had always needed refilled with that same old swill, book after book, year after year. The clichés, tired tropes, the need to love vicariously through another; it all seemed so distant now. For the first time in her life she had something real to write about, as real as her mother melting over these keys all those years ago. She'd do as Rye had. She'd make truth her muse.

She'd manipulated before. Now, she'd manipulate again. He'd torn her world apart. Now, with words, she'd return the favour.

Yet, despite Renata's conviction, her fingers remained locked above the keys as if sealed by rust. The words were there, ready, begging to be born. Her fingers were desperate to give, as the keys were desperate to receive, just like lovers ripe and ready to seal their lust. But nothing came.

She looked over her shoulder, wiping her hands on a wet wipe. Unconsciousness had finally taken Sandie.

Renata peered at the wound stagnating in the girl's knee. Upon the black laceration she saw movement.

Two moths sat upon the exposed flesh, deep in concentration, hard at work, enjoying the task at hand. They were feeding.

Sandie twitched.

Renata stared.

The girl looked down at the wound through half-open eyelids. She jerked, then tightened her hands around the arms of the chair as the insects gorged on her blood. Her mouth dilated like the aperture of a lens, the intended scream replaced by a spray of vomit over her legs. The moths vacated their dinner. She wept.

Renata's eyes widened.

Suddenly the words came.

She would begin with the knives.

Her fingers began typing of their own volition, sentences appearing on the page before she'd even registered the sudden tapping. All she had to do was hold her fingers to the keys and the words erupted before her. The calculation and arrangement of that stunted airport fodder was gone; only truth remained. The same truth *he'd* so arrogantly pursued? Probably not, but he'd get it anyway.

To the typewriter's side sat the beginnings of the girl's diary entries, to the other her mother's fabric scissors, encrusted with Sandie's blood. Renata's periphery collapsed as she typed, the room falling out of focus, until she was staring down a tunnel onto the page. The words were all that remained. That, and the girl's sobbing.

So she wrote.

For Quentin, she wrote.

26

'Good evening, Miss Wakefield,' said Detective O'Connell.

The man stood just outside the porch's overhang, his tatty umbrella doing little to keep him dry. Rain streamed over his raincoat. He burrowed his head into hunched shoulders in a preventative measure of such futility, Renata considered the possibility of its purpose being no more than a ploy for her sympathies. This theory solidified once she saw him register her dark glasses and cane, which prompted him to lower the umbrella and raise his bald head indifferently to the rain.

Through the cataract glasses she watched him work those yellowed detective eyes as he chewed his faithful toothpick. Like his sodden clothes – that same tieless navy shirt and waistcoat he hadn't changed since her arrival in Millbury Peak – his powers of observation soaked up every possible truth, but there were as many holes in these powers as there were in the tattered umbrella. She forced an expression of benign calmness as she writhed inside at the thought of everything that had slipped through the gaps in his abilities. She looked into his eyes and saw where the blindness really lay.

He's no more responsible for the truck or your mother's murder than I am for his god-awful books.

'Your eyes, Miss Wakefield,' spluttered Hector through a face-full of rain. 'What happened to you?'

Quentin's a good man.

Her grip tightened around the cane.

'Cataracts,' she said, 'like my father's. It came on so fast. This is just damage limitation until surgery. I still have some sight, but I'm effectively housebound.'

She stared into his unseeing eyes.

Old fool.

'But…groceries? The care of your father? Can't I help with—'

'I'm sorry, but what's the purpose of your visit, Detective?'

'I was hoping to fill you in on the case.' Hector cleared his throat, moving the pocket watch around in his newly-steadied hands. 'There's been some developments, Miss Wakefield. But if you're busy…'

'Not at all,' said Renata, curling her toes. 'So long as my father isn't disturbed.'

Hector stepped inside and gazed at the gleaming hallway. 'The house,' he said as he removed his coat, 'it's like stepping back in time. This is just how your mother kept the place when you were a girl.' He turned his eyes to Renata's glasses. 'You can see well enough for housework?'

'Just,' she replied. 'Thankfully, I can still administer my father's medication and, yes, get the house back in order. But for the most part my vision's a blur. I'm a bit of a sorry state, I'm afraid.' She forced a smile, fiddling with her striped apron. 'Not sure I'd be able to take anyone in a fight.'

Especially the teenage girl reported missing, last seen four days ago with me. Get to it, Detective.

Hector walked into the spotless lounge, overwhelmed by the transformation. It was like a showroom, immaculate in every regard. Despite the room's return to its former glory, the burnished ornamental silver, polished wooden surfaces, and scrubbed walls all remained dim as a result of the wooden shutters covering every window. Renata glanced at the bookcase.

'Jesus,' Hector grumbled, the smell of bleach and bottled ammonia catching in his throat, 'smells like a chemical plant in here.' He barked a deep cough. 'Haven't smelt anything that strong since I quit the drink.'

'I apologise. We're having a problem with the drains, and, as you can see, we're having a late spring clean, too. Or early, depending on how you look at it.' She smiled nervously. 'Please, come into the kitchen. The smell's not as bad in there.'

A moth fluttered past Hector as he approached the couch. 'Here will be fine, thank you.'

Sandie had been unconscious all evening, ground sleeping pills having featured in the bread stuffed between the girl's vomit-stained lips. She'd been out like a light, hunched over silently as Renata wrote at the desk behind her. Had the detective banged on the door during feeding time, her screams may very well have reached him. She glanced at the bookcase again, a mental image forming of Sandie stirring and hearing the muffled tones of conversation. As for the stench of cleaning fluids, she knew she couldn't trust its masking properties completely.

'I insist,' she said. 'Father's up to his eyes in sleeping pills, but I'd still like to avoid disturbing him.'

He followed her into the kitchen and sat at the table. Renata closed the door and felt her way to the kettle.

'Don't bother,' said Hector, swiping at his face. Another moth. 'I won't be here long.'

'It's no trouble, Detective,' she said, slipping a serrated salad knife into her apron pocket.

'I don't want to take up more of your time than is

necessary, Miss Wakefield.' He ran a hand over his now-sweatless head. Renata sat opposite. 'You've heard the news I assume?'

'News?'

Hector's eyebrow twitched. 'Sandie Rye, the girl whose charity auction you attended. She's not been seen since leaving the event.' He reached for his shirt pocket, then changed his mind. 'You've heard nothing of this?'

Her jaw dropped. '*Sandie*? What on earth... Detective, is she all right?'

'Well—'

'I feel like this town has gone mad,' she cut in, raising a rubber-gloved hand to her forehead. 'Things have been unravelling since my mother's—'

'I know, Miss Wakefield.' Hector sat back. He rubbed his eyes. 'I feel the same. As you're aware, I believe there's a connection between everything that's been happening. This can't be coincidence. It has to be related.' He looked into the tinted lenses. 'Have you *any* idea what may have happened to Miss Rye? You understand, you're a crucial component in locating her.'

Renata had been awaiting a visit from the police. Sandie's mouth had been taped shut near enough permanently, and in the case of an unexpected visitor, she'd planned to wrap even more tape around the bottom half of the girl's face before answering, completely obscuring any muffling or moaning. She'd mastered the technique of replacing the bookcase to its usual spot having entered the cellar, allowing her to render the house empty whilst downstairs, but she thought again of feeding time and the risk of the teenager's mouth being temporarily freed for food. Nevertheless, she'd always been ready to silence her in the event of a police visit, and the regular dose of sleeping pills proved a worthy precaution. Now she was finally being questioned, but by a recently retired, antique of a detective. This isn't how she'd imagined it, and the absence of an official police visit still nagged her.

'Me? Why would...' She feigned abrupt realisation. 'I see. She was last seen with me after the auction. No, I recall her mentioning nothing of note.' She played with the string of her apron. 'Detective O'Connell, you don't think whoever's responsible for everything that's happened to poor Quentin is behind this too, do you?'

Hector leant forward. 'Miss Wakefield, I know you've been romantically involved with Mr Rye.'

She straightened. 'Excuse me?'

'It's not my place to pry – at least not since retirement.' He smiled. Renata stared. 'Miss Wakefield, I've been considering the possibility that someone close to Mr Rye may be responsible for all this. They knew of the flammable film stock and on which truck it would be stored, not to mention where to find Miss Rye, despite her efforts to keep the event a secret.' Hector rose and stepped to the window, popping open his pocket watch with the toothpick. He looked down at its face. 'But there's a greater concern on my mind.' He turned to her as, in an instant, a shroud seemed to fall from his face. The cloak of stoic determination gave way to an expression of fear and disturbance. Suddenly, it was obvious to Renata the man was torn with worry.

'You, Miss Wakefield.'

They locked eyes.

'I'm assuming you're unaware of the other development,' he continued. 'An exhumed grave was discovered in the cemetery by your father's old church.

This grave lay next to your mother's resting place.' He stepped towards Renata. 'I fear for your safety. I always did, but the focus of recent events aren't just on Mr Rye. They're also on you.'

'Whose body was exhumed, Detective?'

He turned back to the window. The pocket watch returned to his waistcoat, the toothpick to his mouth. 'The grave was unmarked. I don't—'

Liar! Damned liar! You know exactly who it was!

'—but I refuse to believe the grave being next to your mother's was a coincidence—'

Blind! You all pretended I'd never existed once I was sent away, now you're too blind to see what's right in front of you!

Her hand clenched the handle of the knife in her apron pocket.

'—there's a possibility your mother's murderer is, for reasons yet beyond me, responsible for this exhumation—'

If you were less focussed on burying the truth you might see more you might see more you might see you might see

She pulled the knife from her pocket under the table.

'—but I have work to do. I'll leave you now, Miss Wakefield.'

Work.

She returned the blade to her pocket.

Yes. I have work, too.

'I know I've already made my feelings clear on this, but I'm going to say it again. Leave Millbury Peak.' He paced the spotless linoleum floor. 'There's a connection between everything that's happened, I know it. You *are* in danger, especially having had romantic involvement with Mr Rye, and this decline of your eyesight only makes you more vulnerable. I beg you,' he pleaded, 'let me see to your father's care. You *must* get out. You're in no condition to be taking care of anyone. More importantly, you're in danger. *Please* consider the—'

Renata stood. 'You're wrong.' He dropped the toothpick. 'I've been no closer to Mr Rye than that of an employee, and I know nothing of his daughter's whereabouts. Being left alone to care for my father: that is all I care about.' She opened the kitchen door, then stood to one side, picking the beige sleeve of her Aran knit. 'I'm sorry, Detective, but I must ask you to leave.'

He froze, mouth open. 'I didn't mean…I just—'

'I know my duty, and I know what I have to do.' Her eyes narrowed behind tinted lenses. 'I have someone to take care of.'

Renata watched the detective trudge down the steps back into the storm. She closed the front door, dropped the cane, and discarded the glasses.

For the first time in her life, she could see.

She went to the bookcase.

I've been told to write about my days here. I don't know why. I don't get why any of this is happening but I'll do whatever she says.

I'm in a lot of pain. She stabbed me in the leg and it's getting sorer. Maybe it's infected. I dunno how to tell. Sometimes she gives me painkillers, but not today. There's moths, loads of them. They're big and they keep landing on me and fuck I think they're feeding. She calls me a moth and I don't know why. I'm so scared.

The pain isn't the worst thing, and it's not being left alone in the dark and the cold for goddamn hours or days – I don't know which cause it's like there's no time here. She sits there tapping all day. I think it's a typewriter or something. I just cry and wait to pass out even though I know she'll wake me when I do.

I'm fed twice a day and given water. I'm not allowed to wash or go to the bathroom. I haven't left this cellar and she even leaves me to piss and shit on the chair before she comes and cleans it up like I'm a fucking baby.

But no, the worst part is that smell. Not even of my mess, but something worse. What the hell is it?! She's actually trying to make it less bad for me by smearing something under my nose. She's driving fucking scissors into my leg but going to the trouble to keep the smell away? What the fuck??? I can taste it, that menthol shit. I've seen stuff under people's noses before but I can't remember where. I don't know what any of this means.

*Now she wants me to write about my 'true self'. I told her I
don't know what the fuck that means but she just said I'd
know with time and to write about my life. I have to do
whatever she says or she might hurt me again.*

*So I was fucking born in San Francisco, California, nineteen
years ago to Quentin and Eleanor Rye FUCK! FUCK YOU
THIS*

*I was born in San Francisco, California, nineteen years ago to
Quentin and Eleanor Rye. I was brought up in a Christian
home. My parents separated after my 17th birthday. It was
hard but God carried me through it like He'll carry me
through this. They separated because Daddy was sick of the
religious stuff and Mom doesn't like the books he writes and
films he makes. I don't get that because it's his work and it got
us nice houses and bought her all the shit she always wanted,
although I guess he did have a gun stuck in my mouth one
time. So anyway, I told her all that and we argued and I
moved out when I turned 18. Now I live in an apartment
Daddy bought me. I'm so grateful for everything he does.
Grateful for Mom, too. I love them both so much. I hope they
know that.*

*I wish they were still together, especially now. Maybe what's
happening to me wouldn't be as bad for them if they were. I
think they split up because they didn't understand each other.
I'll get out of here and I'll marry someone who understands
me. I've also been told to write about my tattoo, and that's it.
They're roses spiralling around my ring finger. They symbolise
my waiting for the right man, someone who will love me and
never leave me. Someone who will understand me.*

I'm so grateful to both my parents, and even though me and Mom fell out, I still want her to know I love her and I'm grateful she showed me Jesus because He'll get me through this and I'll come out the other side even stronger. Jesus went through hell for me, and I'll go through hell for Him. Mom, thank you for teaching me sex before marriage is bad and that drugs are evil and for showing me the right path. When I get out of here, I'll be the best person I can be and I'll work so hard at my acting career and you'll be so proud of me. I love you both to the end of the world.

You want me to write about myself? My 'true self'? Sure. You got it.

I LOVE myself. I LOVE everything about my life – my Daddy, my Mom, and all the opportunities I've been given. I WON'T be broken. Whether by my love for my parents or for God, I WON'T be broken. You hear me?! Whatever you do to me, I WILL find the strength to go on. I WILL make it out of here. LOVE will see me through.

I won't be broken, bitch.

27

Thomas Wakefield did not approve of television. Along with Sylvia's romance novels, it held a high ranking on the list of sins forbidden in the Wakefield house – yet one sat in the attic.

The huge wooden set had been purchased for the sole purpose of watching the Queen's televised Christmas Day speech every year. The ritual would be foreshadowed by Thomas's grunting as he heaved the Finlux out of the attic and down the stairs into the living room, where it would sit all morning. Its bulbous blank screen bulged like an eyeball until, finally, it would awaken at 3 p.m. Following the royal drawl, the television once again faced expulsion for another twelve months.

Nearly thirty years later, it was the Wakefield daughter hauling the set downstairs. The next task would be the positioning of its aerial, those mystical metal antennae her father had manoeuvred with all the focus of a wizard performing an ancient ritual. Would the great, glass eye respond to her clumsy handling of the metal wands?

The electronic snowstorm fizzled into...a boat? Yes, a fantastically affordable Mediterranean cruise. She flicked the channel, a burst of static transforming the ship into a reception desk. Three over-tanned, over-acting hotel receptionists had it out over who was in love with whom.

She looked at the time. Six o'clock.

She cycled through the channels until another desk appeared, this time belonging to a news anchor. Several stories were detailed, first regarding conflicts in lands of which she knew nothing, then relating to scandals involving names she knew even less of. She couldn't remember the last time she'd watched a television. Her eyes were already aching when, finally, the anchor spoke the word she'd been waiting for.

Rye.

'The search for the missing daughter of horror novelist, filmmaker, and philanthropist Quentin C. Rye continues, as police urge anyone with information to come forward.' Renata knelt in front of the six o'clock news, staring into the screen. 'Miss Rye's parents have reportedly taken full-time residency in Millbury Peak, where Sandie was last seen. Mr and Mrs Rye have just given a press conference from the town, where Mr Rye's production company had been filming on location before cancelling all current projects to focus on the search for Sandie. Reporting from Millbury Peak earlier, here's Natasha.'

Renata endured Natasha's introduction before the camera finally panned to a stage blasted by flashing cameras. Chief Inspector Blyth and two colleagues sat with a well-dressed blonde woman laden with jewellery whose red, unrested eyes betrayed her identity as Sandie's mother, Eleanor.

Next to her sat Rye.

He would have been an image of perfect composure had it not been for the eyes behind his horn-rimmed frames, which, like his ex-wife's, gave everything away. To the audience, his stare may have said *anger*, *frustration*, *rage*, but they said something else, too, something evident only to Renata: *knowing*. His eyes told her he *knew*. He knew who had his daughter, and he knew they were watching. Renata leant closer, her face inches from the screen.

'I wuh-want my baby back,' Eleanor Rye stammered, fighting back tears. Renata scowled at the cross around the woman's neck being pawed at incessantly. 'I know someone has her, and I just need to know what they want, what it is we can do for them. Our daughter means everything to us, *everything*...' Blyth placed a hand on her shoulder and whispered in her ear. She shook him off as the tears won out. 'We'll give you *anything*, I swear. Just tell us – *tell us*, *DAMN YOU*.' Her head fell onto Quentin's shoulder. The cross hung limply.

Save for the arm he placed around her, Eleanor's tears barely registered with Rye. His eyes remained unwavering as they poured into the camera. Into Renata.

'Obviously this is an emotional time for everyone,' the chief inspector said. 'Rest assured, my colleagues and I have made Sandie's safe return our highest priority.'

Renata's nose touched the glass as Rye stared back. *I know you have her. I know you have my girl*, his eyes said. Hate swelled on both sides of the screen. Nails dug into her palms.

He stood.

'Furthermore, we want to assure the public that...uh...' Inspector Blyth's words trailed off as he saw the audience's attention switch to the standing man. Rye filled the screen, the camera re-centring and closing in on his stony expression. Renata knelt face to face with him. Time ceased.

Rye finally broke his staring contest with the camera and strode offstage. The Finlux's crackling speakers hinted at the confusion left in his wake; chatter rippled through the audience as the chief inspector tried to calm the room, while Eleanor ran after her ex-husband.

She shut off the television, its screen becoming a mirror in which her own face glowered back. She stood and stepped towards the bookcase. Sandie was out cold again from the sleeping pills, but it had been some hours since her last dose. The girl would be stirring at any moment. Renata slid the bookcase aside. Time to see to the little moth. Time to write.

There was a roar.

...reporting from Millbury Peak earlier...

A familiar roar.

...have just given a press conference...

It hadn't been live.

I know you have my girl.

She grabbed a fresh roll of insulation tape and ran to the cellar. The motorbike soon screeched to a halt on the track outside.

'Open the fucking door. LET ME IN!' The pummelling of Rye's fists was followed by the crisp smash of breaking glass, before he discovered the locked oak shutters. The banging moved around the house to the dining room, kitchen, and back to the front. The yelling ceased as his attention focussed on the ramming of his shoulder against the front door. It crashed open.

Rye stared in.

Renata stared back.

His mouth twisted into a growl. He threw her out of the way and tore up the staircase. 'SANDIE!' he yelled, that once-alien New England twang filling the house. 'I'm here! Call to me, Sandie!' His voice dimmed then amplified as he went between rooms. 'Call out, Sandie! It's Daddy! Tell me where you are!'

Renata listened as the upper level was ripped apart. The ladder to the attic rattled, followed by crashing within the roof. He eventually thundered back downstairs, storming past her to the dining room. He shot Renata a furious look as he charged into the lounge. The house filled with the bellowing of his daughter's name.

The crashing and bawling finally ceased. Heavy footsteps marked his passage back to the hall, where Renata stood patiently at the foot of the stairs. Before he lunged, a wave of recognition washed over her. She'd seen the look on Rye's face before, as a little girl. Those locking crosshairs weren't new to her, but she was no longer a little girl, and fists could no longer hurt her.

He'll never hurt us, not really. Because he can't.

She stood, lips pursed, waiting for the inevitable.

Looking forward to it.

He cracked his knuckles then sprang, one hand pulled back like a coiled spring, the other reaching for her. His fist sank into her face.

Choo-choo.

Renata's head flew back. Her body folded in half as he drove his other fist into her stomach. Her legs gave way. She crumbled to the ground.

'WHERE IS SHE?' boomed Rye, before planting one of his crocodile skin Oxfords into her side. She caught a fleeting glimpse of Fred and Wilma Flintstone peeking out from under his corduroys as she scrambled up the first few steps on her hands and knees. She turned to face him.

She smiled.

'Speak, woman. Open your goddamn *MOUTH.*'

He dragged Renata to her feet and slammed her into the wall, before hurling her across the hall. The rug slid under her stumbling weight, sending her to the ground. Face down, she ran a hand across the wooden flooring, remembering the last time she'd been down here. She glowered over her shoulder at Rye.

'*WHERE IS SHE?*' He knelt over her, nostrils flaring as his hands locked around her throat. '*OPEN THAT FUCKING*—'

She sprang. Rye reeled back as her lips smashed into his, hands clamped around his face. He tumbled to the floor, gazing into the endless stare of her open eyes as her mouth latched on like a leech.

Then he felt it.

Her tongue probed, vying to enter. He paused, in awe at the extent of the bitch's insanity, then opened his mouth. He felt the wet, rank-tasting muscle slide between his lips. He bit down as hard as he could, then threw her across the room, yet, somehow, the tongue remained between his teeth.

His face went white.

It wasn't a tongue.

Rye staggered back, his insides rising in revulsion. He spat the thing onto the rug, coughing convulsive barks as the vile taste expanded in his mouth. He braced himself against the wall as Renata stared from a heap on the floor, her tongue flicking from her mouth like a reptile's. She looked to the rug on which he'd spat the foreign body. He slowly followed her eyes.

It was a finger.

He dropped to his knees. All fight fell from him as he stared at the yellowing digit. A mental barrier rose between him and the finger; its deadened shade, splintered bone, insect-like curl…*it could be anyone's it's not hers it doesn't mean anything this psycho cunt doesn't have shit on you it's*—

The barrier crumbled as the spiralling tattooed roses fell into focus.

He wept.

She rose.

'I'll…the cops…I'll tell them,' he blubbered. 'The cops…they'll make you…they'll…I'll tell them you have her…the cops—'

'No, you won't.' Renata stepped over the lonesome finger, blood streaming from her nose. 'You'd have done so already. My dear Quentin, I know you're afraid.' Her shadow swallowed him. 'You're afraid of what I'd say, what they'll discover about you.'

'I'LL TELL THEM THAT…' Rye's words wilted into a whimper.

'Then please, tell them,' she said. 'Let them come. Let them take me so you can watch the search for your daughter from a jail cell, and I promise you…' She levelled her gaze. '…that search shall not be fruitful.' Silence hung as her eyes drilled into his. 'This was *your* doing. If any more harm comes to me, I swear you'll never see the girl again.'

His lips trembled.

'Understood?'

'What…do you want?'

'That'll become clear with time,' said Renata, turning from the kneeling man.

The front door had remained open as the storm continued to batter the house. The doormat flinched in the wind, sodden with rain. The leaves of a fallen aspidistra quivered in the gale next to the severed finger, upon which bite marks lay visible. It pointed to Quentin C. Rye.

'Don't worry, I'll be in touch,' Renata said, standing by the open door. She wiped her hands on her sleeves. 'Now, if you don't mind, I must ask you to leave.'

Daddy, I heard you shouting my name! I tried to call out like you said but couldn't. She covered my face in tape, my whole fucking face. Cut holes for my nostrils and ears. She wanted me to hear how close you were, Daddy. In my head I was screaming and screaming but nothing came out. I know you're looking for me. Please, please, please keep looking, Daddy. My finger she cut it off it's agony I can't stand it I don't think I

Daddy, I've begged but she won't listen. I'm gonna try here instead.

I won't use your name cause if you let me go I won't tell anyone anything. You could dump me on the side of a road somewhere and I swear on my life and God and EVERYTHING I won't tell. I'm beginning to think you don't want anything cause if you did you'd have told them by now and my parents are rich and you'd have gotten anything you wanted and you'd have let me go. So what is it? You just want to hurt me for the sake of it? Torture me?! You don't even fucking KNOW ME WHY WOULD

Daddy if you ever read this I want you to know I love you. I might lose my mind in here I don't know how much more I can take it's either pitch-black or so fucking bright and the pain it's beyond anything I thought possible and is God even seeing any of this? How could anyone let this happen do other people suffer like this is this just the am I the only I thought they were worse off but this I not like this it's

I hope I do lose my mind. She keeps saying she's going to let me black out for a bit but just wakes me up over and over and over I just want to be in the black for

I just remembered where I saw that stuff wiped under people's noses like she's doing with me I remembered it was on TV that's where on a crime show oh fuck oh God it was in a morgue dead bodies that's where they did it to cover the smell is that it is there a body IN HERE WITH ME FUCK SHE

28

Sandie awoke to the glare of fluorescent lights. She looked at the stump where her finger had been, now treated and bandaged. The encrusted blood and vomit and waste and whatever else had now come to define her body were also cleaned. The gaping wound in her knee was redressed and even felt somewhat anesthetised. A fresh blotch of Vicks smeared her upper lip.

Blurry-eyed, she looked up as a handful of pills were rammed between her cracked lips. Once her mouth was full of candy – yes, just pretend it's candy – the woman held a glass of water to Sandie's dried out mouth. She groaned as the liquid soothed her aching throat. Renata returned to her desk.

'Please…' Sandie croaked. The pretence of intellect had died with her dignity, the awkward shoehorned vocabulary reduced to pitiful begging. 'Renata, please. Just talk to me.' The typewriter continued tapping. 'I'm…sorry.' The tapping paused, then resumed. 'I'm sorry for whatever's happened to make you feel like you need to do this. Maybe I had the life you didn't. I'm lucky, I know that. Maybe I had the…the…' The tapping stopped. '…the parents you didn't, and for that I'm—'

Renata's chair crashed against the concrete as she sprang to her feet, swinging round to stare at the back of the girl's head.

'I'm *sorry*,' Sandie frantically begged. 'I didn't mean…I didn't—'

The telephone rang upstairs. Renata whipped her head towards the door, then back to the sobbing girl. She grabbed the insulation tape and began wrapping it around the girl's jaw. Sandie wrestled against her restraints as Renata stormed up the stairs and into the living room.

She picked up the receiver.

'Hello? Miss Wakefield? I'm sorry to disturb you again. It's Hector O'Connell.'

She swallowed.

'I wanted to apologise for my last visit.' He cleared his throat. 'Staying in Millbury Peak to care for your father, that's noble. It's not my place to tell you to leave.'

Renata switched hands, staring at the bookcase. 'Will there be anything else, Detective?'

'Yes,' said Hector. 'I needed to reiterate that finding your mother's killer is still all that matters to me. I won't rest until they're brought to justice. Sylvia's murder, the truck explosion, this exhumed grave, and now the disappearance of Sandie Rye. It's all linked, and I promise I'll uncover the truth.' He paused. 'I'll visit again soon, and I'm afraid I won't take no for an answer. Your father and I go way back, and I consider it my duty to assist in his care. You're not in this alone, Miss Wakefield.'

Renata opened her mouth, but it was too late. The dialling tone hummed in her ear. She let go of the receiver, letting it clatter against the sideboard as she went to the cellar door.

She stood staring through the narrow gap between the bookcase and the doorway. This girl wasn't the only moth in her world. The detective, everyone like him: all moths. They fluttered and fought for their share of the light, and, like the insect's obsession, knew evil only from within the narrowest realms of understanding. To them, evil was the extinguishing of that light. Yes, that was it. The light goes out, you step up and find the switch. Bring it back so the fluttering may continue.

But for Renata Wakefield, the veil had been lifted. She saw evil for what it was: evil was *good*, and good was *evil*. Yes, one and the same, an arbitrary human construct. Men like Detective O'Connell, blinded by a preconceived notion of duality, were unable to see past a single face of the coin.

I'll visit again soon.

The detective had left her no choice. If he ever stepped into this house again, she would show him the truth. Evil is *good*, good is *evil*. The coin spins on.

But first she would see if she could stop it coming to that.

She slipped through the gap into the cellar, leaving the bookcase partially covering the door. Her eyes followed the fluorescent strips across the ceiling to the end of the chamber and down to the trembling girl. She edged towards the teenager.

'You speak of God in your diary entries,' said Renata, taking the VapoRub from her apron and dabbing it under her own nose. 'He left me, abandoned me. Just like everyone else. I was discarded, forgotten, left to rot in a purgatory of white corridors. What do you think he makes of your plight, child? What would be the sense of him helping you but not me all those years ago?' The girl gazed at Renata, her stare hollow. 'Truth,' she continued, 'it can be a killer. No one's out there for you, least of all God. You apologised for *whatever's happened to me*. The *truth* happened to me, little moth.' She reached for the bloodstained scissors. 'Would you mind if I told you a story?' Renata asked with a smile, snipping the air.

'Pain...killers. Please, more...painkillers.'

'There was a woman,' Renata continued, ignoring the girl's pleas. 'Ballet dancer. This woman gave everything for her art, the only thing that made sense to her. She *bled* for it.' Sandie cringed at the slicing blades. 'Then a double-decker ploughed through her. She splattered on the front like a fly, was mangled like a ragdoll – but she *lived*.' She looked at the girl. 'And although she never danced again, she came to feel more alive than she thought possible. Now that she couldn't dance, time opened up before her. She read, she loved, she travelled. That bus ripped her apart, but it also *freed* her.'

Renata held the scissors by the closed blades and inspected their orange handles.

'You see, I was ripped apart,' she continued. 'I was torn to pieces by the truth, but then it put me back together. And now, well...I, too, am more alive than I thought possible.' She moved behind Sandie's chair and ran her fingers through the girl's hair, swaying and gazing into the light above. 'My dear, all I want is for the truth to put you back together, as well.' She lowered her mouth to Sandie's ear, wrapping the blonde hair around her closed fist, then whispered, 'There was no ballet dancer.' Tears streamed down the teenager's face. 'It's not as easy as that. The only truth that can put you back together is within yourself.' She ran her tongue up Sandie's trembling cheek, tasting the tears and mascara. 'But first,' she breathed, 'you have to let it rip you apart.'

Renata yanked the girl's head back and stared into her eyes from above. 'Tell me you *see*.'

She slammed the handles of the scissors into Sandie's mouth. The sound of dislodging teeth filled the cellar as the butt of the blades smashed a second time, the shock of the sudden onslaught rendering the girl silent until the third blow. She attempted to scream but instead gagged on blood.

In her delirium of pain, she may have thought of all those funfairs, those damned funfairs to which she must have been taken as a child. Maybe she remembered waiting at the popcorn cart while her bucket was filled, staring into the machine, the corn thrown around like teeth in some mad lottery. Maybe, years later, she watched her own teeth flying onto the concrete of her new home in this cellar – her final home – and thought how much fun all those trips to the funfair had been. Maybe it was then, once the pain registered, that she realised her young life was over. The funfair, and with it everything she'd ever cared for: over.

Worlds away, the clock tower struck noon as the girl choked on what remained of her teeth. Renata threw the scissors over her shoulder and pushed Sandie's head forward, broken teeth spraying onto the girl's lap from flaking lips.

The chasm of agony into which the girl now tumbled was evident in her eyes. Enlightened to a new definition of pain, these eyes had awoken in a universe dedicated to nothing but fathomless suffering. Renata rubbed an antiseptic wipe between her fingers.

'Where is your God now, child?' Sandie looked up to a tinkling sound as the woman stood shaking the bottle of painkillers in front of her. She unscrewed the cap and dropped the pills to the floor one by one, where they rattled down an iron drain. Her gaze locked on Sandie's sobbing eyes, soaking up every shade of her suffering.

'I have an errand to attend to, and so you may soon rest,' whispered Renata, picking the bloody teeth from the girl's lap and dropping them one by one into the empty painkiller bottle. 'But first you will write.' She screwed the lid on tight then shook the bottle again. 'Write, dear.'

THURSDAY

6

NOVEMBER

I know now she's going to kill me. She'll either go too far or she'll run out of ways to hurt me. Either way, I'm going to die down here.

I also figured out what she wants, what this fucking 'truth' is she keeps going on about. She wants me to say who I really am, so I will – but not for her. For God.

I'm a sinner. She was right to cut off my finger. Those roses were meant to symbolise the saving of myself for the right man, but it was a lie. The truth is I've slept with more men than I can count. I did it because I felt worthless, despite what I convinced everyone. Thousands, millions of dollars poured into my life and all I can do is…well, what can I do? Turns out I give pretty good head. I did it because I wanted to be worth something. And I was – until morning came.

Then the drugs started. The look on their faces when I hit a line as my big brown eyes looked up at them. Man, I really felt the bomb. No way would they chuck me now. Didn't expect to get hooked. But that great head I gave, and everything else…well, my body became my currency. It was the only thing that would get me more blow. Think I looked pretty good for a junkie. Not so much now.

So there it is, you fucking bitch. There's your truth. But, like I said, it's not for you. God, Daddy, Mom, I'm sorry for all my sins. I hope this counts as confession 'cause I don't think I have long left and I don't wanna burn for all eternity. Forgive me, Jesus. Please forgive me. I repent, Lord. I repent I repent I repent if this is my punishment then let it end take me from here I can't TAKE IT I CAN'T TAK

274

29

Millbury Peak had survived centuries of torrential rain, but an air of concern never failed to linger amongst the townsfolk during such weather. Set on an incline, the town's aged drainage system often allowed a build-up of water on the east side, rendering certain routes impassable and creating miniature waterfalls from street stairways. Tonight, the storm-streaked skies issued forth a downpour of dread-inducing proportions upon the town.

Renata flinched as her cheek tore on the claws of a thorny shrub. Her passage through the undergrowth of this unmaintained marshland of a garden had been slow and arduous, exacerbated by the unrelenting rainfall. The flooded soil hungrily swallowed her shoes underfoot. Renata barely noticed.

She silently congratulated Rye on his performance. His rented manor, its driveway having been full when she first arrived, was serving as the headquarters of the search for Sandie. He knew exactly who had his daughter, but was orchestrating all this purely to show the world the hunt was on. He was going through the motions that were expected of him. In reality, he thought of nothing but what a hermit romance novelist named Renata Wakefield was capable of, and how he may reclaim his daughter from her unhinged grip.

A smartly dressed man and woman clutching wads of papers had stepped out of the side door and huddled under an overhang to suck on cigarettes. Renata had watched, toes tensed in a tight curl, as the pair had examined the papers while shaking their heads gloomily. After gazing into the rain through their final long drags, they had flicked their stubs into the grass and headed for their cars. They'd been the last to drive off into the night.

And now, crouched in the bushes peering through the shrubbery, Renata waited for her moment. Her hands ached from the constant typing. She rubbed her throbbing fingers as the rain fell like pebbles against her face. She'd been acutely aware of the house's rear facing looking out over the garden, with the risk of stray eyes spotting her through one of its many windows. Now, having watched most of Quentin's staff leave for the night, she knew she had less cause for concern.

She was rising from the bushes when the largest ground floor window suddenly illuminated the garden like a stadium. She tugged the soaked scarf over her face and dropped back down into the thicket. From her vantage point behind a dense mass of overgrowth, she could see two figures through the lit window standing over the counter of a large kitchen. She swept the rain from her eyes and squinted, reaching for the details. It was the same drained woman from the televised press conference: Eleanor Rye.

And him.

Renata could feel the solemnity of Quentin and Eleanor's words in the movement of their lips. Without warning, the woman threw her hand across the counter sending empty glasses smashing against the wall and the cross around her neck flailing on its chain. She fell sobbing into her ex-husband's arms. Renata could feel the turtleneck against her face as the woman burrowed into the crook of his shoulder, just as she had done. She could see the sincerity of Rye's actions in the way he pulled her body into his, stroked her blonde hair, pecked her forehead. This was no game, no experiment. The woman in his arms was no guinea pig.

Renata's aching hands clenched into fists.

He held Eleanor in front of him and spoke words that caused the woman's hysterics to abate. As water poured over Renata's face, she watched the pair gaze silently into one another's eyes. She knew what was coming, but was still somehow totally unprepared for it.

Their lips met.

Renata stared through the darkness, gouging her palms. Her waterlogged clothes clung to shivering skin as her hands clenched harder. Sparks ignited in her veins and shot through every capillary. She gazed as the rain battered her, fists from above. She felt the rage inside kick like an overdue baby. Something within had awoken from a stagnant symbiosis; what was once dormant now flared with malice.

She watched the couple's long embrace before Eleanor finally slipped from his arms, kissed his cheek, and left the room. This was her moment.

Renata stood.

She stared as Rye stepped from the side door and stood beneath the overhang, gazing into the rain. It had been hard to tell if he'd seen her when he'd gone to the window to look out after she'd thrown the pebble at the glass, but it was indisputable where his eyes now fell: the trail of tiny, bloodied teeth leading from the side door and down the garden path, glowing in the moonlight like cat's eyes down a motorway.

He'd reached inside to activate a security light, then

stood staring at the trail in horror, trying to make out the blood-spotted white pearls leading down the path, knowing what they were but hanging on desperately to blind denial. He stumbled back, one hand gripping a stone balustrade as the undeniable truth finally hit home. His jaw trembled as his eyes followed the grisly trail, a twisted Hansel and Gretel re-enactment gone wrong, until they met with the dark figure in the shadows. He reached inside to switch off the security light then slowly closed the door, before crossing his arms against the driving downpour and following the trail of teeth to the woman at the bottom of the garden.

Renata, keeping her glare fixed on him, stepped backwards through the rain and behind the vast trunk of a towering elm, leading him further from the house. The distance between them closed. She backed into a brick wall at the foot of the garden, over which red vines stretched like exposed veins.

Rye stood white-faced by the elm, placing a hand against the bark to steady himself. 'Is…she alive?'

'Yes.'

'What are you doing here?'

She rubbed at the pain in her hands. 'You came to my house, now I've come to yours.' She nodded behind him towards the teeth leading up the path. 'Those are just a little punishment for your conduct last time we saw each other.' She reached into her pocket and tossed a single tooth towards him. He leapt back as if it were a live grenade. 'Punishment for you both, I suppose.'

The giant elm shook overhead as a harsh gale picked up around them. The moonlight lit their faces but little else, two floating, wide-eyed scowls staring each other down in the darkness. The wall of crimson vines was just visible behind Renata, those creeping veins emanating around her. She held her hands out into the rain, scrubbing them like a pre-op surgeon, unflinching as the torrents lashed around her. Rye watched the shadow-cloaked figure from beneath the tree, his chest heaving with quick, adrenaline-fuelled respiration.

'I need you to do something for me,' she spoke calmly through the storm. He leant forward to discern her delicate words. 'It's O'Connell. I need you to get him to cease his investigation into the disappearance of the girl. I don't want him bothering me anymore.'

Rye slowly straightened. 'Maybe I'm happy with him investigating.'

'Maybe. But if I tell him about your dirty deeds, then you can be happy about it in a prison cell. I've seen your operation here, your little search committee. I know you have it in your power to make him stop.' He stared, unflinching. Renata huffed. 'Fine, I'll deal with him myself.'

'You knew I'd say no.'

'Yes. I just...' The corners of her mouth turned up. '...wanted to see you.'

He took a step towards her. 'All right, Renata. I'll try. But you have to tell me what it is you want out of all this, out of my daughter. Everything I did, I did it for my work. You're doing this for revenge. What you've put Sandie through, she'll never be the same. I'll never be the same. Isn't that enough?'

She ripped a loose strand of hair from her scalp. 'You know it isn't.'

A fresh torrent swept over the scene.

'What do you *WANT* from me?' he suddenly yelled through the rain. The figure in the darkness remained still, the whites of her eyes piercing through the night's blackness. His tone softened. 'Listen, if I'm responsible for what you've become, then you're responsible for what I've become: *changed*, Renata. What you're doing to my daughter, my sweet Sandie...' He forced his quivering lips to settle. '...it's turned me around. Maybe I'm ill. Maybe I need help. But what I put you through, what I did to you...your mother...I see now how twisted it was. I think I've found my humanity because of you, and I thank you for that. There has to be some left in you, too. Please, Renata,' he clasped his hands together as if in prayer, 'end this.'

End this.

She smeared her sodden hair out of her face. The throbbing in her hands was intensifying – and reminding her of something. A punishment? Yes, her father's Bible. It reminded her of being made to hold that weighty thing for so long, so very long.

'In the beginning God created the heaven and the earth. And the earth was without form, and void; and darkness was upon the face of the deep. And the Spirit of God...' The girl looks up to her father's glare locked upon her. She returns to the pages. '...moved upon the face of the waters. And God said, Let there be light. And, uh, there was light.'

What was it she'd done? Failed to clean her room, maybe misquoted a Bible verse at Sunday school. It didn't matter. All punishments were roughly the same. Noah was not yet born, and so her punishments were frequent. The unusual thing about this punishment was her mother's presence.

There the woman had sat on the sofa, the clicking of her knitting needles trying to keep up with the eternal ticking of the grandfather clock. But the scarf-in-progress draped over her pregnant belly wasn't growing very fast. She was distracted. The girl would risk a glance at her mother every so often from her hard, rigid seat by the window, only to find she wasn't even looking at the knitting. She was staring at the floor in front of her, that wooden smile slipping from her grasp as the hours rolled on, as her daughter was forced to act out her punishment: to sit and read aloud the entire tome.

'And...and it came to pass that in the morning, behold, it was Leah: and he said to Laban, What is this thou hast—'

Her mouth has long since dried up. Grit has formed in her throat.

'Fulfil her week, and we will give thee this also for the service which thou—'

She isn't even through Genesis. She prays for Exodus after every page turn, but knows fine well she has some way to go before that. Even then, she still has Leviticus, Numbers, Deuteronomy...

'And Jacob did so, and fulfilled her week, and he gave him—'

...Joshua, Judges, Ruth...

'And he went in also unto Rachel, and he loved also Rachel more than Leah, and served with him yet seven other—'

...the Samuels, the Kings, the Chronicles, Ezra, Nehemiah, Esther, Job...

'And when the Lord saw that Leah was hated, he opened her womb: but Rachel was barren.'

...Psalms, Proverbs. So much still to go. He can't expect

her to read the entire thing right here, could he? Is that even possible?

'And she conceived again, and…and bore a…son.'

A son.

The girl's eyes rise.

Then her mother's.

Then her father's.

All eyes return as the reading resumes.

Renata rubbed her moonlit hands in the pouring rain, still throbbing from her long writing sessions. She thought of that bulky Bible and the burning sensation shooting through the ligaments of her nine-year-old hands. She'd finally made it out of Genesis, but by that time her voice was nothing but a rasp. She didn't get very far through the opening pages of Exodus before her mother broke into tears. The woman clambered from the couch over to Thomas's armchair, falling to her knees before him, begging for the girl's punishment to end.

'I know you don't agree, but she doesn't deserve this, Thomas.' The woman places a hand on her bulbous, pregnant belly. 'It's a boy, I swear it. I can feel him inside of me. You'll have your son. He'll be here soon and everything will be better. I beg of you, my little girl doesn't deserve this. Please, Thomas,' she clasps her hands together as if in prayer, 'end this.'

Thomas had slowly lowered his newspaper, then stared blankly at the woman as if she'd spoken a foreign language, one of his fingers casually tapping against the crinkled paper in his hands. She'd eventually scrambled to her feet and ran weeping from the living room, her hurried footfall ascending the staircase in the hall.

The girl had stopped reading to watch in a mixture of terror and rage. After her mother's wails had disappeared upstairs, her eyes met with her father's. Her instincts told her to bow her head and continue reading, to avert her gaze immediately like she'd been told to do if she ever looked at the sun.

But she didn't.

She did not resume her reading, instead keeping her gaze fixed on her father's, a raging sun blazing in each of his eyes, scorching and searing her skin.

Her stinging hands had gripped the Bible in her lap, tighter, tighter with every passing second until she'd thought her fingers were going to break. Suddenly, he'd set down his paper and approached the girl warily, hesitantly – *is he frightened?* – reaching down to carefully close the Bible in her lap. He'd then left the room and joined Sylvia upstairs. In more ways than one for Renata Wakefield, the Bible closed for the final time that night.

She still remembered the battle between hate and fear raging in her father's eyes during that stare down. And now, in this rain-pummelled garden, she saw that same old hate and fear warring it out again in Rye's eyes.

He was lying. He had found no humanity. As he appealed to whatever trace of compassion may be left within her, she came to understand that they were as barren of benevolence as each other.

She clenched her aching fists by her side.

'Let her go, Renata,' pleaded Rye through the downpour. 'It's not her you want, it's me. It's always been between us.'

'ENOUGH.'

He froze. Through the darkness he saw her teeth bared

like a Dobermann's, white in the moonlight.

'You want this to *end*?' she growled incredulously, clawing her hands as she stepped towards him. 'It's too late. Things have gone too far, you know that.'

Tears formed in Rye's eyes. 'I…could still kill you, you know.'

'Don't you get it? I *loved* you,' she continued, ignoring his words, 'or whoever that man was. You created him, just like you created me. Why could *I* never be loved? Why could *I* never have what everyone else has? I was so close to ending it, so close to being free when you dragged me back here.' She turned her back to him. 'All of this, it's because of you. It's too late to go back, you know that.'

Rye smashed the tree with his fist. 'TELL ME,' he screamed, tears streaming down his face and merging with the rain. 'Just tell me what to do to get her back. *Tell me*, goddammit. *END THIS*.'

Renata looked back at him over her shoulder. He watched her face fall into darkness as a cloud passed over the glowing moon, obscuring its white light. 'You need to wait, that's all,' she said from the void. 'Just wait.'

'Quentin?' a voice called from the house. 'Quentin, are you out there?'

He turned to see Eleanor standing under the overhang of the side door at the top of the garden. He spun back round to Renata just as the clouds cleared, the moonlight once again lending itself to the rain-swept garden.

She was gone.

30

Renata stood staring at the hair clip. She had to save it. The treacherous things had been slowly escaping over the past months, until now only the current cluster in her head remained – and this final clip. Smearing her hair away from her face wasn't enough. Loose strands still floated in her periphery, but she had to control herself. She had to remind herself what really mattered. She pocketed the final clip and locked the front door, checked the window shutters, and returned to the cellar. The cold air added to the chill of her clothes, still wet from her excursion to Rye's manor, but this was of no consequence. All that mattered was the book.

She'd slipped back into a life of writing with little effort. Inspiration no longer floated out of reach like dust in a sunbeam, instead *insisting* on realisation. Renata was nothing more than the vessel for its delivery.

What's more, the chapters were materialising mostly complete. The first draft of a novel was meant to resemble an over-spiced dish; the essential ingredients were there, but buried within a bloated version of its final form. A dish you could remake, holding back on the spices and allowing the thing to speak for itself, whereas with a novel you had to pick out the offending spice grain by grain. But within the pages churned out by Sylvia Wakefield's typewriter, something different was happening. The thing was coming into existence practically fully formed as fast as a court transcript. With fresh eyes she'd read over previous chapters, pencil in hand, ready to scribble the usual amendments, but had been astonished to find barely anything needing altered.

The dish was spiced almost to perfection.

A blast of inspiration where there'd been none. Focus sharpened to such a degree as to produce a final draft in place of a first. What had changed? What was different? The answer was obvious. It was all thanks to the girl in the basement.

Renata lowered her hands from the keys, took a sip of water, then stepped in front of Sandie. Out cold. She held up the glass and let its contents trickle over the girl's head, waking her from the sweet mercy of unconsciousness.

'Puh-please, Renata,' she stammered, her mutilated gums quivering.

Renata scraped her chair across the concrete and sat in front of the shivering girl. 'I had a brother once, Miss Rye,' she said, picking at the palms of her hands. 'You and I may have been around the same age when he died.'

'*Please*, the *PAIN*, it's—'

'He imparted upon everybody a kind of joy I'd seen nowhere else. To everyone, he was an angel.' She leant forward. 'Everyone, except *me*.'

'I...don't think I can take it much—'

'Only I knew the truth. All the agony of my life, and now the agony of yours, spawned from that truth. Your wounds are nothing compared to the pain I've endured. You've done so well, you still are, but you have some way to go. The truth, my moth, I need you to—'

'I've *TOLD* you the truth. I've told you *EVERYTHING*,' screamed Sandie. 'What else do you *WANT*?' Her body shook against the chair, the cable ties burrowing deeper into the fleshy trenches embedded in her wrists. Renata watched the teenager's rage ebb as her lack of energy caught up with her emotional turbulence. 'Please, I'm begging you. All this, it has to be some…mistake.'

'*MISTAKE?*' Renata screamed. 'The only *mistake* was using my pain as inspiration for a damned *BOOK*.'

'Book? What book? Is this…to do with my Dad?'

Renata stood, rubbing the sides of her head. 'You know, Miss Rye, moths have a remarkable sense of smell.' She gazed at the cloudy nests lining the ceiling. 'The female lures potential mates with a scent that promises sex. I read of an experiment where a male is said to have followed such a scent *six* miles, only to find he'd followed it right into a scientist's pheromone trap.' She turned to Sandie. 'I remember writing to you, little moth, laying that scent and wondering how far you'd flutter. I lit that flame and you didn't disappoint.' She grabbed Sandie's hair and held her head in place, then wiped off the Vicks. The numbness in the teenager's nose began to fade. 'Yes, Miss Rye. It's about your father. He used me as an experiment, used my pain to inspire his work.'

The smell hit the girl.

'I've been the experiment,' Renata continued, 'like the moth in the pheromone trap. Now it comes full circle.' Sandie retched. Her eyes watered. 'Now *you're* the experiment. Your pain is igniting the pages of my gift to him. As he intended for me, I intend for you. We're all monsters, you see, but your father and I truly *are* the same breed.' The girl's bloodshot eyes met Renata's. 'He made me his muse. Now, child, you are mine.'

She rammed a crumpled sheet of paper into Sandie's mouth, forcing her to breathe through her nose, then strode to the back of the cellar, kicking a mouldy Henrietta

Reid paperback out of the way. She opened the rotting wooden hatch in the wall. 'Poor little moth, flew too close to the flame. Let's see what scent awaits you.'

The shape Renata dragged to Sandie could have been a bloodstained sack filled with randomly shaped objects, a leak in the exterior leaving a trail of liquid in its wake. She pulled it by two long, floppy handles. *Funny*, the girl may have thought incoherently, *never seen a sack with those kinds of handles*.

Renata dumped the shape at Sandie's feet like a cat's doormat offering.

Her eyes focussed. The body took form.

The supposed handles were arms, the objects organs still liquefying, seemingly detached from their internal fastenings and knocking around freely. The corpse had marked its route like a slug, leaving a trail of sludge leading to Sandie. It lay at the girl's feet, the remains of its face slumped crookedly.

It stared at her.

Had she not been compelled to determine whether the corpse was her father, she could never have brought herself to regard its twisted, traumatized features, pulped by decomposition, but she had to know.

There were no eyelids. The orbs within the exposed skeletal sockets were completely red except for single white globules in the centre of each eye. Its cheeks were shrivelled inwards, clinging to what little was left of the gaping mouth, the outline of its teeth apparent through the tight, thinning skin. There was little hair, but what strands she saw were white, glued to the grey face over heavily wrinkled skin.

It wore a clerical collar. This wasn't Daddy.

She swung her head away and clenched her eyes shut so

tight that it hurt, but it was no use. The monstrosity was burned in her mind. There was a terrible reality to this thing for which none of the dummy corpses from her father's films could have prepared her. This had been a person. She hadn't known the person, but it had been *someone*, as she was now someone. There weren't many arguments against the probability of Sandie soon becoming the next inanimate sack to leak across this concrete floor.

The girl could hold her breath no longer; she inhaled the puddle of death at her feet. Her stomach convulsed. Renata held her hand against Sandie's mouth, stopping the crumpled paper from shooting out, then winced as vomit sprayed from between her fingers and bubbled from the teenager's nostrils.

Renata wiped her hands on her skirt and returned to the typewriter, where she let her fingers hover over the keys. She listened to the weeping, choking, whimpering, and incoherent blabbering. She listened to the agony and the anguish, to the despair and the rage.

She listened, fingers poised. She listened to the suffering that would provide the only fist she would ever need. She'd never thrown a punch, and she never would. All she needed to wreak true revenge was in that chair, and within these pages.

She wrote.

The human-sludge by Sandie's feet had been her only company all night after Renata finished her tapping and left, but finally the door opened. Sandie's swollen, red eyes burned as the fluorescent strips blazed the cellar with light.

Renata descended.

Her glare on the girl remained unwavering as she stepped through the putrid puddle that had been her father, taking care not to slip. It parted noisily under her feet. Keeping her distance, she cut the cable tie binding Sandie's left wrist and set the open diary upon the girl's lap, then placed the pen on an empty page. 'Time to write.'

'Tuh-truh…'

Renata leant down. 'What are you saying?'

'Truh-uh…'

'Speak up, girl.'

'Truh-truth…'

'Yes, child,' said Renata, 'that's right, but *here*.' She placed the pen in Sandie's hand. 'Please, you must *write*.'

The girl's fingers went limp. Her head dropped, then flew to the side under the impact of Renata's open hand. 'Get a hold of yourself! *Write*.' She reset the pen.

'Truh…tuh…' It fell.

'WRITE, damn you.' Renata set aside the scissors and tightened Sandie's fingers around the pen, manoeuvring her hand so as to remind the girl of the necessary motions.

'The tuh-truh…'

She eased Sandie's hand over the page. 'Come on, you're a grown girl. Snap out—'

'TRUTH.'

The penetration of Renata's cornea took some moments to register. At first she thought the lights had gone out, until she felt the cocktail of ink and ocular fluid weeping down her cheek. Her hands flew to her face as she screamed into the lights above, the pen sticking from her eye socket like a dart from a bullseye.

She dragged her remaining eye reluctantly into focus, only to find she'd fallen into the blackened viscera of her father's remains. She looked at Sandie just in time to see the girl freeing herself with the scissors.

Both froze as their eyes met.

They lunged.

Sandie immediately fell as her shattered kneecap crumbled under her weight. She tumbled from the slab into the mire of decomposition, dropping the scissors. Renata wrestled on top of her, grabbing the girl's throat with a roar and slamming her into the rancid pulp. Thomas Wakefield sprayed across the concrete.

Unreality swamped Sandie's mind as she gazed at the Cyclopean beast throttling the life from her; the sludge in which she was flailing hadn't been human, and this monster wasn't about to murder her. All she had to do was close her eyes and drift as the fluorescent tubes faded and the smell of death died. This hell would become a fading whisper, finally coming to an end. She let go of the monster's claws and let her eyelids drop.

Her hand fell on the scissors.

Her eyes opened.

Renata reeled back as the steel entered her thigh. Sandie tore from the chaos and stumbled across the cellar, pain screaming through her knee as she lurched for the stairs. The woman's howls filled the chamber as she was left thrashing in the pool of decay.

Sandie threw the door open and drove her weight against the bookcase, which slammed to the ground with the girl spread across its back. She gasped as if coming up for air.

There was a crash from the cellar. It wasn't over.

The girl's eyes shot around the room, first to the locked oak shutters over the windows, then to the padlocked kitchen door. She limped to the hallway, scissors in hand, and leapt for the front door.

Locked, of course.

She suddenly remembered the overhangs of the house's exterior. Climbing from an upstairs window would allow her to drop from one of these overhangs, but she had to act fast. The mad bitch would soon catch up. She spat a mouthful of blood and reached for the banister.

Pain bellowed as Sandie heaved herself up the stairs, her severed finger's crusty dressing falling off as she clutched the handrail. She moaned as her bloody stump knocked into the wooden knob marking the summit, then gazed down the corridor in disbelief.

It was like stepping into a different house. While downstairs had been cleaned to perfection, the walls of this upper level were caked in grime, the carpet was blackened with filth, and mildew crawled from the mouldy skirting boards. She locked eyes on the cobweb-curtained window at the end of the corridor, snapping out of her disorientation.

She dragged herself down the musty hallway, too scared to scream, too panicked to cry. Her eyes fell on cartoon animals adorning the door by the window. She ignored them, desperately retaining her focus on the task at hand. Upon inspection, she found the grimy window's lock sealed with discoloured paint. A wail finally escaped her as she battered the lock.

Nothing.

Sandie dropped the scissors and lunged for a dusty side chair. She heaved it behind her before going to launch it through the glass.

It didn't move.

She looked over her shoulder to find Renata's hand grasping one leg of the chair, the other the scissors. Ink trailed from her eye socket over a broad grin.

Sandie thrust the chair back, sending Renata reeling as

its leg speared her stomach. She seized this moment to hobble down the corridor stretching endlessly before her. Finally, her foot met with the top step of the staircase. She would descend, run, find a weapon, fight—

Her heel opened between the blades of the scissors.

The step creaked.

Her Achilles tendon snapped like overstrained elastic, the ground giving way beneath her. As she fell, she may have been dimly aware of the blood trailing behind from her heel, a little like the sack in the cellar. *It left a trail, too,* she may have thought. *I'm going to become that thing. I'm going to die here.*

She landed in a twisted jumble at the foot of the staircase, unable to move. She gazed as Renata floated from above, an angel of death. The angel grabbed her feet and dragged her through the house. As the ceiling of the living room turned into the ceiling of her cell, unconsciousness crept over her.

Death? Please, let it be death, she may have thought. *Take me, God.*

But God wasn't listening. Worse was to come.

Sandie Rye would have known this.

31

Renata stood at the foot of the stairs, patiently waiting for a knock at the front door.

Rye had been right: she'd known he wouldn't comply with her demands to stop Detective O'Connell in his investigation. Why had she wanted to see him if not for that? The teeth were a nice touch – she was getting good at this bunny boiling business – but the truth was that she had *craved* him. Not the same craving she'd felt previously, from before the love turned to hate, but a new kind. Hers was the craving a sniper felt for their target to enter their crosshairs. He'd become her life's purpose, so it didn't surprise her that she desired to see his suffering first-hand – those tears of anguish. Soon, she would witness the climax of his suffering, the very moment his world crumbled forever. Soon, she would witness the end, but first she had to make sure nothing would get in the way of her plan's completion.

First, O'Connell.

'I don't know how this happened or what I'm—' Renata had stammered into the telephone earlier, before thrusting the receiver to arm's length as she'd been interrupted by a fit of coughing from the earpiece.

'Sorry,' Hector said, spluttering down the telephone. 'Throat feels like it's lined with nettles. It's the weather. Seems like this storm's been brewing for decades.'

Truer words had never been spoken.

'I've been lying to you, Detective.

A pause.

'After all you've done to find my mother's murderer, all I've given in return is lies. I'm so sorry.'

'Miss Wakefield, take a deep breath. What lies? What are you trying to tell me?'

'You were right, I am...*was*...romantically involved with Quentin Rye.' She switched hands. 'He broke it off when his daughter went missing. Told me he needed to focus on the search and trying to rebuild his family.'

'I see,' Hector said, the sound of his toothpick being chewed coming through the line. 'And why did you feel you had to lie to me?'

'I was scared. He's capable of...things. Quentin Rye is not what he seems, he's not—'

'Now, Miss Wakefield,' the detective cut in, 'if it ended badly between you two then I understand your anger, but if you're implying Quentin may have had something to do with his daughter's disappearance, I'd ask you to reconsider. Everyone knows the man is doing all he can to—'

'They have her.'

The line went quiet.

'Him and the ex-wife, they have her. Or at least, they know where she is. I saw things during my time at that house. There's more to him than you know.' She made her voice tremble. 'I'm so sorry I lied to you. I need to tell you everything. We need to save Sandie.'

'What did you see at the house, Miss Wakefield?'

'My father...I have to go. He needs me.'

'Tell me everything you know,' Hector demanded. 'This is a missing girl we're talking about.'

'I should never have told you to leave us alone. We need you now more than ever.' She fought back imaginary tears. 'Please come to the house. Detective, I'm so scared what Quentin might be doing to her. I'm begging you…come to the house. God, don't let it be too late.'

The call had ended as she'd ripped the telephone cord from the wall.

And now, standing at the foot of the stairs upon the very floorboards where a five-and-a-half-year-old's beating had set her down this lifelong path of pain, she waited.

Finally, there was a knock.

'Detective,' Renata said, opening the front door. 'Thank you for coming so promptly.' She adjusted her dark lenses, smiling. 'Please, come in.'

Her cane tapped across the wooden flooring as she led him to the living room. 'Can I get you some tea?' she asked, spraying air freshener around them.

'No,' said Hector. 'Why are you limping? What happened to your—' He erupted into a frenzy of coughing. 'Excuse me,' he said hoarsely. 'Like I said, the weather. Wreaks havoc on my throat. That cleaning gunk of yours doesn't help, either.'

Blind old fool.

'Let me fetch you some water.'

Renata stepped into the kitchen before returning with a glass for the detective. He drained the water then sat back in Thomas's chair, placing his pocket watch on the arm. The toothpick remained poking out of his waistcoat breast pocket. 'Miss Wakefield,' he said, lowering his voice as she perched on the couch opposite him, 'you've not been honest with me. Not before, and maybe not now.'

She felt her toes tighten in her shoes.

The man leant forward. The bags under his eyes had darkened. 'I've known you since you were a girl. I don't believe you're capable of any criminality, but you lied to me about your relations with Quentin Rye, and I believe you might have lied to me about them having her.'

She held her breath.

'Miss Wakefield, this is a girl's life on the line. You *must* tell me everything you know. Sandie was last seen with *you*, and I'm even beginning to believe I was wrong to discount you as—'

There was a scream.

The detective's eyes darted to the bookcase, then to the wrinkled carpet by its side. He thrust his hands against the arms of the chair and threw himself to his feet.

Except he didn't.

He remained cemented to the chair, eyes widening as he spotted the ground sediment of the Dexlatine in his empty tumbler on the table. He fought his freezing muscles, but it was no use. The paralysis had him. 'What...what is...' he forced. Renata rose. She pulled the bloodstained scissors from her apron. 'Not...possible.'

'I'M DOWN HERE, *PLEASE.*'

Renata's glare shot to the source of the screaming. Hector watched her limp to the bookcase, one hand clamped against her wounded thigh, the other clutching the crimson-edged blades. She pushed the bookcase aside then hobbled into the darkness. There was a shriek, then nothing.

The woman reappeared. Hector stared in horror as she wiped fresh blood from the scissors. 'Sandie, you...' he attempted, wrestling the words from his mouth, '...you have Sandie.'

The pattering rain filled a moment's silence.

Renata removed the wide cataract glasses and locked the inky crater of her eye upon him. She glared at him with vengeful purpose, a glare that told him everything he needed to know. 'Yes, I have her, but only because you were too blind to see the real monster from the beginning.'

His face tightened under the influence of the Dexlatine. 'What...monster?'

'*HIM*,' Renata bellowed. 'You were charmed by the great Quentin C. Rye, just as I was. But it's not my job to keep people safe, to put beasts like him to justice. You didn't *look*, you didn't *SEE*.' She rubbed her temples. 'And that's the problem. If you people saw more, then my mother might still be alive.'

'Is that what this is about? I've been trying to bring Sylvia's killer to...' His muscles tightened further. Beads of sweat crawled down his face. '...to justice. I'm not the villain.'

'There are no *villains*,' she said, pulling back a strand of hair as she reset a hair grip. She ran her fingers over her bun. 'Just monsters inside us all.' He looked her up and down. 'Precisely, I'm your proof.' Then, lowering her mouth to the side of his head, 'Tell me you *see*, Detective.'

'But what do you hope to achieve with all this? Revenge, is that it? Miss Wakefield, you have to let...let me help you, you have to—'

'I shouldn't have had so much faith in your skills, Detective. I really believed you'd find my mother's killer, that you'd bring justice to her before I left, but I was just as blind as you. I should have opened my eyes so much sooner. Once they were open, you see – once I'd began my *work* – your sickening sense of protective duty for me *still* kept you from seeing what was right in front of you. But none of that matters now.' She picked up the empty glass. 'All that matters is the book.' She stared vacantly into the Dexlatine's syrupy residue. 'It's all about the book.'

'What book? I don't know what—'

'*SILENCE*,' she blasted, flinging the tumbler against the wall. Broken glass tinkled against the sideboard. 'Enough of the lies. You say you don't believe I'm capable of criminality, but *you* know I am.' His face whitened. 'Yes, Detective,' she snarled. 'I remember everything. I killed that little boy in cold blood. I was carted off to that institution, abandoned, forgotten. With *your* help, my father tried to have me deleted, erased. Well, he failed. You all failed.' She leant over Hector, pressing the closed blades of the scissors against his throat.

'Wha-what are you…talking about?'

'NOAH, GODDAMN IT,' she screamed.

His head slumped. 'Blame me,' said Hector. 'Not Quentin. Not his daughter.'

Renata laughed. 'You're as blind as my father.'

'Thomas…where is he? What have you done?' She opened the scissors and pressed the tip of a single blade into his neck. Blood crawled from the steel. 'Renata, please. This isn't you.'

'Yes, it is,' she whispered. 'Finally, it is.'

'I'm begging you, think about this.'

She pressed harder.

'I'm sorry it had to be this way, Detective.'

'Don't do this…*please*.'

She raised her elbow and prepared to thrust.

'Rennie, no!'

She paused. 'What did you call me?'

'Rennie, forgive me, forgive your mother. We never wanted to lie to you. I'm so sorry. Please, Rennie, just—'

'*DON'T CALL ME THAT*,' she thundered.

Tears ran down Hector's cheeks. 'I loved her, Rennie. I loved her more than anything. I just wanted to protect her.'

'What are you talking about?' Her grip on the scissors tightened.

'Your mother, Rennie. Thomas, he blamed her. When she wouldn't fall pregnant, he blamed her. My sweet Sylvia...I loved her, but she chose that *bastard*. I couldn't stand by and let him...let him hurt her.' The tears glistened in his eyes. His frozen body quivered under its paralysis. 'She loved me, too. She was torn. She came to me once he started hurting her. He got his son eventually, Noah could only have been his, but before that...I just wanted to stop the bruises, Rennie. I just wanted to—'

'*What are you trying to say?*'

'We spent time together, Sylvia and I,' he said through tears and sweat. 'She fell pregnant...*we* fell pregnant. I begged her to come away with me, away from him, but she was scared. She thought he'd come after us. Besides, marriage meant more in those days. She was torn with guilt and did what she thought she had to. *We* did what we—'

'LIES. More damned LIES.'

'Rennie, please! You're my little girl!'

'NO.' She flung the coffee table over. '*NO MORE LIES.*'

'Yes, Rennie. No more lies.' He stopped struggling against his paralysis. 'I tried so hard to protect you. I even convinced Chief Inspector Blyth to let me take your statement when Sandie went missing to save you the trauma of police visits. He helped your father, too. He understood why I'd want to save you the stress. I did it for you, Rennie. I did everything for—'

'*SHUT UP.*' She lunged, returning the scissors to his throat. His jaundiced eyes fell deliberately to the pocket watch on the arm of the chair. She followed his gaze, looked back at him, then hesitantly reached for the timepiece.

Its silver had corroded to a sickly yellow, not unlike the whites of its owner's eyes. She turned it around in her hands to inspect the crude racing car etched into its rear, then back around to the SUPERIOR MOTOR TIMEKEEPER – SWISS MADE branding on the front of its cover. Hector's paralysed, tear-soaked face nodded as best it could, coaxing along her inspection. She snatched the toothpick from his waistcoat pocket and, as she'd seen him do so many times before, jabbed it into where the broken spring release button should have been. The cover swung open. Under the glass, placed on top of hands frozen with time, was a faded sepia photograph of two young lovers, their smiling embrace framed by a Ferris wheel in the background. Hector O'Connell and Sylvia Wakefield gazed through lost decades at their daughter.

'We failed you,' he sobbed. 'Your mother and I both failed you. I'm so sorry.' She stared at the photograph. Every cell of her being contracted with shock and confusion and anger at yet another lie revealed to her. She dropped the pocket watch and, trembling with rage, rose the blades above her head. 'I love you, Rennie,' he whispered, then closed his eyes. 'We'll both always love you.'

She threw the blades across the room. They struck the lifeless grandfather clock, coaxing from it a solitary tick. 'You want to know the truth, old man?' She brought her leaking eye within inches of his face. 'Rye *did* murder my mother.'

Hector's eyes opened.

'He killed her to get me back here. It was just the first part of his plan to push me back into madness, all so he could sit and take notes. Inspiration for a damned *book*, that's all it was for. Nothing more.'

The man's face turned red. 'That…can't be.'

She grabbed his head between her hands, his eyes reaching for her – for the truth. 'Your beloved Sylvia,' she whispered, '*Rye* killed her.'

He roared.

She stepped behind the armchair and pushed Hector into the kitchen on the chair's casters. He wrestled against the unseen bonds of the Dexlatine as she opened the larder and shoved the chair inside. His howling died with the sealing of the pantry.

Renata slid down the locked door, dropping her face into her hands.

12

I see it now, that's all there is to say. She tore me apart then put me back together. Now I see everything.

Even if I made it out of here, I'm damaged beyond repair. I'd be worthless to anyone that once loved me — or they'd be worthless to me. She's opened my eyes, and what I've seen can't be unseen.

The world is evil. How couldn't it be when places and people like this exist? God was never listening. She was right. We're all monsters.

My life is a lie. I'm no more real than the characters Daddy made for me. I will end in this place.

For that I am glad.

32

The long grass rippled like waves around Renata's feet in the moonlight. Cloaked in darkness, she waded through the swampy grassland, her outstretched fingers running through dead wheat. Tonight she would cross these fields for the final time. She thought of the bathroom mirror

into which she stares, knowing the fields await her – knowing Rye awaits her. She scrubs her gloved hands under the scolding water, steam ascending from the drenched leather to rise over a face both pale and of a permanent darkness. The blackened eye socket gazes back. Wrinkles have sunk like canyons around her features. She fastens the final clip into her night-black hair, carefully checking for rogue strands. Everything is in its rightful place. For the first time in her life, everything is in place.

No disorder, no disaster.

She pulls the scarf over her head and opens the front door, stepping into the

night, through which she trudged as the heavens opened for one final deluge. She ignored the screaming of her untreated, festering thigh and peered through the lifeless crops towards the clock tower. The world was deteriorating into little more than a blur through her remaining eye. No matter, the end was fast approaching and

so she prepares. Around and around the girl's chair she wraps it like a vast python. There's more than she anticipated, and, to her delight, finds there's enough not only to encircle the chair, but also cover much of the surrounding floor.

The girl awakens. 'Is it…time?'

'Soon,' says the woman, producing a pink mobile phone. She cycles through the stored numbers, an endless list of boys' names, until she reaches 'Daddy'. She hits the call button and listens for

voices through the rain. There were none. The cemetery was empty, save for the crooked stones leering from every direction. Rain fired from an obsidian sky as the tower loomed, its clock face springing to life as lightning flashed, then falling back into darkness.

She fiddled with a clip in her hair as she strode past Noah's grave, the pit now refilled in an attempt to suggest the resumption of normality. There was nothing normal about this place, or this night.

Through the storm she spotted a shape leaning against the tower's stonework: Rye's motorcycle, upon which two helmets sat. Good boy.

'Sandie, is that you?'

'Guess again.'

Silence.

'If you want to see her again, be at the clock tower at midnight.' The line goes quiet, then, 'Bring your woman. And don't bother tracing the call; the girl's still out of your reach, unless you do as I say.'

'Leave Eleanor out of this,' says Rye.

'Do as I ask, my love.' Another silence. 'Midnight, midnight, it's your turn…'

33

Candlelight flickered through the open door at the top of the spiral staircase. Rye stood in the centre of the room with Eleanor sat white-faced on the steps by the glassless lancet window, fingering the cross around her neck, a blanket draped over her shoulders. They watched Renata shuffle into the cylindrical chamber and slink around the stone walls. They stared in horror as she stepped from the shadows and pulled back her scarf.

'Eleanor knows everything, Renata,' Rye said, looking her up and down, taking in the details of her physical ruin. 'Everything I did to push you to the edge: convincing you I loved you, making you remember what you did to your brother. I've even told her what I did to—' He cleared his throat. '—to your mother. Everything, Renata. I've told her everything. And all she wants, all *we* want, is Sandie home safe.' He struck a match then produced his precious notebook, holding the flame to its pages. It dropped to the floor between them, burning. 'I put too much on the line for my work, took things too far just to find inspiration for a novel. I've wronged you beyond forgiveness, but I beg you, let the suffering end.' He took a step towards her. 'For God's sake, Renata. Let Sandie go.'

The glimmer remained in his eyes, that spark she'd so foolishly mistaken for creative energy. Too late it had revealed itself as the spark of evil, that same spark she now knew lay behind everyone's eyes – even hers.

Especially hers.

The spark remained in his words, too. Yes, they were as hollow as ever. Renata now had a sense for deception; like fireflies, his insincerities shimmered in the candlelight. All she had to do was reach out and swat them.

'Do as I say and you'll see her again,' she said, removing her leather gloves and stretching her wrists.

Lightning sprayed the room.

'Anything, Renata,' he said, eyeing her ruined hands. He took another step. 'Tell me what to do.'

'Choose.'

He stopped. 'What do you mean?'

'You know what I mean,' she said, picking the scabs on her palms. 'I can see it in your eyes. The woman or the girl, you can't have both.'

'Renata, be reasonable.' He edged closer. 'Let's talk about this like—'

'Push her from that window and you'll see Sandie again.' Eleanor's eyes widened. Her pawing of the cross ceased. 'The woman or the girl, one or the other. *Push* her, my love, and look upon your beloved daughter again.' Renata's mangled eye gleamed in the candlelight. '*Choose.*'

The bell awoke, shaking the room as it bellowed into the night. Renata peered through the wire mesh above as a streak of lightning lit the stirring mechanism, century-old gears grinding into life to mark the terrible hour. She looked back to find Rye flying towards her, hands outstretched, his roar vying to be heard over the bell.

His fist slammed into her face. They tumbled to the ground and rolled through a pile of rubble, limbs lashing. Her nails slashed across his cheek. He wrestled on top of her and battered her against the stone floor as more lightning crashed, illuminating her deranged grin like a carved pumpkin. Milk bottle chews sprayed from Rye's blazer pocket like confetti as black wept from the crater of Renata's eye socket. She cackled along wildly with the iron cacophony.

The bell ceased.

'Tell her I love her.'

Renata and Rye both froze at the sudden, softly spoken words, before turning round to the source of the voice. Their eyes fell upon Eleanor just as she stepped out of the narrow window into the storm.

Rye leapt to his feet and scrambled to the opening. Hands anchored on either side of the lancet window, he leaned out into the gale and stared down. Through the swirling rain he saw the blanket below dancing upon the lifeless shape of Eleanor. He turned to the crouched figure in the darkness, blood trickling from his slashed cheek. 'You're...a monster.'

'Yes,' she hissed, '*your* monster; and you, my Victor. Like him, you wanted the work to end all works, except *you* wanted to see the breakdown of a human being, all so you could take notes while you watched me like a specimen in a petri dish. You drove me to hell, you killed my MOTHER, all for a *BOOK*.' She paused, massaging the sides of her head as she caught her breath. 'Well, this is your result. Here I am, my love.' Her lips peeled into a sneer. 'Tell me you *see*.'

The candles began to die. Even in the fading glow she saw his spark extinguish as he dropped to the floor, head in hands. Renata stepped from the shadows. 'Your wife was of faith, was she not?' She picked at the toggles of her duffle coat. 'Know that her final moments were filled with the knowledge of eternal damnation. That, and never seeing the girl again.'

'What do you want from me?'

'Midnight, my love,' she said, slipping her fingers back into the leather gloves. She tore out a loose strand of hair, then locked eyes with him. 'Always midnight. Once I've left, remove your wife from the grass below. Lay her to rest in this tower. Then, tomorrow, come to the house. Enter when you hear the midnight bell. No earlier, no later. Do this and I swear you'll look into your daughter's eyes again.'

Renata disappeared down the stone staircase as the final candle died, dropping Rye into darkness.

34

Knives.

Everywhere, knives.

Knives all through her life, carving every last scrap of humanity from her until all that was left was this: an accursed wraith, desolate and obsessed.

Vengeful.

The culmination of her efforts, the climax of her revenge, is finally within reach. Renata Wakefield will descend to the basement one last time, where this endgame will draw to a close. But before her final descent, before her return to the stage on which their concluding scene will play out, she'll stand before the painting. How she'd love to set light to that canvas and watch the waves turn to fire, but she resists. The book is all that matters.

She gazes up at the flood, listening to the silence the storm has left in its wake. Content in the knowledge retribution is ready to be served, she feels the stillness and serenity of the house around her, its walls finally at peace. Harmony is restored.

She sees now that everything comes back to the ocean of darkness above, and to the town of an even deeper dark below. It comes back to the vanquished mist and the storm now spent, to the fallacy of fact and the fickleness of fiction. It comes back to love, hate, light, and shade; to violence and insanity, the alpha and the omega; to the dusk and the dawn, to the truth – and to you.

It all comes back to you.

Even as I write these final pages, I feel you. I imagine the whisperings of the wind are yours as you lurk in the shadows, awaiting the midnight bell.

Everything comes back to you.

My dearest Quentin, I can write no more. Thank you for giving me reason to exist, but that reason has now run its course. This account of our time together, these thirty-four chapters penned by my own ruined hands, finally draw to a close, and so I address you directly, for you deserve nothing less than the truth.

As you can see, I've taken your advice, my love. I've written a horror. Committed to these very pages, written in a cellar to the screams of your child, are terrors beyond anything you could have conceived, for they concern that which you love most: your precious wife and daughter. You pulled me back from the brink, made me believe love had finally found me, only to snatch it away. You forced upon me memories that should have stayed buried, parts of myself that belonged only in the past.

You got your tale, and here it is. This story, our story, is horror born in truth. Just like you always wanted.

This book, finally in your hands, documents the details of your deceit and, more importantly, my reply. It chronicles the seeds of my aberration through childhood, my return to Millbury Peak decades later, our time together, and, finally, your imminent witnessing of Sandie's demise. Your suffering – the finest thing I've authored – hasn't been about revenge, but at long last the granting of that elusive truth-infused story you so craved. I've spared you the formulaic pulp you loathe so; in this book I've so lovingly crafted for you, you'll find no one with which to sympathise, no relief from the artifice of human nature. For we are all beasts, wild and feral,

311

scurrying for the upper hand at every expense. Scrambling for our lives.

Our feud was that of opposing demons, a feud in which our most precious of these feral beasts were caught – my mother, your daughter. I suppose I never really left that night in the clock tower, our first time truly alone. The man I fell in love with never existed, but my love was real. Even through the insanity that's come to define our connection, my love remains somehow true. Which of these few remaining pages will finally allow the conquering of this insanity, of the evil swallowing our worlds? Sympathy, empathy, hope: petty musings which remain on the shelves of every bookshop, flocking around the Quentin C. Rye display like some mad congregation. Evil cannot be conquered, for it defines this vile human condition we call life. Reality is fire, my love, and tonight I bring you that fire.

With the midnight bell you'll come running like the obedient dog you are – no earlier, no later, for you now understand what it means to disobey me. As you run through the house, frantic, panicked, scrambling to locate the distant muffling of Sandie's sobbing, notice this very manuscript on the table. What is that pile of pages? Why does the cover page scream your name in my scrawled hand? At this point, ignore it. Force yourself to ignore everything but that abhorrent darkness beyond the toppled bookcase from where your daughter's animal screams call as steel enters flesh.

Descend, Quentin. Enter your sweet Sandie's chamber of rebirth and bear witness to the fulfilment of my promise that you'd once again look into the girl's eyes.

Then see.

Under the light of a single poised flame, see your work.

See reel upon reel of your flammable nitrate film strewn around your only daughter, waiting for its moment. See the blades of Sylvia Wakefield's fabric scissors lodged in the girl's crusty flesh. See the emerald green dress clinging to her brutalised body. See your darling spawn reborn, a shadow begging for death by light. Then see my instrument of annihilation: a simple lighter, once a token of our love, now my trigger, scarred with words that never found their way to you, yet say it all:

ONE TRUTH: OURS. THANK YOU, QUENTIN.

And before I let the lighter and its flame drop, before the fires of the nitrate film drown her and I, hear the girl's voice one final time. Let the blades twist against bone, coaxing like milk from a cow your child's last words:

Midnight...

Hear them, my love.

...midnight...

Feel them.

...it's your turn...

Then hear the bell.

...clock strikes twelve...

It tolls for thee.

...burn...

The lighter drops.

...burn...

The flames take us.

...burn.

I cannot know the specifics of the end, for the events I describe – my final descent to Sandie, her call to you, my lighting of the flame – will only begin once the closing word of this book is committed to the page. Will you reach for her, my love? Will you scramble through the spreading flames to try and tug Sandie from my grasp, and from the bonds binding her to her fate? Dear Quentin, will you join us as the girl and I melt into one, as the two things you love and hate most in the world fuse together in the flames? You'll know you can't succeed, but let the fires lick your skin anyway. You'll know it's already over, but pull at her blistering flesh all the same. Struggle, please struggle to free your baby from this raging hellfire of your own doing. Whatever your actions in those final moments, know I'll be there in that inferno to seal her and I to our shared destiny, stroking those beloved blonde locks as they turn to dust.

Then weep, my love.

Weep for the charred remains of your daughter. Weep for your dead wife. Weep, then find this, the tale of your family's demise. Will you refuse to read these words? No, the great Quentin C. Rye *must* know the truth. He always had to know the truth.

Quentin, this book is my parting gift; her eulogy, my elegy, our legacy. This is for everything you did for me. For the love, hate, lies, and truth. Always for the truth. For all these things I give to you the end of all that you hold dear. For you. Everything I have done has been for you.

Let it be known that this is for you, my love – my truth, my lie.

This is for Rye.

Gavin Gardiner's lifelong love of horror didn't manifest into this novel until his early thirties. Between the completion of *For Rye* and its publication, he wrote a novella, several short stories, and a selection of non-fiction articles and analysis pieces. These can be found in various online publications and in print via:

www.gavingardinerhorror.com

Before he threw himself into the writing game, Gavin dedicated much of his teen years and twenties to the pursuit of music. Although the nightmares he's since committed to the page have garnered more attention than his songs ever did, he hopes to one day return to music. The writing of horror, however, is here to stay.

He's currently working on his second novel, *Witchcraft on Rücken Ridge*, and has grand plans for the future of his unique brand of horror. He very much hopes you'll join him for the ride, and consider leaving an honest Amazon review for the book you've just read, no matter how brief. Reviews are absolutely integral to the visibility of an author's work, and this visibility will help drive on the creation of further nightmares for your deranged delectation.

He lives in Glasgow, Scotland with his ever-patient girlfriend and ever-demanding kitten.

Connect with Gavin on the platform of your choice:
linktr.ee/GGardinerHorror

Also from Gavin Gardiner…

THE LAST TESTAMENT
OF
CRIGHTON SMYTHE

Crighton Smythe could see how everyone was going to die
– except himself.

A social outcast who relied on his mother to keep him,
Crighton had to use his 'knack' to his advantage when Mrs
Smythe took ill and financial pressures began to mount.
But as his visions started to increase in intensity, and his
hatred of the city around him began pushing him to his
limit, he found himself wondering how much more he
could take.

Then he died.

In his own words, let Crighton Smythe tell you the story of
how he perished. Where is he now?

Discover for yourself.

Visit:
<u>www.gavingardinerhorror.com</u>
to live the nightmare.

More **Burton Mayers Books** titles:

FIONA'S GUARDIANS

When a vampire seduces you, death is minutes away. When she hires you, you'll soon wish you were dead.

It's a truth known to every guardian who worked for Fiona, including Daniel. Aside from managing the day-to-day chores and keeping her protected, he manages an investment portfolio to buy stolen blood from hospital workers.

After 35 years, what keeps him loyal? And will he ever be allowed to leave**?**

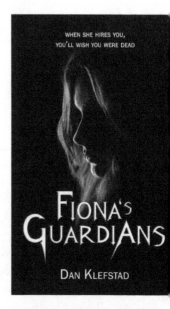

#StoptheGlitch

In a post-pandemic world, the nation is healing its wounds and adjusting to a _new normal_. But the darker threat of a second national cyber-attack looms.

Robin hopes to escape society, using an inheritance to secure a peaceful life off grid in Wales. However, through a series of bizarre circumstances, Robin is pulled back into a life left behind.

CPSIA information can be obtained
at www.ICGtesting.com
Printed in the USA
BVHW081929300321
603710BV00006B/535